TITLES BY NADIA LEE

AN UNLIKELY BRIDE
AN UNLIKELY DEAL
AN IMPROPER EVER AFTER
AN IMPROPER BRIDE
AN IMPROPER DEAL
A HOLLYWOOD BRIDE
A HOLLYWOOD DEAL
THE BILLIONAIRE'S FORBIDDEN DESIRE
THE BILLIONAIRE'S FORGOTTEN FIANCÉE
THE BILLIONAIRE'S SECRET WIFE
THE BILLIONAIRE'S INCONVENIENT
      OBSESSION
THE BILLIONAIRE'S COUNTERFEIT
      GIRLFRIEND
LOVING HER BEST FRIEND'S BILLIONAIRE
      BROTHER
SEDUCED BY HER SCANDALOUS
      BILLIONAIRE
ROMANCED BY HER ILLICIT MILLIONAIRE
      CRUSH
PREGNANT WITH HER BILLIONAIRE EX'S
      BABY
PURSUED BY HER BILLIONAIRE HOOK-UP
TAKEN BY HER UNFORGIVING BILLION-
      AIRE BOSS

AN
UNLIKELY DEAL

BILLIONAIRES' BRIDES OF CONVENIENCE

BOOK SIX

NADIA LEE

To Diane Chardon.

THE BOY

THE BOY IN THE GARDEN IS NO MORE THAN four. He is a handsome child, with bright brown eyes and the silkiest of dark chestnut hair. His black shirt is neatly pressed—thanks to the housekeeper—and his blue denim pants are tidy as well, except for a streak of dirt from the yard where he wrestled with his twin.

He takes hold of his mother's soft, manicured hand with his own, which is sticky with sweat and candy from earlier. She flinches and tries to pull away. When he doesn't let go, she yanks her hand from his grip and stares at her palm with distaste. She takes out a handkerchief and wipes it.

His gaze rises to her face.

"'Ommy?" he says when she ignores him.

She sighs. "It's *Mommy*, not 'ommy." Her voice is impatient.

"I love you!" he declares, not bothered by the correction, looking up at his beautiful golden mother with a cherubic smile.

She shakes her head. "What did I say about manipulation?"

"What's 'anoolation?"

"*Manipu*lation," she corrects him again. "When you say things like 'I love you' you're trying to get the other person to say it back. Manipulation. Putting pressure on someone."

The smile on his face slips. He just wanted her to know how much he loves her.

"You're being needy," she continues. "Needy children are the worst. Why are your hands so grubby?" She opens and closes the palm he held, then wipes it again.

He looks down. "I'm sorry," he whispers.

She doesn't acknowledge him. Instead, she wrinkles her nose and disappears into the mansion.

The boy remains standing in the garden, unsure and alone.

ONE

Lucas

I DO NOT MAKE A HABIT OF REMINISCING about my exes. Nor do I make a habit of stalking our former haunts.

So it is with the greatest annoyance and puzzlement that I find myself back in Charlottesville, Virginia. I have nothing there—no friends, no business interests. Well…there's that house. I really should put it on the market and move back to Seattle permanently, but somehow I can't bring myself to pull the trigger.

For fuck's sake, just sell the place and get the hell out of here. Cut all ties.

Rainwater drips down the pothole-sized windows as my plane slows on the tarmac. The cabin crew hands me a spare umbrella.

My assistant had my Mercedes dropped off
at the airport yesterday before starting her vacation. I claim the car—no luggage to get—and run
a rough hand over my face. My left leg aches. I
should probably move someplace where the sun
shines all year long.

Instead of going to my own house to soak the
throbbing limb in hot water, I drive to the duplex,
park across the street like a fucking stalker, and
watch the sad little building through the rain-
blurred windshield.

She doesn't even live here anymore, but
somehow I keep coming back. Like a damned
boomerang.

*The bitch kicked you to the curb when you were
at your lowest. Fuck her.*

Yes. Fuck her. Forget she exists. Get myself
a hot chick to bang so I can move on. Scarred or
not, I'm young and rich. It won't be a problem to
get a willing girl.

The duplex's exterior could use a fresh coat of
paint and a bit of landscaping, but the manage-
ment company won't do anything until the place
looks like a dump. They know just as well as I do
that college kids don't care all that much about
curb appeal.

The scuffed blue door stays stubbornly shut.
It was raining when we had our first real date and
she let me pick her up from her place.

In my mind's eye, I see the door opening…Ava stepping out… She's in a long-sleeved shirt and old jeans with frayed hems and stitches, and her feet are encased in a pair of black boots she bought on clearance at a department store the year before. I quickly put an umbrella over her to shield her from the icy raindrops and lead her to my car. I don't want even a drop to touch her soft, warm skin.

Idiot.

No matter how much I will it, Ava isn't coming out. She left me two years ago. She couldn't have made it clearer that she didn't want anything to do with me.

A pretty blonde walks by on the other side of the street, a bright orange, white and navy blue umbrella showing her school spirit. Her white UVA medical school shirt stretches across young, perky tits. The skirt she's wearing is short and shows off long, shapely legs. Her canvas shoes are wet, but she doesn't seem to mind.

Med school. Must be smart. And she's easy on the eyes.

But my body remains coolly uninterested. It's as though after the accident, somebody flipped my libido switch off…leaving me deadened to one of the best pleasures in life.

If I were the superstitious type, I'd suspect that Ava cast some kind of dark spell on me before she left.

The muscles in my left leg twinge, and I rub the thigh with an impatient hand. It acts up every time it rains, even when I'm seated. Maybe the pain's making it difficult for me to get interested. I'm not a masochist.

The blonde knocks on Ava's old blue door, and a boy comes out. They hug and kiss. The view twists something inside me.

What the hell am I trying to accomplish by coming back?

I pull out and drive away. It's over.

It was over two years ago.

For a so-called genius, it's taking me an awful long time to accept that fact. I can deal with numbers and patterns. But figuring Ava out... That always eluded me.

No time for this bullshit. Let her go. You have three months left to find a wife.

The muscles in my neck tighten until they feel like steel. The idea of marrying anyone spikes my heartbeat, and the roast beef sandwich I had for lunch churns in my gut. If it were just me, I'd say to hell with everything. But if I don't marry...if all of us don't get married...none of us are getting our grandfather's damned paintings.

I don't fucking *want* a wife. I'm not like my brothers. Pretty Boy Ryder found one—well, he felt compelled to marry his assistant after knocking her up. My twin, Elliot, found a stripper to marry for a year. But I can't let my brothers and sister down. My sister Elizabeth in particular would be devastated.

The paintings are rightfully ours. If Grandpa had had a better lawyer—or a better brain for business—they would've come directly to us rather than our asshole father, who is now using them for his own twisted amusement. Julian is a borderline sociopath who likes to watch people weaker than him squirm at his command. It enrages him that he can't fuck with us—his children from his first wife are too wealthy and well-connected, and Elliot and I made our own fortunes when we were twenty-one.

I drive past the guard manning the gated community in Charlottesville. He gives me a bored nod. The verdant lawn stretches endlessly, trees big with branches that defy gravity. Their leaves are still a vibrant jade, but a tinge of orange, yellow and red has started to creep in, a discordant sign of the end of summer. Homes are stately in stone and brick, with elegant white-framed windows. Beyond them is a golf course, which I've never used.

I only bought an "estate" here because it had an acceptable house for sale. Ava was studying at the University of Virginia, and flying back and forth between the east and west coasts didn't appeal. That's ten hours per round trip I could've spent with her. Seattle didn't have anything for me. Still doesn't, which is why I haven't moved back after finishing my treatment at the UVA hospital.

My home sprawls on one level and has seven bedrooms. Perhaps it was divine providence that the only place available was a single-story house. Going up and down stairs with my injuries would've been difficult, especially on days when I was wheelchair-bound.

I park in the four-car garage. On the other side is a silver Lexus that's barely three years old. I don't drive it, but I make sure it's well maintained.

Get rid of the damn thing. She's not coming back.

Shaking off the gloomy thoughts, I step out. The black, waxed surface of the Mercedes is like a mirror, reflecting the strain on my face. I take the time to smooth it into a calm mask and slip quietly into the house.

"Welcome home, Lucas," Gail says, her voice as gentle as a spring breeze. She eyes me. "Something warm to drink?"

I shake my head.

Her thin-lipped mouth thins further because I'm not letting her mother me, but I ignore her displeasure. In her early sixties, Gail is my full-time housekeeper. Despite my parents' disapproval, I don't insist that she put on a maid's uniform or any such bullshit. She's old enough to dress herself; right now she's in a light blue sweater, jeans and white sneakers.

She goes to the kitchen counter, her cloud-like gray hair glinting under the recessed lights, then almost immediately returns with a white envelope.

"This came for you."

Moments like this, I miss Rachel. My assistant would've thrown it out without bugging me with it, but she's on a well-deserved week-long vacation in the Bahamas.

"You can toss it. It's junk," I say without taking a closer look.

All legal documents that require my attention go to my attorney. Things that matter come to my inbox. My bills are paid automatically through direct debit, and invoices are forwarded to my assistant. Only garish advertisements and pitiful offers of credit end up in my mailbox.

"I thought that at first, but it doesn't look like junk." She hands it to me. "Here. See for yourself."

I sigh and take it. It's as big as letter-sized paper folded in half, and the material is stiff and waterproof. The outside doesn't have any stamps or indication of where it's come from. It merely has a name—LUCAS REED—in all caps.

Maybe it isn't junk after all. "Thank you," I say and take it to my office, trying not to limp.

My left leg is shorter now, even though the surgeons did their best to minimize the discrepancy. I can usually manage to disguise it, but on days when my leg muscles throb, it's hard to hide my uneven gait.

I close the door to my home office and slump in the armchair that faces the cold and black fireplace. The mantel has a framed photo of me and my siblings, taken while we were exiled to fancy European boarding schools. People call it "education," but that's just a euphemism. There aren't any pictures of Ava and me together. We never took any, and I don't remember why. I wish we had.

For what? To burn them? Delete from your phone's memory? Would that have made it clear that she's gone?

I tug at the little red-tipped section on the corner, and the envelope comes apart. Glossy photographs spill out, landing in my lap. I pick one up.

A young female pedestrian on a stone bridge crossing a river. Wind tosses her long and wavy platinum blond hair. The color of her eyes is ice blue, which never seems to fit because they're too warm. Her facial bones are delicate, her lips soft. She's always been frail looking: just a tad too thin, as though she grew up without enough to eat. I can tell that hasn't changed from the way the pale pink dress fits her, a slim white belt cinching her small waist.

My fingers go numb. Ava.

Heart hammering against my ribs, I flip the picture over. Nothing on the other side. I pick up the rest of the photos, but none of them have a message for me or anything on the back.

Suddenly a thought bleeds into my mind. All of the photos are candid shots. Someone's been watching her.

Stalker?

My gut goes cold. My sister Elizabeth has had her share of problems with assholes who didn't understand the meaning of no. But this feels different. Why would a stalker send me Ava's photos?

I dig inside the envelope for clues. My hand grasps a piece of paper.

Le Meridien Chiang Mai, Thailand, it reads. Underneath the name of the hotel are dates—today, tomorrow and the day after—and an itinerary for a flight from Chiang Mai to Osaka via Seoul on Korean Air. The flight doesn't leave until almost midnight two days from now.

If I leave immediately, I can be in Chiang Mai before her departure.

I pick up the photos again. I didn't see them before, my focus being on Ava, but the signs around her are in Japanese. I still remember a few hiragana and katakana characters from back when I spent a semester in Tokyo.

So why Chiang Mai?

I toss the photos on the floor and lean my head against the back of my chair. I never, ever go after exes. *Never.* Not like some lovesick fool with my heart on my sleeve. I might as well cut off my dick and carve LOSER into my face with a rusty nail.

But I'm entitled to closure. It won't be begging if that's all I want…and maybe a pound of flesh for all I've suffered in the last twenty-four months.

On its own volition, my hand reaches into my pocket and pulls out my phone. My fingers move across the smooth surface and dial my pilot, who's ready to go twenty-four seven.

"Sir?"

"Chiang Mai," I say. "ASAP."

I head straight to the garage. No time to pack.

TWO

Ava

*T*HE JOB IS YOURS.

Four simple words that represent a new opportunity.

I walk across the chic, modern lobby at the hotel and step into the waiting elevator to my room on the seventh floor. The school's paying; I would never spend this much on lodging. They're also paying for my flight back to Osaka.

My phone rings with a call from Bennie. I answer and slip into my room.

"Hey," I say. "Sorry I couldn't talk earlier. I was still at the school."

"Don't worry about it. I just couldn't wait, and forgot you're two hours behind. How did it go?"

I kick off my pumps and flex my toes on the

cool, smooth floor. Ahh. So much better. "Got the job! Mr. Liu offered on the spot."

Bennie's whoop is ear-splitting. "*I knew it!* I knew it the minute he offered to fly you to Chiang Mai and put you up in that swanky hotel. You know it isn't normal for them to do that."

That's true. Most schools aren't that generous with recruiting, and usually they expect potential hires to pay a lot of the expenses. But the school owner is very interested in having me work for him.

"Bet he thinks you walk on water," Bennie says.

I chuckle. Bennie's my roommate and my best friend, and always has my back. "Not quite."

"Sure he does. His son was a total psycho when he first arrived and didn't want to speak any English. Then a semester with you, and voila! He improved so much I almost didn't recognize him. I mean, before, he would barely say hi."

"He was just shy." And rebellious. And angry that his father got a new wife. Nicky didn't care that his mother was dead or his father had a right to be happy. The second marriage was a betrayal as far as the boy was concerned. It took me six weeks to make him see that it wasn't. He returned to his family after the exchange program, but he kept in touch.

"Nicky adores you. He never liked English much and had behavioral issues, but those seem to have been resolved," the Chinese billionaire from Hong Kong had said in lightly accented but otherwise impeccable English when we met for the interview. "I think it speaks to your ability as a teacher."

"I'm very flattered, Mr. Liu."

"I believe our school would benefit from having a teacher such as you."

I merely smiled. It's one thing to receive praise, but quite another to agree with it. Asians and their modesty.

"This interview isn't just about you trying to impress us, Ms. Huss, but also for us to impress you. I understand you are happy at your current school."

"It's a great place."

A middle school—which means my students aren't under pressure to take college entrance exams. So many Japanese high school kids seem ready to crumble under the expectations imposed upon them by themselves and their parents. Every time I see them rushing from club activities to cram schools, my heart squeezes a bit.

"You should take the job," Bennie says, interrupting my reveries. "Unless the pay's bad."

"Seriously? And leave a troublemaker like you behind in Osaka?"

He scoffs. "This is probably going to be my last contract. I'm thinking about going back to the States next year."

"You are?" I sit down, slightly stunned. "What about Drew?"

He's Bennie's boyfriend of two years. He comes by almost every day and never forgets a birthday or anniversary. In addition, he brings gifts just because, and from the sounds they make in Bennie's room, Drew's great in bed. Bennie and I have dubbed him *Mr. Perfect*.

"I have to go," Bennie says abruptly. "I forgot I have to submit my grades by tonight."

"Grades?"

"English tests. Due in, like, an hour, and you know how slowly I type."

That's true enough. He's a two-finger hunter-and-pecker. But I'm not dumb enough to believe he suddenly remembered a deadline. Concern for my best friend settles in my belly with unease, but we can talk about Drew tomorrow when I'm back home.

"All right, have fun. I need to puff for a bit then grab something to eat."

"You haven't eaten?"

"Not yet. Two hours behind, remember?"

"That's right. Hey, we should go out tomorrow."

"It's a date. See you."

We hang up.

I toss the phone back into my purse, get up and change into a T-shirt and jeans. Despite being

October, it's surprisingly cool in Chiang Mai… actually much cooler than Osaka. The frequent showers lower the temperature and keep the air comfortably moist but not crazy humid. Mr. Liu told me the hottest months are April and May, when the temperature can hit forty-plus degrees Celsius, which is something like a hundred degrees Fahrenheit. *Ugh.* I shudder. Might as well sit in a steamer.

After shoving my feet into a pair of comfy flip-flops, I take the key from the slot by the door and leave. The lights go off automatically behind me.

My phone pings, and I fish it out. A Google alert notification pops up over my smiling baby wallpaper. I take a moment to gaze at the baby's face—Mia's face—then bring up the message. The subject is Faye Belbin. Some pictures of her in Spain.

I check them out, my fingers shaky. A skin-tight black dress is wrapped around her, almost startling against her milky skin. Despite her paleness, she's a vibrant, arresting woman. Her glossy jet-black hair, wide amber eyes and full, rosy lips make me think of Snow White—the stunning fairy-tale princess with skin the color of fresh snow and hair like onyx.

My mouth dries as I look for a boyfriend in the pictures. Thankfully she isn't draped all over Lucas, unlike the alert I got two weeks ago.

Why do I torture myself like this? It's been two years. It's obvious to everyone, especially me, that she is exactly what a man like Lucas wants on his arm. I was just a girl he fucked in secret because I was willing and he was horny and slumming.

I should unsubscribe from the alerts. I really should. But somehow my finger always hovers over the unsubscribe link without actually tapping it.

Damn it.

My lips tight, I shove the phone into my purse. *Tomorrow*. I swear I'll do it.

It's the exact same thing I've told myself for the last two years.

I exit the hotel lobby and cross the fantastically crowded street toward the Night Bazaar. No matter how preoccupied you are, it's impossible not to absorb the atmosphere. Tuk-tuks blare their horns at straggling pedestrians still on the road after the lights turn red. All of them have bright advertisements for malls and Tiger Kingdom and elephant trekking tours. I haven't had time to do any of that, and now that I'm about to return to Japan, I regret it. *Should've figured out a way to do some sightseeing.*

Still, I file everything away in my head, so that when I get a chance to sit down and finally write my Great American Novel I'll have something to draw on. I don't know if I'll ever set one in Asia, but it's got to be good for my writing to be exposed to different cultures and localities.

I wend my way along the sidewalks. The already narrow strips of concrete are now barely wide enough for a person to pass, with street vendors setting up shop and hawking cheap clothes and merchandise. Naked bulbs light the souvenirs—softball-sized elephants carved out of some kind of black composite, T-shirts with filthy slogans, varicolored dresses. A few women stand in front of massage parlors and call out, "Madam, foot massage?"

It's tempting. My feet are killing me after a day spent in pumps, and the prices are ridiculously low. Only about ten bucks for an hour of massage.

"Maybe after dinner," I say with a smile as I pass by.

Carts selling fresh fruit smoothies are already out. Each clear plastic cup contains overripe mangoes, watermelon chunks, bananas and other tropical fruit I don't recognize. The ladies call out prices, again incredibly inexpensive for something so fresh and scrumptious. Maybe I'll get one of those after dinner, too…if I can still eat. The scent of grilled seafood and meat and curry permeates the air, and my stomach growls.

"Madam, hamburger?" a man says in front of a western-style bar and grill.

"No thanks." This is my last night in Chiang Mai, and I want to try something more interesting and authentic. I can get a burger in Osaka anytime.

Around a corner is a modest-sized restaurant specializing in curry. It doesn't look Indian, though, so I stop to check out the menu.

"Would you like to go in, madam?"

I lift my head at the lilting suggestion. A soft-faced man is watching me with a smile.

"Is this place Indian?"

"No, madam. Moroccan."

Moroccan. That sounds both delicious and exotically intriguing. I smile, about to say yes then stop as my gaze drifts away from the man to something else beyond the smoothie carts I just passed by.

It's a western man. Not unusual; Chiang Mai is one of the major cities in Thailand and there are lots of foreigners. But...

The bold dark slant of eyebrows, the unusually sharp eyes. The masterfully carved bones on his arresting face...and his expensive semi-formal clothing that establishes his station in life and subtly warns people to stay away...

All the air leaves my lungs; the world seems to spin and grow dim at the same time. I can't sense anything over the deafening roaring in my head.

Lucas.

His hair is longer now, and styled differently, with bangs covering most of the left side of his face, but it has to be him. No other man can make me so aware…like an electric current has gone through me.

"Madam?"

I jerk my head back at the man and merely blink at him. Who is this man? Why is he talking to me?

"You like a table?"

Right. Dinner. "No… No, thank you. I'm sorry. I have to go."

I turn and start walking, intent on returning to the hotel. I glance back over a shoulder, and Lucas is still there, standing next to a local merchant. He's alone. But for all I know Faye Belbin is here too, maybe haggling with a vendor over an elephant carving.

Mocking laughter echoes in my head. *Haggling! Ha. That's so funny, Ava. The* women Lucas dates do not haggle. Ever. The kind of women he dates are otherworldly beautiful, sophisticated, wealthy…

Not like me.

It takes no time at all to reach the big intersection. The light's red, and I grip my hands together in front of me. I want to cross *now*, but too many tuk-tuks and cars are speeding past. Unless I don't mind being plastered all over a windshield, I'm stuck until the light turns.

Someone tugs at my shirt, and I almost cry out in alarm. My heart thumping at a hundred miles an hour, I spin around, ready to face him.

"Flower?"

I look down at the young voice. A girl who can't be more than six or seven shows me a long string of small white flowers. Her hand is tiny, her wrist bony and delicate. The dingy pink dress she wears is overly big, and her skinny legs are bumpy with bug bites. Her dark eyes beseech me to buy something. It's obvious if she can't sell, she and her family may not be able to eat. Why else would a young girl like her be out and about at this hour in an area full of tourists?

The light turns green, and the girl's eyes flicker to the people starting to cross. The corners of her lips droop, and I reach into my wallet and pull out a hundred baht bill.

"Here." I hand it to her and take the flowers without thinking. I have to go. *Now.* "Keep the change."

I trot fast to make the light. The girl yells out something behind me, but I don't stop. She's most definitely not telling me I paid her too little. I've seen skewered meat carts selling their goods for no more than twenty baht apiece. There's no way her little flowers can cost more than a meal.

When someone catches me by my shirt, I turn my head over a shoulder. "You can keep the cha…"

My words trail off as I take in Lucas's face, so close to mine that our noses almost touch. I can smell his favorite soap, mint and warm skin, a combination that leaves me breathless. Unblinking, I take in his masculine magnificence. The eyebrow that isn't hidden by his hair is tilted in that familiar arrogant line that says he's too smart and too used to getting his way and that's exactly how he wants his life. The bridge of his nose is strong and straight, the kind that creates a bold profile in men. His jaw has the same hard, square look, like it's been carved from granite. The only soft part of him is his mouth, which is currently set in a flat line.

Suddenly I can't think, can't move. The flowers fall from my limp grasp. But his hand at the small of my back pushes me toward the other side, and we cross before the light changes. My foot catches on a crack in the uneven sidewalk, and I stumble. He catches me, pulling me closer to his large, muscled body, and I cover my face, hoping and praying that I'm hallucinating.

But when I drop my arms to my sides, I still

see Lucas. I still feel his hand wrapped around my biceps.

Why now? Why here?

Why?

"Ava." His voice is the same, gravelly and low. And I shiver as it envelops me like the softest silk.

My breath catches in my throat, and suddenly I can't speak. My stomach roils like a thousand angry bees are buzzing inside it.

I whisper the only word I can. "*Why?*"

CLARITY

Lucas

PEOPLE SAY YOU GAIN CLARITY WHEN YOU'RE about to die—the things that matter most flash vividly through your head, while the things that you fought tooth and nail for over reasons that really won't matter two weeks down the line get dumped.

I've always thought it was bullshit. When you die, you die. What the hell can you possibly be thinking at that moment?

Then it happens to me. I lose control of my Harley, and I'm falling and spinning, leaving what feels like half the meat on my body smeared along the wet pavement. My chest feels like it's on fire, and my leg... *Holy shit...* The pain is so excruciating, the edges of my vision turn black.

But in that split-second, my mind isn't on how I'm going to fix everything that's broken. Or how I'm going to screw my father over.

No. The image that comes is Ava's face.

Ava smiling.

Ava laughing.

Ava gasping my name in climax.

I regret that I haven't spent even one entire night with her in the seven months we've been together…that I haven't tried to be with her more. I know she wants to take our relationship to the next level. She tries to hide it, but sometimes when her guard is down, I can see the longing in her eyes.

I dimly hear a siren screaming somewhere… getting louder.

If I survive this… I'm going to show her the world—and all that the two of us can be together.

THREE

Lucas

WHY?

I don't know how to respond to her question. I asked myself that the entire time my plane was crossing the continental U.S.— and the Pacific—and still didn't find an answer.

Yes, I want closure. Yes, I want my pound of flesh.

But neither are sufficient on their own...or together. And I didn't make my fortune by being half-assed about things.

So why?

I asked myself that question—again—when I finally reached the hotel in the note. The concierge helpfully called Ava's room, but nobody answered. Would I like to leave a message?

No. I had no idea what to say. Instead I asked if they happened to know where she might be. Or when she might be back…

Unfortunately, no. However, as it was dinnertime perhaps she went to get something to eat…? But it would be hard to find her. There are so many restaurants in the area, not to mention street food stalls.

The concierge forgot to mention how crowded it would be. October isn't a high tourist season, but there were so many damned people, so many damned carts and vendors all calling out what they were offering, trying to drum up business. How the hell could I find her in the chaos? And I was assuming she'd gone on foot. She could've taken one of those *tuk-tuk* death traps and gone someplace farther out.

Still, I wandered around the Night Bazaar like an idiot. Most merchants shook their heads when I asked them if they'd seen a blond woman about this tall. Either they didn't see her or didn't want to waste their time with someone who obviously wasn't buying.

But I knew when I found Ava…when my entire body tightened and sharp awareness tugged at me so swiftly that I couldn't breathe with the shock of it. I stopped for a second to regain my composure while my eyes scanned the area. The last thing I wanted was to stagger and lose my balance.

I almost missed her when she made a sharp turn around a corner. I dashed after her, not caring if my gait was uneven or that I was acting without a clear plan. All that mattered was catching her.

Thank god for the red light. Thank god for the girl who delayed her.

Now I breathe in Ava's jasmine and vanilla scent, feel the exquisite warmth of her smooth skin. Her eyes are so large, so dark—twin pools of deep sapphire rather than her usual ice blue. She's close enough that if I tilt my head just a few degrees, I can touch her full, lush lips with mine.

My cock twitches at the thought, growing semi-hard. So. My body isn't dead after all.

Why?

I consider the question. I imagined many scenarios on my flight to Chiang Mai, how Ava would react at seeing me again, but none of them involved *her* asking *me* why.

"Why" is *my* question.

Why did you leave? Why didn't you wait until I was out of surgery? Why didn't you dump me face-to-face? I deserved better than a fucking cardboard box.

When the nurse brought it into my room—apparently Ava left it with the receptionist—it was like the planet fell away from under me. Everything I'd ever given her was inside it—the clothes, the accessories, the fob to the fucking Lexus. Turning away from the nurse, I clutched my chest with a trembling hand as my heart pumped icy bitterness through my veins.

"Dinner," I grate out.

"What?"

"We should have dinner."

She stares at me dumbly.

"Or we can stand here all evening long." My left leg throbs. I ignore the pain.

Suddenly she looks away. "Your date must be waiting."

For a moment, I don't understand. Then I laugh dryly. "I'm here alone."

Her gaze darts back to my face, her face registering shock and something that makes the hair on the back of my neck bristle.

Suddenly the need to corner her grows more urgent. "Dinner."

Letting her gaze slide from my face, she tries to pull away. I change my hold and grab her wrist. I haven't flown for over thirty hours to lose her now. If she's trying to solicit help, that's not working either. People aren't interested in what's going on around them. They're either minding their own business or too busy staring into their smartphones.

Her pulse flutters wildly against my palm. "Fine. Dinner."

She's still not looking at me. Why not? She used to hold my gaze for hours when we were together.

She tugs. "Let go."

"I'm not letting you go."

She lets out a slow shaky breath. I recognize that tell. She only does it when she's nervous or trying to make a very difficult decision.

"Do you have a place in mind?"

I look around and see a bunch of restaurants back on the Night Bazaar side of the street. They're busy but not full.

"There." I jerk my chin. "We can go to any one of them."

Her mouth tightens. "Slumming again?"

A corner of my lips lifts in a sardonic smile. How she's changed… I like that. At least this version is honest.

"One of the restaurants at Le Meridien then."

I half drag her to the hotel, which is right on the street. The security guards smile and greet us, and I wave at them with a grin as though dragging an unwilling woman inside is an everyday occurrence.

The second we step through the four imposing columns of the main entrance, we're plunged into a cool air-conditioned environment. The lobby is contemporary and chic with warm colors and shiny stone finishings. Lots of plushy armchairs and tables are positioned for relaxation and small, impromptu meetings.

A crisply uniformed concierge welcomes us with a friendly smile, palms together in a typical Thai greeting. I nod. "What are your dining options?"

She asks what we want, and I tell her anything is fine, but ideally something nice and expensive, emphasis on *expensive*. I pull Ava closer and put an arm around her shoulders. She feels thin… much too thin for my taste. Why the hell is she so frail?

"My date adores good food," I say in a saccharine voice.

"Well." The concierge shoots me a quick smile for indulging my significant other and recommends *Favola* on the second floor. Contemporary Italian made with Royal Project organic produce.

I give Ava a look. *Does this sound sufficiently gourmet and high class?*

She looks away again, which only makes me more determined.

One of the staff leads us to the restaurant. It isn't that busy, so we're seated immediately at a table past a glass wine cellar that occupies the center of the dining area. The host pulls out a cream-colored chair for Ava, and she sits down with forced good grace. A server comes over and gives us two menus on the table made with wood as dark as that used for the flooring.

"Would you like something to drink, sir?" he asks.

"Water. Plus…" I gesture at the racks of wine carelessly. "A Pinot Noir No. 3 if you have it." Ava reaches for the menu, and I smile. "And we know what we want."

Her chin snaps upward. "I haven't ha—"

"The most expensive appetizer," I say, pinning her with my eyes. "The most expensive entrée. And the most expensive dessert."

"Certainly, sir." The waiter confirms our order, shooting a quick glance in Ava's direction, whose face is now bright red, and vanishes.

"That was uncalled for." Her voice is barely audible, but the force of anger underneath is formidable.

I lean back expansively in my seat. "Sue me."

Our server brings out a large bottle of water and fills our glasses. Then he runs back within a minute with our wine and lets me taste. When I nod, he pours for us then disappears again.

I raise my glass with a mocking smile. "To another meeting."

She picks up hers and drinks without a word

like she's chugging down cheap vinegary junk. If she noticed the excellent vintage, she doesn't show it. But then she was rarely impressed with wine.

After placing her empty glass on the table, she looks away and leans back in her seat, toying with the neckline of her shirt. She's nervous. Feeling guilty about the way she left me? She should be. What she did was a shit move. And I want her to feel terrible about it. That's the least she owes me.

Our server brings out our appetizer. I barely glance at it. My attention is on the woman opposite.

I can't help but notice—again—how much thinner she is. And it's annoying as hell. She didn't weigh much to begin with, and she really can't afford to lose more and stay healthy.

Why should I give a damn? She should be as miserable as I've been.

But I can't help caring. She told me once…

"*Seriously? You actually* like *peanut butter and jelly sandwiches?" She makes a face, her fork hovering over her salad.*

"*Sometimes, when I'm in the mood." I grin. "Why? Did you think my favorite food was caviar or something?"*

Her nose wrinkles adorably. "It wouldn't surprise me if you were born with it clutched in your fists." She shakes her head. "I can't stand them. I even looked forward to Mondays when I was grow-ing up because of them."

"What does a PBJ have to do with Monday?"

"I got to go back to school."

She stretches her legs under the shabby table at the small Greek restaurant and pops an olive into her mouth.

I laugh. "You must've been a nerd." *I gener-ally found Mondays unbearable because my classes were boring and pointless.*

She snorted. "No. It's because on Mondays I was able to eat something other than peanut butter and jelly sandwiches."

"I don't get it."

A mild flush rises in her cheeks. "When I was growing up, that was basically all we could afford. My mom... She tried really hard, but it wasn't easy on minimum wage."

I still can't quite connect the dots, which makes me scowl. I'm usually great *at connecting dots.*

"You can't relate, can you?" *she asks, half-amused and half-sad.*

"Sorry." *Ava seems disappointed somehow, so I do something I don't usually do with women—I explain.* "I grew up in Europe. Boarding schools." *The best money could buy, et cetera, et cetera.*

Sighing, she drops her gaze. "We were poor enough that I got free lunches, and the school *cafeteria served pasta and pizza and…you know. Anything but PB and J."*

I stare at her. I donate regularly to Elizabeth's charitable causes, but I don't understand that kind of poverty. I probably never will. I study her thin frame. I assumed she got her figure from diet and exercise, but now I realize she got it from not eating enough—from hunger. The fact that Ava suffered at all makes me angry, but I stop before showing how upset I am. Her gaze has lost its happy glimmer.

I force myself to say lightly, "Then it's a good thing none of the restaurants I plan to take you to serve that abominable sandwich."

She blinks, then giggles. "Oh yeah. That'd definitely be grounds for a breakup."

As the merry tinkling sound of her laughter washes over me, I vow she will never lack for anything. I will never let her go hungry again.

And I'm not letting her go hungry now.

"Eat." I push the appetizer toward her. "We can talk afterward."

She stares at a point somewhere behind me. "Why don't we just pretend that we ate?"

"Because Ava… I'm hungry, and I'm ill-tempered when I'm hungry. You know that."

"Ah yes. You and your food." Her lips purse for a moment—a sign that she's thinking. Finally, she reaches over and begins nibbling. Then she starts eating with more gusto. Probably it's finally hit her that she really ought to eat more.

I sip my wine and let the excellent flavor coat my mouth. Just what happened to her since she left me? It never crossed my mind that she might not be doing well. In my mind's eye she lives a kickass life, carefree and merry without a fucked-up shit like me by her side.

I wait until we're done with our entrées, noting her clean plate with approval. I give her the rest of the wine, and she accepts. Her face is no longer pale, the alcohol and food giving her a rosy glow.

"Thank you," she says.

"My pleasure."

My well-mannered response rolls out, bred into me by a desperate need to please my mother. But it isn't just a platitude. Watching her eat the food I provided for her is satisfying. Absurdly so.

She puts a hand on her belly. "I can't eat anymore. So…" She starts to push her chair back.

I raise a hand. "We're not finished."

"Lucas… There's nothing for us to discuss." Her eyes slide away.

She's hiding something, something she knows will upset me if I find out. An ugly knot of jealousy starts to burn in my gut.

"Got a sugar daddy waiting?"

Both her eyebrows rise as she swings her gaze back on my face. "Ex*cuse* me?"

"Oh, right. 'Sugar daddy' is offensive. Should I say 'boyfriend' instead?"

She snorts, then shakes her head.

The knot eases. *Not a boyfriend then.*

"Why are you so anxious to get out of here? And why are you always avoiding looking at me?"

Her tongue sweeps over her lips—a nervous gesture, and I can't help but notice the soft fullness of her mouth, with upper and lower lips equally plump and oh-so sensitive. I almost run a hand over my eyes. I so fucking need to get laid.

She makes a show of pulling out her phone to check the time. "I have a flight to catch."

"Which doesn't leave for more than three hours."

"Okay, just how much do you know about my life?"

"You still haven't answered my questions."

She tilts her chin up, meets my gaze, and says, "I'm looking at you now." She sighs to good effect, but there is an unnatural stiffness to her that betrays her. She might be a decent actress, but I grew up with Ryder Reed, who's a freaking brilliant actor. After a moment she adds, "Was I supposed to stare at you the entire time we were eating?"

"No."

"Lucas, I have to go—"

"Is it the scar?"

My hair usually hides it, but the cover isn't perfect. I push it out of my face so she can see the whole ugly jaggedness on the left side of my face.

She inhales sharply and her hand flies to her mouth. "What happened?"

The question severs the tight rein I have on my temper. My voice rises. "What the hell do you mean, *what happened?*" I drop my hand, letting my hair conceal my disfigurement again. "You were there."

She shakes her head. The luminous sheen of unshed tears in her eyes is like pouring oil over a fire. What gives her the right to look so stricken when she dumped me like so much trash? *How dare she?*

Maybe I underestimated her acting skills.

"You came by the hospital and left me a *box.*" I don't mean to sound so damn bitter, but I can't help myself. It festers like a wound that won't heal.

"I was giving you back the things you gave me." Her voice is hoarse.

"They were *gifts.* You were supposed to keep them."

Then the fucking box wouldn't have sat in a corner of my office and taunted me for months.

You weren't enough. None of the things you gave her—none of the things you could have given her— ever mattered.

Failure. Failure. Failure.

"It wasn't right for me to keep them, given the circumstances. I couldn't take anything from you."

"But you did. You took something from me, and I want it back."

The blood drains from her face, leaving it sheet white. She sways, knocking over her half-full wineglass. The Pinot Noir spills; the stemware shatters against the floor. The red drips over the table's edge, soaking her shirt and jeans, but she doesn't seem to notice.

Alarm clangs through me.

"Ava!"

She starts to slump. I jump up to catch her lest she fall on the broken glass.

My arms wrap around her. She's so damn slight, so fragile. Her skin feels too cool, her breathing shallow. Her heart is racing like a terrified sparrow's.

Our waiter assesses the situation and comes over with a broom and dustpan. A busboy appears with a couple of hand towels. I help Ava up, not caring that the wine is staining my clothes.

"*Ava.*"

She blinks a few times and looks up at me.

There's some life in her eyes now, and I let out a shuddering breath.

"I have to go," she whispers almost soundlessly. "*I have to go.*"

"Ava."

She shoves me with more strength than I would have thought possible from such a small body. I stagger, my body tilting backward. The stiff muscles in my left leg protest the abrupt movement. As I step back, she grabs her purse and runs.

"Ava!" I start to rush after her the second I regain my balance.

"Sir." The waiter physically blocks my way. "The bill."

Ah shit. I reach into my pocket, pull out my money clip and hand him a couple of hundred-dollar bills. "That should cover it."

He glances at the money, but doesn't move. "This is not Thai baht."

"It's U.S. dollars."

"But, sir…"

"You have currency exchange places everywhere! Do it and keep the change."

The waiter wets his lips and shakes his head. "We cannot accept foreign money in this restaurant. If you want, you can exchange at the concierge desk."

Oh for fuck's sake! I throw my Amex Centurion Card his way. "Charge it. I'll be right back."

Before he can protest again, I dodge around him and run out. Ava's gone. I search the elevator bank, but she isn't there either.

I drive my fingers into my hair and bite back a curse. I *have* to talk to her. Something I said—the thing about wanting what she took from me— scared the shit out of her.

I have to know what she did two years ago.

FOUR

Ava

Y OU TOOK SOMETHING FROM ME, AND *I want it back.*

He can't know. How could he? I've been so careful. Used my middle name. There's absolutely nothing that can tie me to it.

But what if he found out anyway?

My belly churns dangerously as Lucas's words ring in my head. My fingers are shaky, and it takes me two attempts before the door unlocks. I shove the card in the slot by the entryway and run straight for the toilet.

The second my knees hit the cold floor, everything comes up. I retch until there's nothing left, until my stomach and throat are so raw it hurts to breathe. My legs feel like quivering gelatin, and I slowly sit back and stare at the wall.

Lucas has money, and he's very well-connected. Google told me he's related to some very powerful people.

If he really wanted to, he could figure it out.

I jerk my torso back up and dry-heave into the toilet. There's absolutely nothing left in my gut, but I can't stop. By the time I'm through, I'm completely wrung out. I collapse on the floor, feeling like a corpse.

Why did I tell him I had a flight to catch? What if he follows me to the airport?

I need a simple game plan, something I can stick to no matter how emotionally upset I am.

Deny everything. Pretend ignorance. Distract him if I have to.

Besides, it's not like he has any room to talk or get upset. What he had his brother say to me…

He has no right to barge back into my life like he's entitled to something.

Anger reenergizes me. I push myself up. I need to get back on my feet and keep living my life. *Fuck Lucas.* Fuck him and his money and his gifts and his entitlement. I've been fine without him, and I will *continue* to be fine without him.

I flush the toilet, rinse out my mouth, splash some cold water on my face. I'm still pale, except for the red splotches on my cheeks. My eyes look listless, and now that the lipstick's worn off, my mouth is almost ashen.

This won't do. I look weak and pathetic. And the wine stains on my shirt and jeans just add to the air of slovenliness.

I change into a fresh set of clothes—a fitted pink button-down shirt and black jeans—and reapply my makeup. I'm not great at applying cosmetics, but I know enough to make myself look okay, like I haven't just been ambushed by the former love of my life.

Lipstick goes on last. I finally settle on a bright red. It's bold and aggressive, just the color I need to feel like myself again.

That done, I toss everything into my suitcase. I don't have the mental energy to organize everything neatly like I did when I arrived. But it doesn't matter. I'll have to wash most of it when I get home anyway.

I drag my rolling suitcase out of my room, my chin held high. The entire time I'm checking out and requesting the concierge to grab me a cab, nobody approaches. My eyes scan the lobby, but I don't see anyone except a few Chinese tourists lounging by the tables closest to the Latest Recipe restaurant.

In spite of that, the base of my skull tingles as I climb inside the waiting taxi. *Relax, girl. Lucas is gone. Stop being paranoid.*

I look back to make sure. There aren't any cars following us.

See?

He probably decided I was too crazy and split. Now that I think about it, my reaction was a bit over the top. Knocking the wine over and breaking the glass? Almost fainting? Running out of the place like my clothes were on fire?

I acted *insane*...which turned out to be perfect. Nothing repels a man better than a woman who looks like she's off her meds.

By the time I reach the check-in counter at the airport, I almost feel normal again. I slide my passport on the scratched and worn surface toward the airline representative. She takes my ID and types a few things on her computer, the keyboard clacking loudly. A frown tightens her forehead.

"Miss. Um... There seems to be a problem."

Shit. "Is the flight delayed?" I really want to make my connection from Incheon to Osaka.

"No, but... You are not on this flight. Are you sure you're supposed to fly today?"

"Yes." I pull out my phone and show her the email I received with my flight information. "See?"

"Mm." She nods. "But our system does not have you as flying today or...any day." She purses her bright pink lips. "Let me check something. I'll be right back."

She spins her wheeled chair, gestures at a middle-aged Thai man in an ill-fitting dark brown suit and gives him a thirty-second spiel in Thai. He listens, nodding a few times, then talks into his radio.

Come on. I have to be on this flight. I have to get out of here today.

Finally, the man comes over. "There's been a change in your itinerary," he says, his English slightly halting but still confident. "Do you mind if I take you to the new gate?"

"Sure. Please," I say, relieved.

"Don't forget your passport."

"Right." I grab it from the counter and walk with him.

He takes me past the main international terminal's security and immigration control. We get to a small, private area where a glossy black suv is waiting. "Please get in."

Unease trails a cold finger down my spine. "What is this about?"

"It will take you to your new jet." He smiles winsomely. "There's been a change of plane."

I eye him. My imagination says he's part of an elaborate plan to kidnap me or worse. But the logical part of my brain says he's just an airport employee doing his job. He has a plastic security badge with his headshot and name clipped to his jacket, and the lady at the check-in counter obviously trusted him.

Get real. I'm just not important enough for anyone to go to this much trouble. This is what I get for having low blood sugar—nonsensical thoughts. I should save them for my stories, although I haven't finished any.

"Thank you." I flash him a quick smile to disguise my ridiculous suspicions.

He opens the rear door, and I climb in. He follows, settling next to me and shutting the door.

The car moves smoothly along the asphalt, passing by shuttles, an airline catering truck and a huge jet bearing an Air Asia logo.

"Would you like something to drink?" the man asks.

Startled, I look his way and see a selection of alcohol and juices laid out on a built-in shelf. I don't really want anything, but I haven't eaten. Well. I did, but nothing stayed down…

"Orange juice, please, if you have any."

He pulls out a bottle from the silver ice bucket and twists the cap for me. I murmur my thanks and sip the juice. My throat is still raw, and the acidic drink burns on the way down. After a few mouthfuls I put the cap back on and place the bottle in the cup holder.

The car finally stops. My guide clambers out first and holds open the door. I climb down, then stare at a sleek private jet gleaming under the airport's huge halogen lights.

"What is this?"

I might be young and naïve, but I wasn't born yesterday. Airlines do not put you on a private jet just because there's been a problem with your flight.

He looks at me like I'm an idiot. Maybe my crazy imagination has been right all along. This really is some elaborate scheme to kidnap me. I take a step ba—

"Ava."

Every cell in my body freezes at Lucas's voice. I spin around and see him walking toward me.

He's changed into different clothes, too. The undone collar of his black shirt shows the strong column of his throat and a hint of muscular chest. His black linen trousers fit him perfectly, hugging his lean, tight hips and thickly muscled legs. He looks expensive, aloof and untouchably self-possessed.

What the hell is he doing here?

Blood roars in my head, my stomach churning. It's good that I didn't drink more of the juice. I turn to the man from the airport.

"I can't fly on that jet."

He frowns. "But…your assistant arranged…"

My assistant? Hysteria bubbles inside me. "I don't have an assistant."

"But—"

"I'll take it from here." Lucas hands him a few bills. The white background and brownish ink tell me they're thousand-baht notes, worth about thirty bucks each. "Thank you for your help."

The man smiles, his face relaxing into a jovial, pleased mask. "My pleasure, sir. Have a good flight home."

He gets inside the SUV, and the car pulls away.

"No!" I take a couple of steps after the vanishing vehicle.

Lucas's hand circles my wrist. "Too late. They're not coming back."

"What the hell is the matter with you?" I rage, yanking my arm. But his hold on me is like a manacle.

The dark eyebrow cocks, slanting arrogantly. "Is it so wrong to want to reduce the carbon footprint?"

The non-sequitur brings my brain to a screeching halt. I can't process what he's trying to say, and my panic recedes into the background for the moment.

"What?"

"Your ticket's gone, and I have extra room on my jet."

"I suppose my ticket being gone has something to do with my 'assistant'?"

He doesn't respond but I know.

"What do you want? Wasn't dinner enough?"

"Board the plane, Ava." His tone is firm and commanding. "You're delaying our departure."

"It'll be a cold day in hell before I get on that plane of yours."

He smiles with the ease of a man used to getting his way. What I wouldn't give to wipe that expression off his face.

"Is that so? I guess they'll need to break out the blankets in Hades tonight." Before I can respond, he picks me up and tosses me over a shoulder like a sack of rice. Blood rushes to my face, but that isn't the only thing making my cheeks heat.

"*Put me down, you bastard!*"

I lash out with my legs, trying to hit him in the ribs or wherever it's going to hurt enough for him to stop this, but he wraps an arm around the backs of my knees, effectively stopping me. My head bounces on his back, and I pound the thick slab of muscle there, but I might as well be smacking a rock.

"You're making a scene, Ava. Bad girl."

He smacks my ass with his free hand. It stings enough to make me see red with outrage. I flail around, trying to get down or hurt him or even better—accomplish both.

"Keep doing that and I'll drop you. Which will hurt."

"Like you care!"

"But I do. Very much."

The softly spoken words seem oddly sincere. And for some absurd reason I believe him.

"Then let me down," I say quietly.

"Not until you're on board."

He takes the steps up to the plane. His gait is uneven. Did he hurt himself? Or did I manage to hit him hard enough to make him limp?

A tiny part of me says he deserved it, but I feel bad anyway. I don't want him injured. I just want to be left alone.

"Welcome aboard, Mr. Reed," comes a friendly greeting in a professional female voice.

Oh my fucking god. *Kill—me—now.* "We have a crew member here?"

"The plane's not going to fly itself."

I cover my face with my hands. I don't drop them when he puts me back on my feet. I don't resist when he sets me in a plushy leather seat and buckles the belt.

This has to be a nightmare. A horrible dream induced by anxiety and guilt and nerves and wine and stress. If I can just wake myself up, I'll be back in my hotel room after a refreshing nap. I'll go to the Night Bazaar and have that curry I saw in my dream.

Yes. That's exactly what I'll do…just as soon as I wake up.

"Would you like something to drink?" the cabin attendant asks.

I open one eye and peer upward. She looks back at me with a professional, polished smile as though she hasn't just witnessed my being hauled on board like a sack of cornmeal.

Okay. I need to face the reality that Lucas did indeed carry me onto this infernal jet like a… possession, and the people who work for him are unlikely to help me get off it.

"What do you have?" I ask in my calmest voice.

"She won't touch anything other than Dom," Lucas interjects. There's a glass of champagne on the armrest next to him, and a little movie plays in my mind: me snatching the bubbly and tossing it in his face.

"I'll have what he's having," I say with a sweet smile for the cabin attendant.

The woman's composure stays intact. "An excellent choice."

I accept the proffered champagne served in a real flute—I've never been served in an actual glass when flying—and take a tentative sip. The carbonation tickles my mouth and nostrils, and the wine goes down smoothly with a hint of vanilla and honey.

I look everywhere but at Lucas as I nurse my drink. The interior of the jet is teal blue and mahogany with light cream-colored leather. There are four plushy seats that recline all the way back until you can lie flat. A workstation's built into the other side, and there's a well-cushioned bench behind us for casual relaxation and chatting. I spot a door in the back, probably leading to a private room.

Everything gleams and looks hideously luxurious. This is my first time on the plane, but Faye Belbin's undoubtedly been on it more than once. The notion clenches around my chest, making it impossible to breathe.

She looks like she deserves to be pampered with a toy like this. You? Well. Look at you.

Yes. Look at me. In my cheap clothes that I picked up on sale.

I put the champagne down.

"We'll be taking off in ten minutes." The cabin attendant smiles at Lucas as she speaks, and she continues to keep her focus on him.

My stomach burns. It can't be a good idea to have alcohol so soon after throwing up.

"Once we reach cruising altitude, I'll be serving you a light snack of chicken satay, salad lightly tossed in pineapple vinaigrette, vegetarian fried rice and figs stuffed with goat cheese and honey-glazed walnuts. And seventy minutes before we land—"

"We can discuss the other options later," Lucas says smoothly, interrupting her monologue.

"Certainly, sir." She takes his empty glass. I hand her mine although it's still half-full.

"Dom not good enough?" Lucas asks.

I stare directly at him. "No. I didn't want to hang on to it during takeoff."

"You don't look good."

I tilt my chin, my mouth firm. "I'm fine."

I'm more than fine. Lucas is welcome to play whatever game he wants, but I have my own plan. I don't have to do anything except wait until we hit cruising altitude and nap—or at least pretend to. We're flying red-eye, and there's nothing unusual about wanting to sleep until we land.

I relax my muscles, one by one, and force myself to feign a calm I don't feel.

THE GIRL

THE MOTHER LOOKS DOWN AT THE CHILD. The toddler is barely two, but she's skinnier than a spaghetti noodle.

The father of the child does not wish to marry. He is often away on work, and he worries about losing benefits. The mother worries too. They can't make ends meet without EBT and what little assistance they get from the government.

At least he gave the girl a name. "I love her, and I love you for giving her to me," he said.

"Would he have said that if you were a boy?" the woman whispers to the girl. "Would he have married me? Men love daughters, but men *love* sons. Strong sons to carry on the line."

The girl looks at the woman innocently, then grins.

She stares at her child, unsmiling, and sighs. "Why bother? You still aren't a boy. Should of known it would happen when I learned it was a girl in my belly. Men always want sons. Your grandpa did too." She shakes her head. "He was so disappointed when he got me instead."

The girl extends her arms toward the mother, asking to be held. The mother gets up. "I gotta do the dishes," she says. "Always more stuff to do."

As she walks away to the kitchen, she mutters, "Should of aimed for a boy. Every man wants a boy."

FIVE

Ava

I CLOSE MY EYES THE MOMENT THE PLANE REVS up for takeoff. I keep them closed as the plane speeds down the runway…then tilts upward, reaching for cruising altitude.

When the plane finally becomes horizontal again, I open one eye and hit a button to turn my seat into a flat bed. As soon as I can stretch out, I turn my back to Lucas and tuck my hands under my head.

"It's not going to work," Lucas says.

"I can't hear you. Because I'm sleeping."

"If you don't talk to me now, I'm taking us all the way to America. That's a damn long flight. I'm sure it'll give us a chance to chat."

I jackknife up and glare at him. "Are you kidding me?"

"Nope."

"You can't do that," I hiss, keenly aware of the cabin attendant's presence.

"Sure I can." He sweeps an arm around. "It's my plane."

"That's *kidnapping!*"

"And I care because…?"

"I'll press charges!"

"Please do. But you'll press them in the States." He reclines his seat and relaxes. "Besides, who's going to believe you've been kidnapped? Kidnappers don't use private jets."

Anger heats my face. "Are you fucking serious? Your being rich doesn't make what you're doing lawful."

He shrugs. "Flying a friend home was perfectly legal last time I checked."

"You bastard!"

He smiles, but the dark gleam in his eye remains implacable. "Thank you. It warms my heart to know you have such a high opinion of me."

Smacking my forehead with the heel of my hand a couple of times, I think fast. Back at the restaurant, he said I took something from him. I freaked out because that announcement felt like an ambush. I won't overreact again. *But what if he knows?* I have no clue what I'm going to do if he does. I just know I can't go to the States right now.

I cross my arms. "Fine."

"Let's eat."

"I'm not hungry. You have the singular effect of killing my appetite." And I don't want a repeat of what happened earlier. I doubt my stomach lining could survive another round of vomiting.

The muscles in his jaw flex. "If the scar on my cheek bothers you that much, I'll sit to your left."

I stare at him. "That's not what I meant."

He stares back. "Does it matter?"

I look away. Nothing matters except getting him to take me to Japan and then leave me alone forever.

He unbuckles and moves to a seat facing me. Stretching out his left leg until the foot encroaches into my personal space, he tilts his head and looks at me with tooth-grinding insolence. "You will eat."

Before I can bristle at his high-handedness, he signals the cabin attendant, and she quickly serves us a tray of the food items she described earlier.

When I don't move, he stabs a piece of fruit with his own fork and hands it to me. "Eat." Then he smirks. "Afraid it's poisoned?"

"That's a possibility." But I take the fork and bite into the proffered fig, which is stuffed with goat cheese. I acquired a taste for figs in Japan, but I've never had one prepared like this. It's extra sweet…and the pungent taste of goat cheese goes well with the gooey meat of the fruit.

It's really quite good. It would go well with the champagne they served earlier.

"Why did you bolt the way you did?" Lucas asks.

I almost choke, but manage not to by taking a quick sip of water. "It was the food. It made me nauseous."

"Bullshit. We had the same thing, and I was perfectly fine."

"Maybe for you, but it wasn't for me."

"You're evading the topic."

"What makes you think I still owe you my time and mental energy after two years?"

"The accident that left my face scarred also mangled my body. Cracked ribs and a broken leg tend to lay a man flat despite his best intentions."

I tilt my head at the bitterness darkening his narrowed eye. "It didn't take you two years to recover."

"No, thank god."

My throat closes up, and I can't eat anymore. I put my fork down. "I was there."

His eyebrow arches.

"At the hospital. My roommate Erin…"

"The nursing student," he murmurs.

I'm surprised he remembers. "She was at the hospital for some class." The instructors required the students to follow doctors and nurses around to observe and learn. "She saw you come in on a stretcher and left me a message. When I got there…"

Lucas's mouth twists as he brings a glass of some kind of amber-colored liquor to his lips. "I must've looked like shit."

"Your injuries had nothing to do with my decision!" I breathe out roughly. The abject mortification of the moment floods through me, as though the meeting took place minutes ago rather than a couple of years. Not even my father's betrayal made me feel so cheap and dirty. My hands shake from the bitter memory.

Lucas pales. He's staring at me like I'm an enemy he'd like to stab with the butter knife clenched in his hand. "What does that mean?"

"Why don't you ask your brother? The really nasty one."

He lifts an eyebrow. "Brother?"

"Surprised I know about your siblings? I guess you must be, since you never introduced me to your family in the seven months we were together." And I was too stupid to wonder about that, accepting his explanation that his family lived far away and was too busy to keep in touch. "Blake," I bite out the name. I'll never forget that piece of work—how he made me feel:

He looked down his nose and spoke to me in a silky but venomous voice.

"*You're Lucas's mistake, a gold digger trying to swindle money out of him when he's down and vulnerable. Better women than you have tried, sweetheart, so get the hell out of here before I ruin you. Oh, you object to my description? Should I prove how right I am then? It'd be my pleasure to dig into your past and see what kind of dirt is hiding behind that pretty face. A girl like you probably has more dirt than Mount. Everest, and I'll make sure everyone knows about it. By the time I'm through, you won't be able to suck a cock for a dollar.*"

"Blake." Lucas runs a hand down his face. "Fuck."

"He made me realize you and I had nothing together." Worse than nothing. Lucas had never told his family about me—I was some kind of *dirty little secret.*

He looks up at the cabin ceiling briefly. When he speaks, his voice is soft. "Ava, we had something good together."

I shake my head. "What we had was sex—good sex, but just sex."

"Damn it, Ava. It was more than that for me."

"Really? Then who's Faye Belbin?"

Shock flashes in his gaze. In a different situation with a different person, I might be pleased. "What, you thought I wouldn't find out?" I let out a dry laugh to disguise the sick feeling growing in my chest. "I got smarter after my meeting with your brother, so I looked you and your family up. It's amazing how informative Google can be. Turns out you *aren't* some college instructor like you led me to believe, and Faye's been the woman on your arm every time you attend a high society function."

"Ava, she's nothing," Lucas says, apparently recovered.

"Nothing? Really? Do you take 'nothing' to balls and premieres and expensive parties?"

His eyebrows pinch together, and he reaches for another drink. "I occasionally need someone as a date, and when we were together I didn't want to ask you to miss classes because of my social obligations."

Anger courses through my veins like acid. "Are you shitting me? You're actually trying to blame *me* for taking her to those events?" I clench my hands, resisting the urge to throw my water at him. "Would you have been okay if I'd taken a guy to a party because I didn't want to *bother you?*" I ask, even though I know he'll lie and say, *Yes, I'd have been perfectly fine with it.* A man like him always has a few slick words to justify what he does.

He stares at me for a while, then finally says, "No."

"Sure, lie throu—" I stop abruptly. "'No'?"

"No."

I'm deflated…but only a little. "Well, then, that makes you a hypocrite."

"I know, and I'm sorry. But I swear Faye and I are just friends now. Nothing happened."

"Nothing…" I cross my arms. "So you never slept with her? Not ever?"

"Not while I was with you."

The bitter knot I've had in my gut since finding out about Faye eases a bit before I remember he hasn't always been entirely honest with me. "Not while I was with you" sounds like he's claiming he was faithful to me for our seven months… but it might also mean he slept with her during those months but when I wasn't physically with him. After all, he did take her to those parties, and Faye is a seriously beautiful woman. Hell, I might be tempted if I were a man.

I shake my head. "Well, none of that matters now. I made the right decision to leave you."

His eyes sharpen. "Ava."

"It's been two years, Lucas. You can't just," I cast around for the right word, "unilaterally decide to come back and impose yourself on me."

A dull shade of red colors his cheeks. A vein throbs in his forehead, a clear sign that his patience is wearing thin. "Was it fair then that you *unilaterally* decided to dump me when I was at my most vulnerable? I have no idea what Blake said, but you never gave me a chance to explain."

"Because you were deliberately staying away from me." If he'd come for me as soon as he was out of surgery… Maybe we would've ended up differently.

"I stayed away because I didn't want to look clingy and pitiable. I was waiting for you to come back."

"Then why now?"

"Someone let me know where you were. Once I knew…I couldn't stay away."

"Then pretend you don't know anymore. That's what I want." I dig the heels of my palms into my eyes. "Lucas, I really need some sleep. Now that we've talked, can you just land in Osaka and let me off?"

He presses his lips together. "We are not finished."

Every cell in my body tenses, ready for a fight.

"But I'll let you off in Osaka."

I sag in my seat. "Thank you."

This is a victory. I got to say my piece, and he's going to let me go, contrary to his announcement.

But somehow I don't feel triumphant.

SIX

Lucas

I WATCH THE TAXI DISAPPEAR INTO THE EARLY Osaka dawn…carrying Ava away. It's an effort not to run after it. I hate that she's vanishing right before my eyes.

But she's not really gone. You know exactly where she is now.

The talk I planned to have with her didn't go as anticipated. Truth be told, I'm still reeling a bit. I had no clue she'd met Blake—or found out about Faye and drawn the worst conclusions imaginable.

It's clear enough what Ava thought was going on between Faye and me. Clear…and fucking unfair because nothing's happened between us. I haven't touched Faye in five years.

But Blake…

I have no clue what he's done. Thanks to his snotty mother, he's related to the Pryces, one of the richest and most well-connected families in the world. He carries himself with a superior attitude, and being the oldest, he's patronizing on top of everything else.

I pull out my phone and call him.

"Blake," he answers.

"What the hell did you do to—"

"I do a lot of things. Be more specific."

I hiss out a breath. "Condescending asshole."

"I did something to a condescending asshole? Sounds like he deserved it."

"No, *you're* the—" I tighten my hand around my phone, wishing it were Blake's neck. "What did you do *to Ava?*"

Blake's voice is flat. "Ava?"

"Don't play dumb. You know exactly who I'm talking about."

"Actually, I don't." There is genuine bemusement in his quiet tone.

Is whatever he did so insignificant that he doesn't remember? It's a real possibility with Blake. He's excellent at compartmentalizing things, and a lot of those things go into a box labeled "beneath notice".

"She's my…"

It is now my turn to stop and consider. Exactly what was Ava to me back then? We were exclusive, fucked often and spent some time together although I made sure to return to my own place every night. I also paid some of her expenses, even though she wasn't exactly "kept". No. She was too independent and too angry about me paying for anything to be a kept woman.

But she wasn't precisely my girlfriend either. What we had wasn't really dating…

Finally I settle on: "She's a woman I started seeing almost three years ago. She broke it off two years ago, and now I find out you're the cause."

"She specifically blamed me?"

"Yes. She did."

"I have no idea who or what you're talking about. I don't meddle in other people's love lives. You know that."

I do, but… "She wasn't lying."

"Neither am I." Blake's voice is cold and sharp. "I don't know how well you know her, but I don't appreciate either of you dragging me into your relationship mess."

I scowl. He is definitely not lying. He's too self-righteously angry. Did Ava lie? Or maybe she misunderstood…

"Why are you talking with this woman?" Blake says. "Are you going to propose to her?"

I snort. If I asked her to marry me for a year, she'd brain me with that handbag she carries everywhere. "No."

"Then forget her and go after someone with more potential."

"I'm not going to marry for a year for the portraits. Dad's not going to control me like that," I say, feeling a wave of petty annoyance.

"Not even for Elizabeth?"

Trust Blake to hit below the belt. I could deal with my brothers not getting the damned portraits, but my half-sister is another matter. She's just too damn nice to become collateral damage. After all, how do you look the other way from a woman whose goal in life is to change the world one hungry child at a time?

"Not even for her," I insist, just to be contrary.

"You know Elliot got married, right?"

I laugh dryly. My twin is the last person Blake should bring up if he wants to change my mind. "Oh yeah. Huge sacrifice for him, marrying a hot stripper. I bet he auditioned her—missionary, doggy style, up against a wall. Blow jobs. All the positions to get the position."

"I think you're wrong. She didn't look like some cheap ho you can buy with a few bucks."

I snort. "How the hell would you know? You have the sensitivity of a bull on Novocain."

He grunts in response.

"Let's say you're right about the cheap part. I bet he still had to test her for STDs."

"You're a cynical bastard."

"Pot, stop calling the kettle black." This isn't helping. "I gotta go."

"Where are you?"

"Overseas. I have things to take care of."

"This Ava girl?"

"Yes."

Blake sighs. "I'm not going to tell you to get hitched just for the portraits. Grandpa didn't paint them so Dad could use them to leverage us around."

"But…?" There's always a *but* with Blake.

"But if you are going to do it, find someone who understands how things are. A woman who won't be hurt when you can't give her the world on a silver platter in some garish romantic gesture." He hangs up.

An image of Faye flashes through my mind. She fits Blake's requirements to a T. She's widowed now, but she used to be married to a rich land developer. While he was alive, she hosted big events by his side, looked gracious and beautiful on his arm when the occasion called for it, and didn't start or spread rumors. Most importantly, she doesn't push or demand. She accepted my decision to end our affair with good grace, and we've remained friends.

If I explain the situation to her and ask her to help, she'll marry me, no questions asked. She'll also sign whatever prenup my lawyer drafts.

But a sixth sense tells me if I marry her, it will mean losing Ava forever. She won't give me another look even if I divorce Faye once the year is up.

Faye has nothing to do with anything, you dumbass. Ava doesn't want *me*. If she did, she wouldn't have dumped me the moment she faced Blake or learned about Faye. She would've stuck around until I was out of the OR and had a chance to explain.

Much to my bitter bewilderment, Ava's very presence made me feel something other than barren coldness, even when she was delivering cruel blows about how I was unworthy of her time and attention. If that makes me pathetic, fine. I'm sick of living an empty husk of a life. Until I met—and then lost—her, I was never, ever aware of this horrible chill that nothing except Ava can thaw.

I want to be free of her so I don't need to be around her to feel. That's the least I deserve.

Twenty-four weeks. One week for every month she left me. Surely that will provide enough familiarity-bred contempt to wash my hands of her forever.

Plan fully formed, I make a call.

YOUNG DREAMS

"HEY SWEETHEART."

It's a warm, soft greeting, but the girl doesn't look up. Her father has missed her birthday again. He always misses her birthdays. School plays and Christmases, too.

She's sitting on the edge of her small worn bed. The mattress is so old it no longer has any bounce. He squats in front of her and puts a hand on her knee.

"Sweetie, I'm so sorry." He sighs. "Daddy had to work."

"You always have to work," she whispers, her gaze cast down.

He looks away, then reaches behind him and presents a glossy pink, black and white bag bearing a store logo. *Victoria's Secret*, it reads. "Here you go."

When she doesn't reach for it, he pulls a doll out of the bag. "Look. Isn't it pretty?"

It's a girl doll with blank eyes. Her dress is pink and frilly, and there is a slight scuff mark on her right cheek.

"She's hurt," the father says. "Nobody wanted her, but I thought you would want to be her friend."

She takes the gift. Her father can't buy her anything new and nice, she knows that. He's doing the best he can.

They are poor. That will not change no matter what. This is not about her being a girl.

Apparently interpreting her acceptance as forgiveness, he sits next to her on the bed and puts an arm around her skinny shoulders.

"I'm so sorry, sweetheart. Daddy has to work or we can't eat."

"I know."

Her mother has two jobs. The kids in her school call her poor even though most of them get free lunches just like her anyway.

"I have to leave before dinner," he says.

"Work again?"

He gives her a tired smile. "Yeah. But I'll be back soon."

She nods. He's always away. He says the money is better if he travels.

She wishes he didn't have to travel so much. But he said if he didn't, then her mother might need to take on another job.

Her mother is always so tired. The girl doesn't want her mother to work more.

Later that day, the girl clenches her hand around a few old and worn bills and coins. They're sweaty from her palm.

Six dollars and fifty-six cents is all the money she's saved from her allowance. When she gets an allowance.

Swallowing hard, she places everything on the scarred dining room table where her mother puts down two plates of PB and J sandwiches. Both have crusts since they can't afford to waste even a crumb.

"What's this?" the mother asks.

"Can you buy me some lottery tickets?"

The mother stares at her. "What for?"

"To win money. I heard Brian talk about it in school."

Brian is a jerk who loves to talk in a stuffy-nosed voice she hates, but he knows a lot of things she doesn't. He said his dad was going to buy ten tickets. When his friends asked why he wasn't buying any, he looked at them like they were morons. "Kids can't buy lottery tickets."

Three hundred million dollars in the jackpot.

She can't count that high, but she knows it's a lot of money. Enough to make her family really rich—*millionaires*, according to Brian.

Millionaires don't have to work so much. Millionaire dads can stay home and not miss birthdays and school plays and Christmases. And millionaire families don't have to eat PB and J all the time.

If her family just had more money, they'd be all right.

SEVEN

Ava

I'M DEAD TIRED BY THE TIME I REACH THE small apartment I share with Bennie. Private jet or not, I didn't get much sleep on the flight. I was too tense and too aware of Lucas.

I reminded myself over and over about how he used me, but it wasn't enough. My entire body was prickling like it was being enveloped in heat after being out in particularly grueling cold weather. Much to my mortification, the flesh between my legs throbbed as I remembered the decadent, insatiable things he used to do to me.

I press the spot between my eyebrows and breathe out. I'm just tired. That's the only reason I'm letting myself feel anything other than disdain for Lucas.

I forcibly evict all thoughts of Lucas and concentrate on the present. Our apartment is a 2LDK—two bedrooms plus a larger area that serves as a "living-dining-kitchen". Not that it's really large; the place is tiny by American standards, actually smaller than some of the shared dorm suites in college. But space is at a premium in Japan, especially in a big city like Osaka.

I step into the entryway, take off my shoes and call out, "Tadaima."

It loosely means "I'm home" in Japanese. Since it's local custom to say it every time you come home, I've started saying it too.

There's no responding "okaeri", so Bennie's probably either asleep or out. He often sleeps in on the weekends, and on the rare occasions he gets up early, he goes out. He says hanging around the apartment feels like being stuck in a hamster cage."

I go to my room. Unlike Bennie's, mine doesn't have tatami-mat flooring. There's a kind of synthetic, slightly cushy wood-like material instead. It's actually pretty easy on the feet. There's no bed in the room, just a low table with a seat cushion underneath. A small closet with sliding paper doors has my clothes and the futon set I pull out every night. I set down my suitcase, unroll the futon and pass out on top of the blanket.

When I open my eyes, it's semi-bright in the room. My thin curtains don't block the sun very well. A good thing too; otherwise I would've overslept every morning I've been in Japan. I hate getting up early.

I take my phone out to check the time. It's a little after four p.m. I have an alert—a new email from my foster mother, Darcy McIntire. She lives in Virginia with her husband Ray. I lie back on the futon and read it.

Subject: Holiday Plans?

Ava,

It's been so long since we last saw you. How are you?

We are doing fabulous. Mia is also doing well. We're attaching her latest photos for you to look at. She looks a lot like you, especially the eyes and mouth. Ray keeps saying she's going to break some hearts when she grows up. I agree.

Unable to wait, I click on the four photos she sent along with the email. They show a toddler who is a little over seventeen months old. She's in a pretty pink dress with pink, blue and white ribbons in her dark hair. Mia is my foster parents' adopted daughter and absolutely gorgeous. And Ray's right about Mia's eyes and mouth. I smile, tracing the adorable lines of her smiling lips, then run my fingers over her face lovingly. She looks happy, with fat cheeks and bright blue eyes. She's perfect, raised by perfect parents.

I go back to the email.

We were wondering if you're thinking about coming home for the holidays. If Thanksgiving is difficult, we wouldn't mind Christmas or New Year's. I know trans-Pacific isn't easy, but we'd love to have you back. We miss you so much, Ava.

If it's difficult booking a ticket this late, we'd be more than happy to help.

Love and miss you.

Darcy

Darcy's offer to "help" sends a pang of guilt through me. When she asked last year, I told her I couldn't go because it was too expensive to buy a ticket so late. It was a lie, of course. I just didn't want to return to Charlottesville. Back then she didn't push, obviously trying to spare my pride. But this time she isn't going to be that delicate about it.

After all, it's been sixteen months since I left.

Suddenly I'm wide awake. I rest the phone on my chest, screen down. Darcy and Ray don't know

I had the interview in Thailand. A job there would put me even farther away.

A fierce longing pierces my heart. Why not just go home permanently? Who cares if I'll be unemployed? Darcy and Ray won't mind if I stay with them while I look for a job.

But…

I tighten my mouth. It'd be stupid to go home when I have a job in Japan and a nice offer in Thailand. The economy is horrible in the States. It's better to stay where I am.

Better to stay. Mentally repeating that a few more times, I get up and drag myself out of my room.

The TV is on, its volume low. An old Bond flick with Sean Connery is playing on the flat screen.

Bennie is parked on the couch. His neatly cropped brown hair is streaked with magenta, the color a sign of his rebellion against the ultra-staid administrators at his high school. Left to his own devices, he'd have longer hair with jagged edges, but the conservative Japanese prefer that he be more mainstream and clean-cut. The girls in his classes swoon over his dark brown eyes and chiseled looks, but they don't know he has zero interest in women. Bennie isn't leading-man handsome, but he is charming with a crooked half-smile and animated manners.

His pedicured feet bare, he is dressed in a pale gray long-sleeved cotton shirt and artfully frayed blue jeans that show off his body. He works out regularly to maintain his physique. In his hands is a phone. He's busy texting, probably planning something for tonight.

"Hey. I got you an onigiri from 7-Eleven in case you were hungry," he says, barely turning my way. His eyes briefly flick to the screen where Connery is beating the crap out of some bad guys.

"Thanks." I go to the kitchen—just big enough for one person—and grab the triangle-shaped rice ball wrapped in a sheet of black seaweed. He got me the salmon one, which is my favorite. I take a bottle of sports drink from the fridge and sit next to him on the hand-me-down couch we got from an expat who was returning home.

"How was the trip?" Bennie asks, eyeing my wrinkled shirt and jeans.

"I'm…" I frown. "I don't know. I saw Lucas."

His eyes widen until it seems like they take up most of his face. "You saw *who?*"

Bennie knows plenty about Lucas since he was the one who patted my shoulders as I hunched over and cried my eyes out. He also has very strong opinions about Lucas now.

"Lucas." I don't bother to call him an "ex." That's reserved for men who I had real relationships with.

"The guy from my fourth year at UVA." I unwrap the food and start nibbling on it.

"Yeah, I remember. The guy who gave you the car. He's here?"

"Chiang Mai. He was, uh, on my flight."

His mouth hangs open. "Flying *economy?*"

I shake my head and give Bennie a condensed summary of how Lucas basically kidnapped me so we could "talk".

"Wow. Two years later and he wants to have a conversation?" Bennie snorts.

"I don't know what he wants. Closure, maybe? He freaked me out for a moment when he said I took something from him, but he didn't bring it up again."

"Holy shit." Bennie lowers his voice. "Do you think he knows?"

"I don't think so. I didn't get that vibe."

"Or maybe he doesn't care. I mean, you think he might, but given the kind of man he is, he might be relieved you didn't try to involve him or get any kind of financial support."

My nails dig into my palms. "I'd rather die than take a penny from him." Especially after his brother accused me of being a gold digger.

"You go, girl," Bennie says. "Besides, who trusts a man who shows up after two years to talk? He can't be up to any good."

"I know, right? He even tried to make it sound like being photographed with that Faye woman was for *my* benefit." I give him the gist.

"Oh my god. *So* typical. Bullshit with a capital B to gloss over all the things he did wrong and make you feel like shit for dumping him… when really you were totally justified in doing it! I saw Dad do that to Mom time after time. But no matter how horribly he hurt her, she could never leave him. It's just"—he sighs, deflating slightly—"frustrating."

I reach out and pat his hand. Bennie is continually upset about his parents. His father was quick to anger, alcohol an accelerant to his temper, and he swung his fists indiscriminately when he got mad. I was there one time when he sprained his hand. Not being able to make a fist, he used his feet.

But the day after… He was always such a gentleman the day after. It amazed me that he could be so…nice and apologetic.

"A punch isn't the only thing that can hurt," Bennie says. "There are other ways to inflict pain. They don't leave any bruises, but they hurt more because they don't heal as fast…or as completely."

"I know," I whisper.

"Let me know if there's anything I can do to help. I feel responsible," Bennie mutters, shoving fingers into his messy brown hair. "If it hadn't been for me egging you on, you wouldn't have slept with him."

I flinch with shock. "That is so not true."

"Yeah it is. You said you weren't interested, but then I told you to live a little and screw him." He heaves a sigh. "Should've known better."

"Nobody knows the future. If we could, we'd all be millionaires."

"Still…"

I raise an eyebrow. This is a little too strong of a reaction to my old romance gone wrong.

Bennie's phone rings. He scowls at it but doesn't pick up.

"Who is it?"

His lips purse. "Drew."

"Soo…why aren't you answering?"

Bennie and Drew are inseparable. Or were, anyway, until I left for Thailand. Then I recall how oddly Bennie behaved when we were on the phone earlier.

"It's complicated."

"Maybe I can make it less complicated." I rest an elbow on the back of the couch and cup my chin in my hand. "Come on, talk to me. Is Drew upset that you're going back to the States?"

"Like he has any reason to be mad. *He's* going back to England."

"What…? When was this decided?"

"Right after you left. Apparently, *Mum* wants him back home. He asked me to go with him, but I don't know. Flying to Europe is expensive, and it seems ridiculous to go all the way there just to…" He shrugs.

"You might like it," I say carefully.

"I heard it rains a lot. And the food isn't that great. After having sushi and sashimi in this country, I don't know about fish and chips."

"Pretty sure that's not all they eat. Besides, think about the good points. For one, they speak English."

Bennie is terrible with languages. He still bemoans the fact that the locals in Osaka can't speak English because he sure as heck isn't learning Japanese. A few simple greetings are about all he can manage. It's pretty incredible, given how social he is, and I'm sure it's one of the reasons why he isn't entirely happy here.

"That's a plus…" He nods, but I suspect he's merely trying to placate me. "I'm just not feeling confident about the whole thing."

What the heck is this about? Bennie loves to go to new places. He's the one who said we should get jobs in Japan.

"Are you sure?"

"I haven't really decided yet. Drew thinks if I'm not going to be working at the school, I should go with him, but why should I? I'm not some boy toy he can just haul around."

I don't know what to say…and I don't understand why Bennie's acting like this. He adores Drew.

Bennie continues, "I'm just restless, that's all. I may change my mind about going home anyway. I don't have to tell my school until after New Year's. Plenty of time to think things through."

He closes his mouth and returns to the movie, but his eyes aren't focused anymore. I finish my onigiri. He isn't telling me everything, and it obviously has something to do with Drew. But what can it be? I've never once gotten an odd vibe from him, ever. In fact, he's so nice that if he weren't taken—and played for my team—I might've dated him myself.

I wash down my snack with the sports drink. "We still going out tonight?"

"Of course." Bennie finally smiles. "There's a new bar about fifteen minutes from here. We should check it out. Everyone says it's pretty cool."

"Great. You want to use the bathroom first, or should I?"

"Go ahead. I want to finish this movie."

I get up, squeezing his shoulder to let him know I'm one hundred percent behind him. It's the least I can do for my best friend, and I hate it that I can't do more.

EIGHT

Ava

THE BAR TURNS OUT TO BE WORTH THE walk. The fact that it's only fifteen minutes—on foot—is a bonus because in Japan you can't even ride a bicycle after drinking. Outside hangs a simple white sign containing a black circle made with a single rough brushstroke and a highly stylized ideogram. Underneath are two English letters: WA.

The crowd is about twenty-five percent expat. The long, dark wooden counter and tables and stools are mostly occupied, and a group of young Japanese women in stylish outfits is playing pool. The sound system adds to the cheery atmosphere with a selection of Japanese and foreign songs.

Hips loose, Bennie moves toward the counter to get the attention of one of two bartenders, black canvas shoes treading along the faux wooden flooring. His light beige top and artfully frayed jeans showcase his tall frame, and more than a few women slant their eyes to check him out. *If they only knew.* He says something to the bartender and raises two fingers.

Looking at the way some of the women are dressed, I'm glad I'm in my new dark crimson number and black ankle boots. I got the thigh-length dress on sale last month, and Bennie insisted I wear it out at least once before the weather gets too cold.

A couple of Japanese men at the counter are leaving and I snag their seats. Bennie quickly comes over with two bottles of Asahi Super Dry. "To your new adventure," he says. We clink bottles.

"I haven't decided yet, but…"

"As if. You're totally gonna go."

I smile, but I honestly have no clue what I'm going to do. I take a quick sip of the cold beer, then look around. "Not bad."

"I know, right?" He flips through the menu. "Hmm… How about chicken fingers and fries? I need some junk food in my life."

"Go ahead and get it. I'm hungry."

I flag a bartender and give him our order. He nods.

I sense a few gazes on me, but shrug them off. I'm sort of used to it at this point. Platinum blond with blue eyes has its advantages and disadvantages in Asia. One of the latter is that people sometimes stare. I even had a child touch my hair, then flee when I turned around.

"Hallo, Bennie."

Bennie's shoulders tense as an arm wraps around him. Drew lowers his head and whispers into Bennie's ear—probably something embarrassingly sweet. Drew's dark brown hair looks exceptionally soft under the warm glow of recessed lights in the bar. But he pulls back pretty quickly and frowns at Bennie.

"Something wrong?"

"No." My roommate pastes on a smile. "I was just surprised. I didn't know you were going to be here."

Drew's frown deepens. "We *did* agree to meet here on Thursday…"

"Right. We did."

"You weren't answering my calls or texts, so I thought perhaps you were ill or some such." Drew turns to me. "Ava. Back in town already? I had no idea, or I would've called you instead to make sure our lad here was all right."

"Just got back." I smile to hide my unease. I do *not* want to get between the two of them when I can't even manage my own personal life.

Drew is the same age as Bennie—twenty-five—and has high cheekbones in a slightly narrow face. His sharply defined features make him almost pretty, and his eyes are the color of a deep lake on a sunny summer day. His body is leanly muscled from regular workout sessions, and the black shirt and slacks hint at the nice physique underneath.

To top it off, he's smart—graduated top of his class at Cambridge. I don't know why he's teaching English in Osaka when his degree could open a lot of more lucrative doors in England.

"I left my phone in my room and totally forgot," Bennie lies. "Sorry."

"'s okay, love."

Drew keeps his arm around Bennie's shoulders, and Bennie sends me a look full of pleading.

What does my best friend want me to do? If Drew did something wrong, maybe I could yell at him, but it doesn't look like he's done anything. He's just being his usual affectionate self.

Bennie stands up. "Potty break. Back in a flash." He pulls away from Drew and disappears down a small hallway in the back.

"Is he really all right?" Drew asks me.

"I guess," I say carefully. Every word feels like a potential mine—for me to step on and betray my friend somehow. "Why?"

"Seems a bit off."

"He probably has a lot of things on his mind. Hey, I got the job in Thailand."

A genuine smile splits Drew's face. "Excellent. Congratulations."

"Thank you, but…" I tilt my head in the direction Bennie disappeared to.

"He doesn't want you to go."

Did Bennie tell Drew about his own potential decision to move back home? I can't remember. "He probably doesn't want to be alone in Osaka."

God, I'm going to go to hell for this. I hate misleading a guy as nice as Drew.

"Yeah, I completely understand. I'm also returning to England." He purses his lips. "I asked Bennie if he wanted to visit with me, but he refuses to discuss the matter."

"Wow. That's unusual because he told me he'd love to travel more. I'd love to have a local person guiding me when I go to another country."

Damn it. I need to stop babbling. I turn to my beer. If I'm drinking, I can't talk.

"Would *you* like to come along then?" Drew asks suddenly, leaning closer.

"What?"

"You can come with Bennie if that'd make him feel better."

Oh crap. I take a long swallow of Asahi, then thank the bartender profusely when he places the platter of chicken and fries in front of me. Anything to buy some time.

Finally I say, "I don't know if I can afford

it. My foster parents are pressuring me to come home this holiday."

Not that I've decided to go or not. But if Bennie doesn't want to visit England for whatever reason, I don't want him to have to. Picking up a piece of chicken, I make a mental note to check airfares to the States for the year end, hoping there are a few cheap tickets left to grab. I hate putting stuff on credit and paying the exorbitant interest.

Drew waves away considerations as mundane as *expenses*. "No need to worry about that. Everything would be fully paid, for both of you. Just show up and be your usual cheery selves."

The chicken forgotten, I stare at him. "You can't be serious."

"As the proverbial cardiac arrest," he says.

"I…" Drew is a teacher just like us, and it isn't like he has the seniority to draw a bigger salary than we do. So where is he getting the money to fund everyone?

I put the chicken down and take another long swallow of beer. I can't process why he's doing this. "I don't know… Going to England—"

"Won't be possible," comes Lucas's cold voice.

Shit. The beer goes down the wrong way, and I start coughing.

"Lucas," I gasp as he pats my back with a surprisingly gentle hand.

Even as I sputter, it feels good to have him

touch me. The spot on my back tingles, a heat that has nothing to do with the alcohol slowly spreading through my body.

Dear lord. I'm in trouble.

"What the hell are you doing here?" I manage to rasp. "Shouldn't you be back in America by now?"

Which is precisely where he belongs. But no, he's here—in this small bar in Osaka—in person.

His dark brown hair is slightly damp, as though he's just gotten out of the shower or been rained on. Since it's clear today, my money's on the shower. A dark gray button-down shirt and black slacks add an austere harshness to his presence.

He smells fresh and clean with a hint of soap, and my heart picks up its tempo as liquid warmth pulses through me. I don't understand why something as ordinary as soap can smell so incredible on him…and turn me on. My hands curl into fists so I don't do something stupid like bury my nose into the crook of his neck and inhale.

Drew cocks his head. "Do we know you?" The tone is mild, but there's something underneath that isn't.

"*You* don't." Standing behind me, Lucas rests his hand on my nape, and my entire body prickles with needle-sharp awareness. "But Ava does, and

I say she won't be going to England or anywhere else with you."

Drew stands up, his eyes on Lucas. "Ava, are you actually friends with this person?"

How I want to say, "No, throw him out," but I know better. Lucas isn't the type to just let people boss—or toss—him around, and he has means and connections. Google says that his half-sister is on a first-name basis with the ambassador of Japan and often entertains equally important people. He could probably get all of us deported just for embarrassing him.

"I knew him back in the States," I say neutrally.

Drew narrows his eyes. Hostility is positively *pouring* off him. "Is that so?"

Lucas arches the eyebrow, then dismisses Drew like he's a candy wrapper. "Ava, we didn't finish our earlier conversation."

Is he serious? I'm about to tell him there's no way we can continue the conversation unless I have a lobotomy, but his hand tenses around the back of my neck. Not forcefully enough to hurt, but enough to admonish.

"We can either talk here or someplace more private."

I sigh. "More private."

"Good choice," he murmurs so only I can hear

him. The hand slides down to my back, creating a trail of fire.

I get up. "Drew, I have to go. Tell Bennie I'll see him at home."

"Ava, pet." He's still looking daggers at Lucas. "You needn't talk to anybody you don't want."

"It's all right." I give him a quick hug, feeling Lucas's scorching gaze on us. "I'll see you later, Drew."

NINE

Lucas

TAXIS ARE EVERYWHERE IN JAPAN. I HAIL one and instruct the driver to take us to the luxury hotel the Centurion Concierge booked for this impromptu stay. I can sense Ava glaring at me in the twilight of the cab's backseat.

"I said someplace private, not your hotel room." Her voice is low but no less forceful for it.

"Don't worry. I won't do anything you don't want me to." I give her a cool stare. "I never did anything you didn't beg for."

Her cheeks flush. "Because you never told me the truth."

"Ava."

She glances at the driver. "Not right now."

"He won't understand."

She snorts. "Some drivers speak English surprisingly well."

I frown. That may be true; our cabbie understood me when I told him where to go. I have no desire to give somebody an earful of our history. Making the tabloid headlines is Elliot's hobby, not mine.

The lights from the night streets illuminate her profile. I wouldn't say she's classically beautiful. Her nose is a little bit too upturned and her chin is a little too pointed, with a hint of the stubbornness that rivals that of a singularly cantankerous mule. But somehow her features come together to create an arresting façade. Her eyelids are at half-mast now, mostly hidden by the long lashes. Although there's tightness in her mouth, her bee-stung lips look so damn soft. I run my thumb along the side of my index finger, wishing it was her lower lip I was touching instead.

With a considerable effort I tear my gaze from her face.

Not the right time, and not the right move. I've waited two years. Surely I can wait a few more minutes.

I inhale and realize what the problem is. Her scent is permeating the atmosphere—jasmine and vanilla. It's intoxicating, inescapable. And I *want*.

I want, I want, I want because I've waited for so damn long.

Almost there.

When we pull up in front of the hotel, I pay the driver wordlessly. A uniformed doorman rushes over to open the door for Ava.

I tell him, "No bags," and lead Ava toward the elevator to the top floor, where I have a suite reserved for a couple of days. A uniformed butler welcomes me back in lightly accented but smooth English, and I dismiss her with a curt nod. She leaves, closing the door behind her.

Ava stands in the middle of the sumptuously appointed suite. "So this is how you really live."

There's a cool censure in her tone that throws me off. "It's just a hotel room."

She laughs. "Right. Just a hotel room."

"A penny for your thoughts?"

"I think you can afford more than that." She gestures around. "Just *look* at all this stuff. And the way you treat the staff…"

My eyebrows pull together. "What?"

"You act like you were born to have your every whim and desire catered to."

"Ava, it's a hotel. It's their *job* to cater to me. And they're getting paid handsomely for that service."

Her mouth twists, but she doesn't say more.

Jesus. What the hell are we doing? I didn't bring her here to argue about how I treat the staff.

"Something to drink?" I ask with a calm

I don't feel. "There's a wet bar, and if you want something warm, I can call the butler and have her make you something."

"I don't want anything." Her mouth shuts so fast I can hear her teeth click.

"Not if it's from me, you mean."

"Astute."

"Not astute. Just remembering our history. You always fought tooth and nail over every gift I ever gave you. Perhaps you would've been more amenable if they'd been dipped in gold first."

She treated them like tokens of ill-intent, and it still fucking hurts.

"I never wanted any of those things, dipped in gold or otherwise, not that that ever meant anything to you," she says bitterly.

The throb in my left leg worsens—it always tenses up and gives me trouble after long flights. My temper starts to fray.

"If I want to give a woman something, she'll damn well take it and thank me."

"Then you should've fucked someone who would've damn well taken it and thanked you because I'm not her. Can I go now?"

"Who the hell was that guy?"

She looks at me blankly. "What guy?"

"The one at the bar who offered to pay you to join him in England."

"Drew?"

"Yes! Drew! Who apparently can pay for an entire damned trip, when I can't even share a flight with you." I sound like an asshole, but I can't help it. Jealousy is my least favorite emotion, and I'm feeling it all the way to my bones.

"He's a friend..."

A friend who was sitting entirely too close to her. A male friend who undoubtedly wants to get into her panties. A friend who isn't bad-looking... an unscarred and undamaged *friend*.

The impressions drip into my consciousness like acid. My hands clench, and I wish the bastard were here so I could punch him in the face and break his perfect nose.

"...and you're nothing."

The softly whispered words shatter my control. How can she toss me into the "nothing" category when I wanted to be her *everything* the moment I glimpsed her?

Ignoring the ache in my leg, I take two long and slightly uneven strides toward her. My hands cup her head, palms to cool cheeks, and my head dips.

My mouth slants over hers. Her lips stay closed, although she doesn't pull away. I don't want to force myself in. I want her to let me in, beg me for it.

Left without a way to get inside without bruising her tender flesh, I give her a few licks, coaxing her. Her jasmine and vanilla scent leaves me breathless with need. The feel of her smooth, soft lips… *Jesus.*

She lets out a low moan, and her lips part. Seizing the moment, I sweep in with my tongue. At the taste of her, I groan. She's just as sweet and lovely as I remember… No, even sweeter. I'm a man lost in the desert who's discovered an oasis. I can't stop drinking her in. The more I have of her, the more I want.

I'll never get my fill.

The thought is fleeting, stirring unease, but lust burns away all sanity. My hand fists in the warm silk of her hair, and I kiss her hard.

She clutches my shoulders, pulling me closer. She devours me back, her lips fused to mine. Her tongue strokes the inside of my mouth with a familiar boldness that boils my blood.

I want… Oh how I *want*…

My other hand is at the small of her back, drawing us together. She adjusts, fitting her body closer and cradling my erection in her lower belly the way she used to when she was turned on and wanted my cock sliding deep inside her.

The need to take her, to mark her as mine again, is becoming unbearable. Suddenly she pushes me away. The unexpected move almost makes me lose my balance, breaks my hold on her.

Ava breathes harshly as she stares at me, her eyes wide and impossibly blue. As control slowly returns to her, her kiss-swollen mouth sets in a tight line, as though she's rehearsing nasty things to say the moment I speak. She expects me to gloat, but that isn't my style.

I step forward, my hand reaching out, but she flinches and turns away. Her face is drawn and slightly pale—except for a red flush in her cheeks. She has to be jet-lagged from the red-eye, and she probably hasn't had more than a snack since landing in Osaka. She has a habit of skipping meals when she's tired or stressed. I noticed she didn't take a single bite of the chicken she ordered at the bar.

"I haven't had dinner yet, so I'm going to order something," I say.

"Go ahead. I'm not stopping you."

Good fucking god. Pushing down my mounting irritation, I call room service and order a rare Kobe-beef steak, chicken tenders and fries.

She crosses her arms. "That's a lot of food you're getting."

"I took you away from having your dinner, so it's the least I can do."

"No need. I lost my appetite the moment you showed up."

As soon as she finishes, her stomach rumbles. Her face turns bright red, and it's all I can do not to howl with triumph. I school my face to impassivity. "Your belly seems to disagree."

Her face turns even redder.

"Ava. Sit down." Without waiting for her, I take the sectional. She seats herself across from me in an armchair. Now her legs are crossed, too.

"I've made a decision."

"Oh, goody. As long as it involves you going back home tonight and never contacting me again."

"I told you, you took something from me. We never got to talk about that."

She goes still and slightly white. Her teeth bite into her lip and she looks at the curtains. "What is it you think I took from you?" Her voice is thin, almost inaudible.

I go on full alert. Her reaction is muted now, but I can't help but think of the way she freaked out in Chiang Mai. She's definitely done something she's afraid I'll find out about.

Unease knots my gut.

Focus on what I want first. If I get that, I'll have the opportunity to figure it out.

"Half a year," I state firmly.

"What?" She turns toward me, dropping her hands in her lap. "How did I steal half a—"

"No. I *want* half a year. With you. Twenty-four weeks."

"And just exactly how did you arrive at that number?"

"A week for each month you stayed away."

She snorts. "Perhaps you should ask your brother to stay with you for twenty-four weeks."

This again. Now I'm glad I had that call. "I already spoke with Blake."

"Oh?" Her eyes are sharper now. "And?"

"He said he didn't do anything to you."

TEN

Ava

I GLARE AT HIM. "YOU'RE KIDDING, RIGHT?"

"I trust him. It's not his style to interfere in relationships."

"Of course! Why would you ever doubt your awesome brother? Let's doubt the *gold digger*."

Lucas inhales sharply. "I never considered you a gold digger. You know that."

"Right. That's why you kept showering me with money and gifts…and a freaking Lexus. Because I'm *not* a gold digger."

"I gave you those things because I wanted to help. And you needed a new car anyway. That rat-trap you were driving was a time bomb."

My mouth twists at the familiar argument. The beat-up, dilapidated Nissan, as far as Lucas was concerned, was going to give out on some deserted road frequented only by serial killers and rapists. I give a sudden and theatrical mock-gasp, as though I just recalled something, and cover my mouth with a hand. "Oh, and I forgot. I'm also supposed to be your mistake!"

And a dumb one too from the way liquid heat lingers in my veins. God. How can I still respond to Lucas like that? My body should know better.

"*Ava,*" he growls out my name in a warning. "I've never said you were a mistake."

The old mortification surges, and I feel my cheeks and chest heat. "Not to my face, you didn't. So what? You think saying that crap behind my back makes it better?"

His mouth parts. "I didn't—"

"If *you* didn't talk about me as a mistake or a gold digger, why did your *brother* call me those things the moment we met? How did he get that impression?"

"I already told you I spoke with him, and he said he doesn't remember saying anything of the sort. You're mistaken."

I stare at him. He's so, so earnest, his gaze direct and steady. This is how he was able to get me to succumb to him in the first place. I couldn't turn him down when he looked at me like that, like he meant every syllable.

So why did Blake say those things? Did he really deny everything to Lucas?

I feel like my world is upending again, my resolve weakening. The truths I knew are no longer true, and I only want to believe what Lucas is telling me.

Don't be an idiot.

Fool me once, shame on you. Fool me twice…

I can't afford to repeat the past. I drop my eyes. "It doesn't matter anyway."

"The hell you say."

A knock interrupts him. He curses under his breath and answers the door. It's room service.

The man keeps his gaze straight ahead and brings our food in. If he senses the tension in the suite, he doesn't show it. He lays everything out, confirms that the order is correct, has Lucas sign a slip and disappears.

"Eat," Lucas says, retaking his sectional.

"I told you, I'm not hungry."

"Humor me, Ava."

The cold, quiet rasp of his voice lets me know he's close to his breaking point. I grab a fry and nibble on it, while he helps himself to the steak. If he's disappointed by how small the portion sizes are, he doesn't show it. Japanese people consume not even a third of what Americans routinely polish off in one sitting.

"As I said, I want you back for twenty-four weeks."

"If you need a fuck buddy, surely you can get Faye Belbin to fill the role," I say.

A tinge of something that looks like satisfaction glitters in his gaze. "Jealous?"

"You wish."

"I told you, I didn't sleep with her while I was with you. She and I were over years ago. Ask her to confirm if that will help."

I laugh. "You haven't been listening to anything, have you? *I don't trust you.* I don't trust the people *around* you to tell the truth, Blake being the most recent example."

"I trusted you." He speaks quietly and evenly. "I didn't come to Osaka to fight, Ava. And I can't stay in Japan for long, so you'll have to quit your job and come back home with me."

Both my eyebrows rise. "Are you out of your freaking mind? There's no way I'm quitting my job for you."

"Teaching isn't your calling. You told me you wanted to be a writer."

"Teaching is what I do so I can eat and put a roof over my head."

"I can give you money, enable you to write full-time. Surely you can write a book in twenty-four weeks."

I have to laugh. "It's not quite that sim—"

"Fine, whatever, it takes longer. I'll continue

to provide for you until you make enough to earn a living from your writing. How long does it take to write a book? A year? Two?"

Bastard. He's using what I told him in a moment of particular closeness to leverage me.

"I'm not the girl I used to be, and people's dreams change. I'm not going back to you. I can never go back to what we had."

He frowns. "What was so objectionable about it?"

My mouth slackens. "What *wasn't* objectionable about it?"

"What we had was perfect."

"For you, maybe, because it was on your terms. It was about you fucking me whenever you wanted."

He gives me a look. "Ava. If I'd fucked you whenever I wanted, you would've never left your apartment. Mainly because you wouldn't have been able to walk."

I flush, and an unwanted heat winds through me. God, he used to be insatiable. I often wondered how—and why—he habitually left before the night was over, because his eyes always seared me with undisguised lust every time he walked out.

"I'm older now," I say, hating that my voice seems weak even to my own ears. "I need more than just a good lay to have a relationship with someone…and you can't give the other part to me."

He finishes the last bite of his steak and leans back, ignoring the veggies on his plate. "Okay, let's hear it. What do you need?"

I laugh again. *This man.* "You think you can make it happen if you know what it is?"

"Of course."

"Well you can't. You aren't capable."

He steeples his hands. "If you're upset about Faye, I already told you it's over, and I don't plan on touching her, ever. As for your issue with Blake, I'll make sure you never see him again."

A realization dawns on me. "You never wanted me to meet your family, did you?"

He eyes me a little warily. "No."

My pulse accelerates, and my hands start trembling. I clench them, but that isn't enough. I jump to my feet. "You bastard! If you wanted to make me feel cheap and dirty, congratulations. You've succeeded." My vision blurs, and I realize I'm crying. I snatch my purse and run.

"*Ava!*"

I ignore his shout. The door closes behind me, cutting off a string of curses from him. Thankfully there's an elevator waiting, and I rush inside and smack the buttons for CLOSE and LOBBY. When the elevator takes its sweet time, I jam my thumb against the CLOSE button repeatedly. *Come on, come on!*

The doors finally start to draw together. I hear uneven footsteps, and see Lucas's stark face in the diminishing gap.

"Wait!"

I step backward. The doors shut just in time, and the car starts descending. I sag against the wall behind me.

Tears leave hot tracks down my cheeks, and I dry my face with a sleeve. What the hell is wrong with me? Why cry when I've always known what he thought of me, what I was to him?

I keep my head lowered, humiliated and embarrassed that I'm wasting emotional energy on a man who doesn't deserve it. I climb into a taxi and give the driver my address. As the car pulls away, I see Lucas running across the lobby toward the front doors.

He bellows my name. Although I can't hear it, I can read his lips.

Very deliberately, I turn away and close my eyes. But it can't stop the tears from staining my cheeks or my heart from bleeding all over again.

ELEVEN

Lucas

*F*UCK!

What the hell just happened?

The taxi vanishes beyond the intersection, and I smack a fist into the opposite palm. The doorman looks at me warily. He's probably debating whether he should call the police or the closest mental institution.

He asks something about a taxi, and I wave him off. I don't have the time or energy to deal with the man.

I stare at the road where her cab vanished. My heart says to go after her now, but my head tells me to give her a little space to pull herself together. She isn't going to listen to a word I say until she's calmer.

My teeth dig into the inside of my cheek, drawing blood. Normally I would listen to my gut, but I can't afford to at the moment. I've screwed up one too many times following what's in my heart. The wisest course is to regroup and decide on my next move.

I make a sharp one-eighty and return to my room. My left leg hurts like a bitch, but I grit my teeth and do my best to avoid limping. I need to soak it in hot water and get it massaged or it won't be of any use at all tomorrow.

God how I hate my fucking leg. If I were just a little bit faster, I would've been able to catch her back in Chiang Mai…and here. Then it would've been *my* decision whether or not I let her go, not hers.

I wrack my brain for what could've triggered another of Ava's extreme reactions. She was upset at the possibility that I might've been unfaithful. But I'm not a cheater. I would never hurt or demean Ava that way.

I already told her I spoke with Blake, and he emphatically denied it. Not that he doesn't have the capacity to say some horrible shit, but he isn't the type to deny it afterward. He'd own it, and proudly at that.

Is it because I told her I wasn't letting her meet my family? She obviously doesn't like Blake, so it's only logical to keep them separated. Was it that terrible, enough to make her cry?

I seriously don't get it.

I draw an extra-hot bath, strip and sit down gingerly in the tub. I stare broodingly at the scars along my leg. They still look like something out of an old Frankenstein movie, much worse than the one on my face. Since I threw out all the shorts I own, nobody—except the medical staff who treats me—has seen the foul, raised tissues.

Meanwhile Ava's legs are perfectly smooth... flawless, in fact. She often looks away when we talk. Maybe she doesn't want me to notice something in her expression. Or maybe she just doesn't want to look at my facial scar, even by chance.

What would she say if she were to see my leg?

Disgusted, I tilt my head upward. Of course she'd be grossed out. No reason not to be horrified.

The heat gradually loosens the tight muscles in my leg—the psoas, the quadriceps, the gracilis, the sartorius... I became an expert on thigh anatomy during my time in rehab. The tension in my shoulders and neck also slowly eases. Sweat beads on my forehead, and I reach for a cold bottle of water.

My phone rings, and I lunge for it, idiotically hoping it's Ava. Of course it's not.

Elizabeth. I consider ignoring it, then change my mind. She'll just call me again later. She can be such a pest.

I put her on speaker. "Yeah?"

"Hello to you too, Lucas."

I make a face at the gentle rebuke, even though it's delivered in a voice sweet enough to belong to an angel. My half-sister is a stickler for etiquette, but who can fault her for being polite?

"Hello, Elizabeth. How are you?" *There.*

"I'm doing well. Thank you, Lucas," she answers primly.

"And to what do I owe the pleasure of this call?"

She laughs. "You're overdoing it. I just spoke with your assistant, and she told me you're in *Japan.*" I can tell from the tone that my sister didn't quite believe it. My fault—I've had Rachel make up excuses to avoid certain obligations in the past.

"If you're calling to see if I'll confirm that, yes, I am."

"I see. Well, that explains why you missed the dinner."

"What dinner?"

"You forgot?"

"I...don't have my calendar with me." But I do vaguely remember hearing about it and giving her something other than a "hell no" in response. So it's got to be about The Pryce Family Foundation, which she runs. If it were a family function or something, getting together with my relatives, I would've definitely scrubbed it from my memory.

"Didn't I already pay for a ticket?"

She sighs. "It's not just about giving money. You have to show up."

"You must be sick if you're worried about stuff like that."

"I'm worried about *you*."

"You're worried I'm going to miss the deadline." I don't clarify. I don't need to.

"That's not it. You were really upset at Dad's place."

"And you weren't?"

She's quiet for a moment. "I don't want to argue, Lucas. It's just that…everyone's counting on you, and I don't know if that's healthy. For anyone."

"Everyone's counting on everyone. Besides, what about you? You haven't dated in four years."

"No need to worry. I have a list of candidates."

"You're kidding." This is news. I thought she'd find a real husband, not some guy to stand in for a year. "Who?"

"None of your business."

"Well then. You won't be too upset if I tell you it's none of your business how I go about meeting the deadline."

She lowers her voice. "Are you going to marry a Japanese woman?"

I snort. "There *are* other reasons to travel."

She sighs. "I saw Faye at the dinner. She came alone."

The gentle rebuke in Elizabeth's voice says she expected me to escort Faye. "That's too bad, but even if she'd asked me, I would've bailed."

"At least our family was represented by Ryder and Elliot. They attended with their wives."

The muscles in my jaw slacken. "Really?" Ryder and Elliot are the last people to attend charity functions. They prefer to give money, but stay out of the spotlight. Actually that isn't entirely true. Ryder enjoys the spotlight, but it has to be *his* spotlight. And he likes his parties wild, with lots of drunk, topless women. Unfortunately Elizabeth disapproves of such delightfully amusing spectacles.

"They seem happier," she says.

"You met Elliot's wife?"

"Yeah."

"Is she really a stripper?" The sordid background information about Elliot's wife made a splash not too long ago. And my twin has been on edge, calling to warn me about a mutual acquaintance who also happens to be a royal asshole— Keith Shellington, the embezzler.

"Yes. But before you jump to any conclusions, she's really lovely. I couldn't be happier for both of them."

It makes me think of Ava and her furious reaction to what I said about my family. Given that I have no idea what brought that on and I don't want to discuss Ava with Faye, Elizabeth is the best source of female insight I have.

"Can I ask you something?"

"Sure."

"Would you be upset if a man you were dating said he didn't plan to introduce you to his family?" I quickly add, "You really don't like his family."

"Well… If I didn't like the family, I don't think I'd be that upset about it. Why?" She gasps. "Are you seeing somebody who hates us?"

There is a subtle change in her voice, something I've never heard from her. It's not exactly cowed, and it isn't disbelief either. The closest thing I can think of is cautious.

I shake my head. What is up with women and their overwrought behavior? "She's not a psycho or anything. And it's not you she doesn't care for."

"Then who?"

"Blake."

"Oh." She stays quiet, but that's my sister. Say nothing if you can't say anything nice.

"Maybe he was having a bad day," she finally offers.

"Doubtful." I snort. "Anyway, don't strain yourself trying to come up with reasons justifying why Blake isn't a saint. I don't want to give you an aneurysm." I sink deeper into the hot water.

"I promise not to have an aneurysm if you'll tell me about her."

"*Elizabeth.*" My voice is low but firm.

She sighs loudly. "Fine, I won't pry. Still, it'd be nice if you told me what's going on after I gave you my thoughts."

I can hear the pout in her words. I allow myself a small smile.

"Thank you, Elizabeth."

"You're welcome." She hesitates. "You know you can tell me anything, right? I'm always here for you."

I rest the back of my head against the rim of the tub. "I know. Thanks." Closing my eyes, I disconnect the line.

WHAT IS WRONG WITH HIM?

THE SECOND THE BOY SEES HIS TWIN WALK into the giant mansion they call home, he launches himself, his small fists tight and shaking with rage.

"You butthole!" the boy yells, spittle flying from his cherubic mouth. He's bitter, and "butthole" is the worst word he knows.

The twin raises his arms to block the blow. "I'm sorry!" he shouts. "I thought you were gonna be there."

"You lie!"

"Mom said you were waiting for us."

"Liar!"

The boy keeps repeating it. He can't believe his mother left him home and took his twin to Disneyland. She *knows* how much he loves the amusement park...how much he adores her.

"Stop that, both of you!" comes a sharp rebuke. "Goodness, what's wrong with the two of you?"

"I told you he was going to be upset!" the twin says to their mother, gesturing wildly.

She is not having any of it. Hands on her hips, she turns to the boy.

"What did I say about acting out, Lucas?"

"You told me if I was good—"

"Were you good?"

"*Yes!*"

"No," she corrects him coldly. "Remember last week when you made a mess of my dress?"

The boy remembers, and it's unfair that she's upset about that. It was just mud, and it came out. He saw the housekeeper clean it.

"I wanted to hug you, Mommy."

"Well, you shouldn't have done that. I've told you a thousand times to stay away when you're dirty."

Suddenly this is too much for him to handle. The boy bursts out crying, tears pouring down his cheeks.

"Other moms don't mind when their sons hug them!"

"You are not like other boys," she snaps. "You cling. You demand. You don't care about anyone but yourself. Actions have consequences. It's time you learn that."

"Mom," the twin says. "Stop."

"*I hate you! I hate both of you,*" the boy screams.

"What is *wrong* with you?" the mother says. "This behavior is appalling."

He wipes the tears and smears snot on his cheeks. "I *hate* you," he sobs.

His mother wrinkles her nose. "You're a sight. Go to your room and wash your face. Now."

She turns away and disappears down the hall.

The twin approaches the boy and starts to put an arm around him. The boy shrugs it off.

"I hate you, too, Elliot," he whispers before running out into the garden in the dusk.

But he can't help but wonder…

What *is* wrong with him?

TWELVE

Ava

THE SECOND I UNLOCK THE DOOR AND STEP inside my apartment, Bennie jumps off the couch and runs toward me, his bare feet slapping the floor. He's in a loose charcoal T-shirt that says *I like mayo sand* across the chest in bright hot pink and a pair of black lounging pants he ordered online last month. In his hand is a phone, clutched tightly.

"Thank god, you're home!" he breathes out. "I was debating whether or not to call the police."

I tilt my head. "Why?" I slip off my shoes and go toward the living room. The NHK news is on TV, the sound muted.

His face goes cold as I pass. He grabs my upper arm. "What the hell did he do to you?"

"What?"

"You've been crying!"

I thought I'd wiped my face pretty well in the taxi. I guess not. "It's nothing."

"How can you say that when *Lucas* dragged you away? If I'd known he was going to show up, I would've never left your side. You have no idea how much I yelled at Drew about that."

I collapse onto the couch, suddenly tired. "Please. It wasn't his fault."

"Like I'm supposed to believe that?" Bennie sits down next to me. "It totally *is* his fault for not stopping your ex."

"Bennie…" I don't have the energy to fight him. "He couldn't have known. And I told him it was okay."

He is still looking mutinous. "I'm trying to be fair, Ava. I just… I just feel like Drew *should've* known." Bennie takes a few deep breaths. "So what did the asshole want?"

"He…" I stop, not wanting to talk about the kiss and the shameless way I responded to him. "Apparently, he wants me back."

Bennie's jaw drops. "Is he on crack?"

"Didn't look like it."

"Did you tell him pigs would be singing 'Hallelujah' before you'd let him touch you again?"

"Not exactly. But he knows…now."

"He's such an asshole. And just so…wrong for you. The stalking, the harassment. And why show up now? He didn't do a thing to get in touch for two years!"

I shrug, feigning nonchalance. "I don't know. But he said he couldn't stay in Japan for long, so he's going to leave."

Then remembering what he asked me to give up, I laugh dryly.

"What?"

"He asked me to quit my job. No, he actually *told* me to quit my job and move back to the States with him."

Bennie's eyes bug out. "Is he out of his freakin' mind?"

"Yeah, that was pretty much my reaction too."

"Wait." He puts his head closer to mine conspiratorially. "Do you think he knows? About"—he lowers his voice—"*you know*."

My heart seems to skip a beat, but I shake my head firmly. "No. No way. He didn't say anything about it. Besides, how could he know? He probably left Charlottesville after his surgery, and even if he didn't, he doesn't know Darcy and Ray. I doubt he made the connection."

Bennie thinks it over. "You're right. It's not like anyone looks that closely at random people's kids." He puts an elbow on the back of the sofa.

"So did you confront him about what his brother said?"

Bennie's fists are tight. He's still angry about the way I was treated by Lucas's family, especially his oldest brother. Elliot wasn't so bad. He merely stood there while Blake ripped into me.

"I did, but apparently Blake has denied everything, and Lucas believes his brother."

"What a lying piece of shit. So he *is* close enough to believe his brother after all."

When I asked Lucas about his family when we were dating, he told me they weren't that close and that he avoided talking to them. Now I know the truth. And it hurts like hell. "Well, it doesn't matter." Maybe if I fake nonchalance long enough it'll become real. "I always suspected he wasn't being honest about everything. Now I know, so I can move on."

"Girl, you've already moved on. You're here, away from him, and you're figuring out your life."

"Right." I flash a quick smile for Bennie's benefit. But if I have indeed moved on, why did I hesitate when Darcy asked me to come to the States for the holidays…and why am I considering moving farther and farther from home?

Since I don't have an answer to either question, I go wipe the makeup off my face, change into pajamas and rejoin Bennie in the living room to watch some silly TV personalities making fools of themselves. I'm tired, but I can't seem to shut off my brain. When I finally go lie down on my futon, I toss and turn, obsessing about Lucas's wicked mouth and his outlandish demand that I move back home with him.

THIRTEEN

Ava

"OHAYO GOZAIMASU!" I SAY, AS I WALK INTO the teachers' office the next morning.

Sato-sensei repeats my greeting with a small incline of her head from her desk. She's a petite Japanese language teacher. Though she's in her mid-thirties and has two children, you'd never know it from her smooth golden skin and the twinkle in her dark eyes. She's in a conservative black dress and a white sweater. Once every few months she'll get a wild hair and wear something dark blue.

"You're a little early," she says.

I'm twenty-five minutes early. I didn't sleep much last night, but I couldn't bring myself to linger in bed once the raucous neighborhood crows woke me up before six. "I wanted to review a few things before class."

"Ah. As it happens, Kouchou-sensei mentioned that she would like to see you…"

I smile, despite a bit of apprehension slithering up my spine. Kouchou literally means "school principal," and everyone calls the old bat by her title rather than her name, Yukiko Tanaka. Older than a T-rex's femur, she's as cold as her namesake—snow—and doesn't like foreigners that much, although she recognizes the necessity of having them in her school to teach English.

Sato-sensei would never presume to give me a direct order, but the implication is clear: I need to go and see the dragon-lady before doing anything else.

A young secretary guarding the Kouchou's inner sanctum smiles nervously when I walk in. This is not a good omen. Yamamoto-san's expression determines what's waiting for you in Kouchou-sensei's office, and that smile means, "I'm so glad it's you, not me."

"Good morning, Ava-sensei. Please go in. Kouchou-sensei wanted to see you."

"Yes, I heard. Thank you."

I wipe my damp hands on my pants surreptitiously and step past the threshold to the dragon's lair.

Kouchou-sensei is seated at her desk, her black glasses almost too overpowering on her narrow, powdered face. Her hair is steel-gray and pulled back into a tight bun, and she's wearing her usual white button-down blouse. Under the desk will be a black pleated skirt that stops at mid-shin and white pantyhose. I've never seen her wear anything else.

"Please sit down," she says in accented English, gesturing at the empty seat across from her. It's a well-upholstered chair meant for making important visitors feel at ease, but it doesn't have that effect on me.

"You wanted to see me...?"

"Yes." She folds her brittle hands on the desk and takes her time. She isn't doing this to figure out how to say what she needs to say in English. Her command of the language is excellent. She spent years studying, not because she wanted to communicate with foreigners, but she saw it as an intellectual challenge.

After a few moments I glance at the clock on the wall. I have perhaps twenty minutes left before I need to get going.

"I have heard some...disturbing things about your conduct, Huss-sensei," Kouchou-sensei says finally.

"Excuse me?" Of all the things I imagined...

"One of our staff saw you entering a hotel… with a man."

The way she speaks… It's like I butchered a baby bunny and drank its blood.

"Did this staff member also mention it was *not* a love hotel?"

Japanese people have meetings in respectable non-love hotels all the time. I don't see why Kouchou-sensei is being so weird about it.

She purses her thin lips briefly. "Yes. But it *was* late at night. Also, you were wearing a dress that showed…quite a lot of your body."

The dress I had on showed some leg. But her tone makes it sound like I paraded nude into the lobby.

I have a feeling I know who the staff member is. "I'm not certain what you and Mishima-sensei think happened, but I was with an old friend from America." My mind rebels at the fact that I'm calling him "an old friend" but I'm not going to tell the disapproving Kouchou-sensei that he is my ex-lover.

There is a slight flicker in Kouchou-sensei's eyes that tells me I was right. "Then what were you doing at the hotel?"

It takes a lot of willpower not to laugh at her ridiculous inquisition, but bureaucratic bullshit is unavoidable in Japanese schools with their medieval attitude about sex.

"We went up to his suite and ordered room service for dinner. And that's it." But the second the words leave my lips, I know I've made a tactical error.

Kouchou-sensei is looking at me sadly. "You went to his room."

"Yes, but I left before the dinner arrived. I had an urgent call—"

"You were in his room with him?"

Argh. The woman is like a dog with a bone. "For less than an hour."

"Huss-sensei." She sits back. "Appearances must be maintained if one is a teacher."

"I swear nothing happened." Just to make sure she understands, I say, "There was no sex. We just talked."

She nods, but her eyes are sweeping me from head to toe. The skin around my neck starts to warm. Her silent judgment is like a fist around my throat.

"If there's nothing else, I do need to prepare for class." I glance at the clock. Ten minutes.

"Of course, the students come first. We will continue this later."

I give her a bland smile and leave. We will *not* be continuing anything later. She has no right to act like I've been a slut. I know why she's putting my behavior under a microscope. I'm a foreigner. As far as she's concerned, if she isn't careful, I'm likely to exert a negative influence on impressionable Japanese youth.

I'd bet my working visa that if I were Japanese, Kouchou-sensei wouldn't have put me through the "aren't you a little slut" interrogation.

The teachers' office is almost empty. I spot a mug on Mishima-sensei's desk, which sits at the other end of the room, and vow to have a quick conversation with her. If she has a problem with me, she can say it to my face instead of running to her BFF Kouchou-sensei.

I skim the notes left by the substitute teacher. Since I did most of the lesson prep before I left for Thailand, it doesn't take much time to pull hand-outs and teaching points for the day. My primary focus with the first-year junior high students is to break their attitude that English is by default difficult. Secretly, I agree that English isn't an easy language for Japanese people to master. The grammar and thinking are totally different. But if I can't get my students to at least believe it's a challenge that *can* be overcome, they won't even try.

After the third period, I have a break. I go to the teachers' office to start grading the mini-essays my students wrote over the weekend, then stop short. There is a huge bouquet of blood red roses in a crystal vase on my desk. Their heady scent fills the utilitarian teachers' room and brightens the drab space.

The school secretary, Kanagawa-san, is looking at the flowers with admiration tinged with something that I can't quite identify but don't like. "Very beautiful. Is today a special occasion, Ava-sensei?"

"Not at all," I manage, though my mouth feels like it's full of sawdust. "I'm surprised myself."

Lucas. What are you trying to do now?

I go to the flowers. I'm almost tempted to throw them away, but I can't. They're just too beautiful, not to mention if I did toss them out, it would draw attention from my coworkers. I pluck the stiff note stuck to the bouquet.

I'll give you until tomorrow.

–L

The nerve! He can wait until the sun goes cold. I'm not quitting my job.

Sitting down, I rip the note into little pieces under the desk and toss them in the trash bin next to my chair, then turn my attention to the essays. I start reading the one on the top of the stack from first period, then feel an odd vibe in the air.

I look up, but all the teachers seem to be focused on their own work.

Huh. I turn my attention back to grading. I don't have time to mess around. The more I get done now, the less I'll have to take home with me.

Then I feel it again. What's going on? Did I spill something on my sweater or something? I look down but my clothes seem as pristine as they were when I left home…

Sato-sensei occupies the desk next to mine. I lean over. "Is there something wrong?" I whisper.

She puts down her pen while casting a furtive glance at the other teachers. I almost roll my eyes. She actually hunches a bit, until she starts to resemble a turtle trying to go back into its shell. "Mishima-sensei had a break during the second period. And she…ah… You see, she mentioned…"

You've gotta be kidding. "About me going to a hotel with a man?"

She blinks, then relaxes a bit. "Ah. You know," she says, obviously relieved it won't be necessary to explain in embarrassing detail.

"If she's that concerned, she could just talk to me directly."

"Yes." Sato-sensei sucks on her teeth. "But that is not our way. She wants to be…not so direct. Being direct is"—Sato-sensei laughs nervously—"too awkward da yo." She puts an emphasis on *da yo.*

"So it's better to tell on me, like a three-year-old?"

"Eh?"

"Nothing. Thank you for explaining the situation."

She peers at my face. "Are you angry?"

I want to bitch-slap Mishima-sensei, but I won't because that woman is old enough to be my grandma. I bare my teeth in what I hope is a reassuring smile.

"No. Just…relieved to know what's going on."

She nods. "I think it is not a large problem, but some older teachers worry about the image. Well, you are American, so…we can't expect you to be like Japanese teachers, ne?" She sits back up.

I can't decide if Sato-sensei is trying to be insulting or helpful. I decide on the latter. "No. Of course not."

Just then I see the originator of my problem walk by in the hallway. I get up and go out after her. "Mishima-sensei!"

She stops and turns, looking like a barely rehydrated mummy—all skin and bones and as thin as a tarp. Her clothes—a pink sweater and ankle-length navy skirt—flap limply around her short frame. Her mouth is flat as usual. I've never seen the woman smile, ever. But the eyes are extraordinary—they glitter with almost frightening intensity, like those of a hawk before swooping down upon prey. She has a reputation among the students for being terrifying.

"Can I talk to you for a moment?" I say.

She looks at me coolly. "Most certainly."

"I heard you spoke with Kouchou-sensei."

"It seemed like something she should be aware of."

"Why didn't you come to me first if you have a problem?"

"It is obvious you did not realize it was a problem. If you did, you wouldn't have done it. And I am not your mother. Nor am I in position to officially correct behavior." She peers at me, the corners of her mouth curving downward.

I force my hands to relax. "I did nothing to be ashamed of."

"Do unmarried teachers in America often go to hotels late at night with men?"

There. That judging tone. And late at night, my ass. NHK news was on when I came home, and it runs from nine to ten.

"Is it customary for elder teachers to gossip about others behind their backs?"

Red shows on her powdered cheeks. "I can't believe you are talking back to me."

"I can't believe you not only spoke with Kouchou-sensei, but to every other teacher in the school except me. I find that petty and immature, if you must know."

"Do you think you can talk to me like this? I've been with this school for over ten years."

"Then perhaps as my elder, you should have set a better example and guided me, don't you agree? Next time you have something to say about me, just say it to my face."

"This is why we can't accept foreign attitude."

Normally I would've ignored her because it's not worth the fight. Mishima-sensei has been around a long time, and seniority carries a lot of weight in Japan. But with a job offer in hand, I don't feel like biting my tongue just to satisfy this superior busybody.

"You know what? At least foreigners don't jump to conclusions and spread ugly rumors. Are you happy that you made all the other teachers look bad by association?"

This barb hits home. She flinches. Japanese people are so focused on the group identity rather than the individual's.

"You are American. You are not like us."

"I'm still a teacher at this school," I call out over a shoulder as I walk away.

Even though the parting shot feels great, I know I'm finished at the school. They won't fire me, but they probably won't renew my contract. It's okay though. I have a position waiting for me in Chiang Mai.

And there's Lucas. He's willing to support you so you can write.

I smack myself inwardly. What the hell is wrong with me? I'd rather just never be a writer.

Accepting what he's offering would be admitting that I deserve to be treated like a cheap prostitute men fuck in an alley, trousers down around their knees.

GIFTS

THE GIRL HIDES BEHIND THE BATHROOM door and peeks through the gap. Her mother stands in the living room with her arms crossed. Under her feet, what's left of the carpet is brown, and the walls are so dingy it's hard to believe they were white at one point.

The mother is petite, with pretty green eyes and pale golden hair that's almost silver. The pictures of her on the bookcase show her as radiant, her skin smooth. She is now not even ten years older than those photos, but her cracked hands are rough with calluses, and deep lines bracket her downturned mouth.

"What are you doing here?" she says harshly, her voice husky and raspy. Cigarettes are the only vice she can afford with any regularity. They also give her energy when she's tired.

"Baby, I'm sorry." The girl's father spreads his arms. "I had to work on our anniversary. I tried to get the day off, but it was impossible. You know how Bob is."

The mother's lips tighten. "Bob's an asshole. You tell me where he is so I can give that man a piece of my mind."

"Now, baby, don't do that. If you cause trouble at work, I'll lose my job. Then what?"

"I don't know, Beau. Is it worth it? It's not like trucking pays much. I'm tired of working two jobs to make ends meet."

"I'm sorry." He takes her hands in his nicer, softer ones. "Here." He reaches into his jacket pocket. "This made me think of you."

He gives her a black box. It has no label or brand, and inside is rather sad with a pair of golden earrings shaped like strings of hearts. Still, the mother's face brightens. "They're pretty."

"Just like you." He reaches out and runs one hand softly along her hair. "You're the only one for me."

Smiling, the mother lets him lead her to the only bedroom in the apartment. Their moans and grunts keep the girl awake for a long, long time.

142

FOURTEEN

Ava

TUESDAY PASSES WITHOUT INCIDENT. Teachers still eye me speculatively, but I pretend it doesn't bother me. Neither Kouchou-sensei nor Mishima-sensei has bugged me since then, so I act like Monday never happened.

Even if I have a job offer, I still need to finish out my contract with the school, and I don't want to have any pointless tension here.

Thankfully Lucas doesn't bother me with another bouquet of nonsense. Hopefully he's flown back to America by now, where he belongs…with Faye Belbin. The idea stirs a crazy cocktail of jealousy inside me, and I breathe deeply to calm myself. It's better this way. Don't I know that?

But Wednesday morning Mishima-sensei comes and tells me that Kouchou-sensei wants to talk to me again. I raise my eyebrows. I haven't gone out or done anything that could be construed as inappropriate, so I don't know what Kouchou-sensei can possibly want to talk about.

"Before your first class," Mishima-sensei clarifies.

"Arigato gozaimasu."

I make my way to the office. Yamamoto-san fidgets when she sees me. She won't meet my eyes.

A bad sign. What's the problem now?

"You can go in," Yamamoto-san says.

I murmur my thanks and walk inside. Kouchou-sensei is again seated at her desk, and she offers the same chair. I sit down, feeling a bit of déjà vu. Maybe I'm hallucinating. That wouldn't surprise me. I haven't been sleeping well—thanks to Lucas's sudden reappearance and demands—and I could be dreaming with my eyes wide open...

Her thin hands are on the desk, folded neatly. "It's come to my attention that there is a problem other than the hotel incident."

I stare at her. What crime have I committed? My Facebook account has nothing that could come back to bite me in the butt. I didn't even start one until I left the States, mostly so I could keep in touch with Darcy and Ray. Bennie and I used LINE and Skype to communicate with each other until I joined him in Osaka.

When I don't give her the reaction she was obviously expecting, Kouchou-sensei asks, "Is it true you're cohabiting with a man?" There is a subtle emphasis on *cohabiting*, as though I've been hosting and participating in orgies or something.

"If you're asking me whether I have a room-mate, yes, I do."

"And this roommate... Is he a man?"

"Yes. He's my best friend. He's been my best friend since I was a small child."

"But he is a man."

I can see where this is going. "Yes."

"And he is not related to you."

"No, but he's like a brother to me. We grew up together."

Her forehead wrinkles. "Yet he is not your brother, correct?"

"Correct."

She stares at me as though surprised at my frank answers. "You must realize how this appears."

"He is homosexual. He looks at me the way you look at Mishima-sensei."

I'd bet my gaijin card that that hateful busy-body is behind this. She's probably pissed off over our confrontation and wants to show me who's boss.

"But do you see him the same way?"

My mouth parts. The question is so preposterous it takes me a moment to process. "Like I said, he's my best friend, and he is not at all interested in women that way. How could I possibly see him as a…romantic partner?"

"Men and women cannot be friends."

"Of course they can."

"Even if that is the case, there is the matter of appearance. Teachers are the moral pillars of society. A young unmarried female teacher cannot cohabit with a young unmarried man who is not related to her."

It's on the tip of my tongue to ask if it's acceptable if the man in question is a young *married* male adult who isn't related to her, but I swallow my sarcastic comment. That would be pouring gas on the fire.

"This isn't Edo-jidai, Kouchou-sensei," I remind her, referring to the medieval Tokugawa Era when the shoguns ruled the country.

She gives me a bland look. "Very fortunate for you. Foreigners were not allowed in Osaka during that period." She lays her hands on the desk, her spider-leg fingers linking loosely. "Regardless, your female students may look at your behavior and assume that it is acceptable to cohabit in such amoral manner. And your male students may feel that it is natural for them to expect women to cohabit with them. This will not do. I cannot allow it."

"What are you saying?" Is she going to try to put me into some kind of dorm or some—

"I'm afraid I will have to terminate your employment."

My mouth parts, and it takes two attempts before I can gasp, "*What?*"

"Your contract has a clause that specifically prohibits you from behaving immorally, which you have done." She pauses meaningfully. "Twice."

I feel heat traveling from my chest to my face. Goddamn it. I cannot believe how narrow-minded Kouchou-sensei is being. Mishima-sensei probably egged her on to get me fired. I clench my trembling hands into fists and stiffen my body. I will not show weakness.

"You're going to say I'm guilty without a hearing? Giving me a fair chance to defend myself?" I ask.

She looks at me like I'm slightly slow. "I gave you a chance, and you admitted to everything. I don't know what more you expect. I have been more than fair."

Shit. This is it. I'm not Japanese, I'm not a permanent employee, and I don't get the consideration that a unionized teacher here might get. The situation galls me.

"We have a substitute teacher to replace you today. I do not expect you to teach." Kouchou-sensei puts a subtle emphasis on "expect," making it clear she will not allow me to have any further contact with the students. "Now. Very sorry to have to say this, but it is required that you will leave."

"Fine," I say, shaken by how coolly and swiftly I've been dismissed.

It's going to be okay, I tell myself. I still have the job offer in Chiang Mai. I'll just go there. The pay's comparable to my current school, and given the low cost of living in Thailand, the money will stretch much further.

I go back to the teachers' office to grab my bag and the few personal items I have in my desk. Sato-sensei looks at me with concern, but the other teachers avoid meeting my eyes. Heads down, don't make waves. The Japanese way.

As I start walking toward the subway stop, I pull out my phone. These aren't the circumstances under which I would've liked to take the new job, but I do my best to look at the bright side. Bennie's considering going back to the States, and what would I have done by myself in Japan anyway?

Mr. Liu likes me, and so does his son. I should be all right in Chiang Mai.

I open my email app. A new message from the school in Thailand regarding the offer is waiting for me in my inbox. I tap on the subject line—*Re: Your Offer.*

Dear Ms. Huss,

We regret to inform you that we are rescinding our offer, as new information has come to light about you. Thailand is a traditional nation that values moral conduct, and it seems you may not be a good fit at our school.
To clarify, our decision on this matter is final.

Sincerely,

Nigel Jackson
Headmaster

My vision dims for a moment, and I stare at the email, unable to process it. Is this some kind of cosmic joke?

When Nigel and I had tea together with Mr. Liu, both the men were sweet and complimentary. What changed? What "new information" is he talking about?

Maybe the same thing Kouchou-sensei grilled me about this morning…?

I stop in the middle of the sidewalk, my arm dropping limply to my side. I assumed Mishima-sensei was behind Kouchou-sensei finding out about my living situation, but maybe I was wrong. Mishima-sensei may be a busybody, but she probably has better things to do than follow me around looking for lapses in moral rectitude.

I'll give you until tomorrow.

I got that note from Lucas on Monday…and today's Wednesday.

I start shaking from head to toe. Every cell in my body is vibrating with tension and searing fury. *He has no right!* No right to screw up my life. The first time our orbits crossed, he crushed my heart. This time he's destroying my ability to be self-sufficient and independent. He's trying to demolish my pride, reduce me to a hole he can stick his cock in whenever he's bored or horny.

I'll kill him first.

I hail a cab. The driver stops and opens the door with the automatic lever thing all Japanese taxis have. I slide in and give him the name of the hotel where Lucas was staying earlier. If my guess is correct, he won't have left the country yet. No, he's too busy pulling strings to ruin my life.

My phone beeps with another new email alert. I jump for it, hoping and praying that the school in Thailand changed its mind.

But the new message is from Google. It's about my dad's "other" family. The *real* one.

Elle—the daughter who counts—is engaged to some lawyer she met in Boston where she works as a financial analyst. They look so happy in the photos she posted on her blog. Her fiancé grins at her with a soft gaze full of love, his arms around her waist. Elle is blond like me, although her eyes are green like her mother's. She looks into the camera with a confident smile.

Well, why not? People apparently adore her. Most likely nobody's trying to wreck her life. And her fiancé is looking at her like she's his dream come true.

Though we aren't close—hell, she wishes I didn't exist—we are half-sisters. My vision starts to blur. What does she have that I don't? Why does she have everything while I can't even try to make something of myself without someone pulling the rug out from under me?

A lone, slightly startling drop of moisture lands on my phone.

I dry it off and put it back into my purse. Then I wipe away the rest of the tears on my face. Lucas is *not* worth this. I am *not* giving my enemies the satisfaction of seeing me suffer.

I pull out my compact and travel-sized tissue packs. I'm not going to face Lucas with smeared mascara and eyeliner, either. I repair the makeup as well as I can and put more powder on my nose to hide the redness there. Except for slightly red-rimmed eyes, I don't look awful. I apply a fresh layer of blush.

When the taxi stops in front of the hotel, I pay the fare and get out. The doorman bows with a polite greeting, and I nod and trot to the elevator. I remember exactly which suite belongs to Lucas.

A "Do Not Disturb" sign hangs outside the double doors, clear evidence that he's still in town. Not that many people spend thousands of dollars a night on a suite like this.

Fucking bastard.

I knock loudly and wait. When nobody answers, I bang with a fist, and press my ear to the door.

Did Lucas already check out?

But that doesn't make any sense. He's gone this far to get what he wants. He isn't going to leave before he's achieved his objective of dragging me back to America to be his exclusive whore.

"Don't you *fucking* play games with me!" I pound on the doors with enough force to make them shake.

Suddenly they open, revealing Lucas in nothing but a white bath towel around his trim waist. His hair is damp and slicked back, revealing both eyes and the scar on his unfairly handsome, freshly shaven face. A drop of water clings to his chest, just above his left nipple, which is pierced. I used to play with the silver ring there, making him shudder in reaction. I loved the way he responded helplessly then, the flesh between my legs going slick every time.

152

The memory makes my breath catch, and my own reaction intensifies my fury. I should be finding him disgusting, contemptible for what he's done to me, all because he's horny. Why me? Why doesn't he just go fuck someone else?

He has an insatiable appetite. He's probably not alone.

The thought sends blithering jealousy through me, and suddenly I can't control myself anymore. If he wants to fuck me, he should at least have the decency to keep his dick in his pants around other women. Or maybe it doesn't matter. He only cares about what *he* wants, not my feelings.

Without a word, I shove past him into the room, on full alert for any sign of a companion. The suite is as I remembered, and I don't spot anything, not even a scrap of lace.

His dark eyes flicker with surprise as he turns around, his hands pushing the doors closed. "Ava."

I spin around to face him. "Don't you Ava me, you *son* of a *bitch!*"

"What's this about?"

"You fucking bastard. You told the school about me living with Bennie, didn't you?"

Shutters come down over his eyes, making him appear impossibly aloof. He radiates the self-possessed calm and arrogance that can only come from an unshakable conviction that he is entitled to everything he wishes for.

If I needed proof of how different—how *incompatible*—we are, I only need to see this side of him.

"Do you have any idea how the principal at my school treated me? She acted like I was a harlot! A *slut!* Then I got a message from the school in Chiang Mai where I interviewed telling me they're rescinding their offer now that they know I'm an *amoral whore.*"

The muscles in his face tense, his alert gaze on mine.

"So great. Congratulations. You just destroyed my career and means of supporting myself. I hope you're happy."

"Ava, that wasn't what I was trying to do," he says tightly.

"Really?" I pull back exaggeratedly, then fling my arm out. "You sure could've fooled me."

"If you want to be independent, I can arrange for that. I can give you money—no strings attached. A million or two should be enough to set you up…unless you want more."

My breath heaves, blood roaring in my head. This is just like him, to think everything can be resolved with money and things it can buy.

Not just any money, but *his* money. *His gifts.*

"I don't want your damned money."

"It's a gift."

"You mean payment for being your whore." I pick up a vase with a single red rose from the low table by the window and hurl it at him. He ducks before it can connect with his face.

"What the fuck?" he yells.

"You're saying 'what the fuck' after throwing money at me? You crushed my hea—" I catch myself. I am *not* letting him know I actually loved him back then. "You cost me my current job. You got me fired from a school where I haven't even started. What do you want to destroy now? My pride? My spirit?" My fists shake at my sides. "I don't think I was ever that good of a fuck, so what's your problem? Ego couldn't take that I left you, and now you want me to pay on my knees? Would that get you to leave me alone?"

"This isn't about sex or hurt feelings or ego! It has nothing to do with those things."

He crosses the living room until he's standing only a hairsbreadth away from me and wraps his big, warm hands around my arms. I can smell the soap clinging on his clean, taut skin, and I hate myself for noticing.

"I would never work this hard just for sex, Ava. This is about how I feel about you."

How I feel about you…

How cheap is that phrase? How empty?

A lot of people have said that even as they knew they were betraying me. Dad said it. Mom said it. Ex-boyfriends said it.

Don't you know how I feel about you?

How can you not know how I feel about you?

Like it's some kind of character flaw that I can't figure out how little they cared for me.

"Feel? *Feel?* You feel *nothing* for me!" I yell in a voice so raw that my throat hurts. "I'm just a dirty little secret you don't want your family to know."

"Is that what you think?" he asks hoarsely.

"What else am I supposed to think? You did everything in your power to ensure your family and friends would never find out about me."

"It's not like that." He closes his eyes for a moment as though gathering his thoughts. "I wish I could just…rip my heart out and *show* you all the crazy things I feel about you."

The earnest tone of his voice finally penetrates. But I'm not anywhere near ready to let go of my anger and outrage. I cross my arms across my chest. "Well, why don't you just settle for an explanation? And if I don't like it, *I'll* fucking rip your heart out and show it to *you*. How about that?"

His Adam's apple bobs. "I never wanted you just for your body. I wanted you the moment we met because of your loyalty and kindness."

"Oh, for fuck's sake! And how could you have known those things about me?" Lucas and I met at a Chinese restaurant near UVA where I was waitressing three days a week. He asked me out when my shift was over.

"Because I watched you with Mrs. Ling and overheard that conversation about how you were helping them manage the restaurant after she broke her hip. Not even her own son came back for that."

"Because he has a career in New York."

"Which he put above his parents. But you didn't, even when Mrs. Ling fretted she might not be able to keep you much longer."

Talking about it takes me back. "Her husband wanted to close the restaurant and retire. He was fed up with the business."

"And their son wanted them to as well. But you were more concerned about her condition, how stressed she was, than your future unemployment." Lucas gives me an earnest look. "Do you have any idea how rare and precious that is?"

I don't know how to respond. I never imagined he was watching so closely.

"When I'm with you," he says, "I feel like I'm in possession of the most precious jewel in the world. And you're right: I don't want anyone else to see it. Because if they do, they'll covet you and want to take you away. I want to hide you away, keep you under lock and key, so I never lose you."

A dull shade of red has tinged his cheeks, and his face is set in hard, unyielding lines, daring me to reject the truth of his words. There's tension in the way he's holding his body, and I know he wants to shift his weight, squirm, look away—anything but stare me in the eye and wait for my reaction.

It's my turn to swallow. In those months we were together, I never imagined he could be this vulnerable, that I might have this much power over him…and now, that I would still have such influence.

Suddenly it's no longer in my heart to be angry. I put my hands on his cheeks.

"I do have a mind of my own, you know," I say quietly.

His gaze is skeptical. Not because he doesn't believe me, but rather he doesn't believe I'll stay with him. He worries I'll somehow find him lacking.

I recognize the look; I've felt that way myself. My heart aches. I don't know what or who caused him to think this way about himself, but I hate them for having done it. This kind of self-assessment is pure hell.

"No one is going to take me away just because they want to," I add. "The only person who can make me leave is you."

"Then tell me what I did wrong so I can fix it."

I shake my head. How do I explain to him when his brother said all those horrible things to me at the hospital, they stirred up my old insecurities and sense of worthlessness? I don't want to relive a second of my past.

Apparently interpreting my silence as my refusal to give him a chance, he tightens his hold on me. "I'm not letting you go."

Determination glints in his eyes. He dips his head, his tongue brushing against my mouth. My hands are still on his cheeks, and if I want, I can push him away. But I can't bring myself to reject him after he's revealed such vulnerability.

He's never done that before, and I want to show him how much it means to me.

When I meet his tongue with mine, a deep groan tears from his throat. Our lips seal together. I slide my palms up until the fingers tunnel into his damp hair. He tastes like homecoming and Lucas and everything I've missed over the last two years.

"Ava," he whispers, his warm breath against my face.

I shiver. My heart is bursting, and I can't articulate all the emotions churning inside at the moment. The only thing to do is act.

I pull him closer. Through the layer of my thin sweater, I feel the heat radiating from his bare body. I glide my hands along the strong lean lines of his neck and back. My fingertips tingle as they relearn the beauty of his body.

His hands release my arms to skim along my torso over the sweater, tracing shoulders, ribs, the small of my back. When they reached my waistline, they tug gently, untucking my top. He slips his hands underneath and touches my belly, and I gasp at how hot his bare skin feels against mine.

"You have no idea how I've wanted this. How I dreamed of it," he rasps into my neck.

I tilt my head to give him easier access. "It's been so long."

"You haven't…been with anyone else?"

"No. They weren't you," I say, unveiling a facet of my own vulnerability. It seems only right after what he's revealed.

He rests his forehead against mine and lets out a shuddering breath. "It's been so long for me, too," he says in a shaky whisper.

A tiny hope stirs inside me.

"After you were gone, it's like my body went into some kind of…hibernation. Nothing—no work, no woman—could wake it up. I barely felt alive."

Suddenly I understand. "This is what you meant when you said I took something from you, isn't it?"

He nods.

Relief leaves me staggering. And with that, I feel free. "Then let's make this count." I pull his head down for another kiss.

FIFTEEN

Lucas

YES, YES, LET'S MAKE THIS COUNT. LET US make this count until we can't imagine not being together like this again.

I'm no longer restrained. I devour Ava's mouth, starved for her sweetness. A blistering lust pulses through my veins—I'm alive again, at last!—and I shake with the intensity of it, my skin taut and hot.

I pull the flimsy pale blue sweater over her head, and immediately dive in to kiss the sensitive spot just under her ear. This close, I can sense the tiniest quiver running through her, the quietest hitch in her breath. And her reactions are glorious, like the sun finally peeking through dark, stormy clouds.

My hands are clumsy with need, but I try to rein in my raging lust. There's no longer a question about my interest or ability to perform. The only thing is to make it good for Ava, who also hasn't been with anyone for two years.

I want to be the best for her.

My thumb brushes against the soft underside of her breast through the lacy bra. It's thin enough that I can see her rosy nipples clearly. They pebble under my gaze, and my mouth waters. It's been so damn long, but I know exactly how to make her burn. Every fantasy I've had in the last two years starred Ava…and me, doing all the things I know will make her cry out for me.

I flick the straps off her shoulders and push the bra down. The elastic bands trap her arms, and I love how her tits rise and fall. They aren't large, barely a mouthful, but there are no breasts finer than Ava's. Blue veins show under the nearly translucent skin, and I let my tongue flutter over them.

Her breathing grows shallow with anticipation, and my erection twitches in response. My dick's so hard, it's almost painful.

Still, I take my time loving her beautiful tits, then fan the tightly beaded tip with hot breath. The muscles in her belly jerk, and I pull the nipple into my mouth.

She cries out, "Lucas!" and her knees buckle.

My mouth sealed over her breast, I hold her close, sucking the sensitive mound like my life depends on it. She's so damn addictive, so damn perfect. Her heady jasmine and vanilla scent grows stronger, and my head spins as I grow drunk on her.

I pull away, then give the other breast the same attention. Ava whimpers deep in her throat, sweat misting over her warm, flushed skin. Her mounting need stokes my lust, my dick tenting the towel around my waist. It's maddening not to just rip everything off and drive into her, but I keep myself together. I want to feel her come first.

Swinging her into my arms, I carry her to the bedroom and place her on the edge of the mattress.

I unbutton and unzip her black slacks, pulling them down along with her magenta panties. Her legs are shapely and smooth, nothing marring their beauty. I place a long, open-mouthed kiss on her inner thigh.

"Kick off your shoes."

Panting, she toes off her flats. Her feet are narrow and delicate, just as I remember. Pearlescent pink lacquer coats the small toenails.

I pull her clothes all the way off and toss them over my shoulder. Then, very deliberately, I kiss her from one delicate ankle bone all the way to the knee, then along her inner thigh. She is warm and oh so soft.

Her musky scent grows thicker as I get close. My heart knocks against my chest, my blood so hot that I feel like I'm boiling inside out. She is starting to tense in anticipation as well, but I break off to give worshipful attention to her other leg, since every inch of her deserves to be loved and adored.

By the time I'm back up to mid-thigh, Ava is gripping the edge of the mattress, her knuckles white. Her breasts quiver with every shallow breath she takes.

"Lucas…"

"Relax, Ava. I'll make it good for you."

This time, when I reach the slick heat between her legs, I close my lips over her heated flesh. Her sweet taste floods my mouth, and I growl against her. She cries out, widening her thighs shamelessly. Her wanton reaction drives me, enslaving me to the need to make her shatter.

I suck on her swollen pink folds, tonguing the bundle of nerves, and push a finger into her quivering pussy. She's so fucking tight, it's almost like it's her first time. In some ways I feel like it's *our* first time. It's been so long, and we're both desperate for each other.

Her muscles grip my finger, and my cock throbs almost painfully, the primitive need to thrust into her almost overwhelming. I control myself, sucking her clit hard while pushing another finger into her. I tunnel into her pussy over and over again, stretching her and bumping the sweet spot inside her every time.

Her spine arches, and she screams piercingly as she comes. She's clenching the edge of the mattress so hard that it's vibrating under my chin.

Heady satisfaction and triumph fill me. Instead of letting up, I intensify what I'm doing to her, determined to drive her to another climax. She screams again, this time louder. Her knees come up, angling her pelvis, pressing her pussy even more tightly against my greedy mouth.

I feel drunk with her heat, her taste. Her platinum hair sticks to her glistening cheeks and neck. She's breathing like she's run a thousand miles.

I raise myself up, placing my hands on each side of her, and lower my head to take her lips. Warm and soft, they part instantly. She pulls my tongue into her mouth and strokes it with her own, while her fingers reach around my waist and tug at the knot keeping the towel together. It pools at my feet.

I gather her up and place her in the center of the bed. My dick is so hard and so hungry for her, my cockhead is dripping with precum. She reaches between our bodies and wraps her hand around my aching shaft.

"Ava…"

"I love the way you feel, I love the way you're so ravenous for me." She licks my mouth. "Let me make you feel good just the way you did me."

She pushes against my shoulders, and I give way. I can't deny her anything at the moment. I would carve out my heart if that's what she wanted.

The sudden gasp of horror slashes through my lust, like someone threw me into the Arctic Ocean. She doesn't have to say a word. I know what's wrong.

My scars.

If the scar on my cheek looks bad, the ones on my leg are something from a horror movie. Long, white and jagged, they mar so much of my leg there isn't enough unscarred flesh left to cover a paperback book. I know I'm emotionally messed up, that something's not right with me, but before I wrecked my bike I was at least outwardly perfect. Now the outside is a mess, too.

I make fists resisting the urge to cover up. That would betray too much of myself.

"The accident?" Ava asks in a low voice.

"Yes."

"What happened?"

I shrug, feigning a nonchalance I don't feel.

The accident was probably some kind of a divine sign that it was time my appearance reflected how flawed I am inside. "It was raining, and...I lost control of my Harley."

"That's terrible."

I don't want her fucking pity. But what an *idiot* I've been. I should have anticipated this and planned accordingly, rather than smashing her life to pieces in my blind need to have her back again.

She places a hand on my left thigh, between the scars, and brushes her cheek against them one by one. "I'm so sorry, Lucas."

Somehow I don't detect any pity in her voice, just simple empathy and sorrow.

Her soft breath and hair fan along the jagged lines. She kisses every inch of them as though they're something precious.

My eyes are suddenly hot, and I realize that they are prickling with unshed tears. Tremors run through me. I can't think of anyone who's ever loved me, not like this, not enough to embrace my...obvious imperfections. My heart pounds, so full of emotion. And at this moment I would die for Ava.

"I know you don't like them," she says, "but they're perfect to me because they're part of you." She reaches up and lightly tweaks my pierced nipple.

Her gentle words shatter my control. I can't wait a second longer.

"Are you on the pill?"

She flushes. "No. You can't get them in Japan."

"I don't have any condoms." *Dammit.* I should be better prepared, but sex hasn't been on my radar for a while.

Ava gives me an impish smile. "Mmm. A challenge, but there's no way I'm letting this"—she runs her hand lovingly along my thick, hard shaft—"go to waste." She licks her lips.

She pulls my dick deep inside her mouth, hollowing her cheeks. My eyes roll up as knife-sharp pleasure runs through me. Digging my hands into her hair, I place my feet flat on the bed and start thrusting…shallowly, careful not to gag her.

But what I'm doing only seems to excite her more. She bobs her head, pulling me all the way down her throat. A soft purr vibrates through her.

"I'm about to come, Ava," I say.

She only increases the suction on my cock.

Holy shit. If this is a hallucination, I never want to be sane again.

With a guttural cry, I come. She drinks me down, eager, as I explode inside her mouth.

After a little time, she raises her eyes and meets my gaze. They're full of soft emotion, and I suddenly realize what I've been trying to deny to myself all this time.

I love her.

SIXTEEN

Ava

I STEP OUT OF THE SHOWER, WRAPPED IN A
fluffy white robe. While I was washing, Lucas
ordered some late brunch items from room
service. Apparently, a butler has taken my clothes
to unwrinkle and freshen them up. I would normally feel a bit shy in a situation like this—the
butler undoubtedly knows what we were doing—
but right now I'm basking in the afterglow of hot
orgasms.

Standing at the table, Lucas pulls out a chair
with a gallant grace I find irresistible. The grim
tension that hung around him like dark clouds
is gone, replaced by an air of replete satisfaction.
He's put on a shirt and slacks, and looks delicious,
smelling slightly of soap and the musk from our

time in bed together. I feel my body quicken again, and it's all I can do to not squirm.

"I wasn't sure what you wanted, so I ordered a little bit of everything," he says with a boyish smile that makes me melt.

As I sit down, he reveals food on multiple plates covered in steel domes. I gasp at a full platter of lox with all the trimmings, caviar, egg omelets with bacon and sausages and potatoes, a bowl of fresh berries, a plate of thinly sliced roast beef and a bowl of salad lightly tossed with what smells like a vinaigrette dressing. There is also a large basket of warm, freshly baked bread.

"Are you trying to feed the entire city?" I tease as I place a stiff white napkin on my lap.

"I think the Osaka metropolitan area would need a bit more than this." He considers, taking his seat. "Or maybe not. Japanese people don't eat much."

"I see you've become acquainted with the portion sizes here."

"Reacquainted. But yeah."

That makes me pause. "You've spent time in Japan?"

"Only about a semester. It was an exchange program I did." He shrugs. "Eat. Please. I feel like it's my fault that you've lost weight in the last two years."

"It has nothing to do with you. I've just been really busy."

Busy hiding things from him, my subconscious whispers.

Not wanting to ruin the moment with my secrets, I smack the thought aside and take a big forkful of the egg omelet. It's fluffy, with lots of cheese, and cooked to perfection.

"I want to make this official. Move back to the States with me. Ava, I might be the most infuriating man you've ever met, but I'm open to reform. Just give me a chance."

I hesitate. I want to say yes. But it's not that easy, not anymore. I half shrug. "You aren't *the* most infuriating man I've ever met in my life…"

"I swear I'll take care of you. I'll do everything I can to make up for the job you lost. I'll help you get a new job, introduce you to people."

The intensity of his gaze sears me. He isn't just saying this to have me as a regular bedmate again. He really wants me back, and he really wants to make this work. I wish I knew why, but I'm afraid to ask. If he doesn't say, "Because I love you," what will I do?

However, staying in Japan is no longer an option regardless of what he says. I wouldn't stay even if I got another job offer here in the next ten minutes.

"If it's about the hassle of a trans-Pacific move, I can send a moving crew immediately to your apartment and have them pack everything," Lucas offers. "We can probably leave by tonight. The plane's ready."

My mouth parts. This is all much too fast and too sudden. "Lucas, I can't just drop everything and go."

"Why not? You don't need to give the school any notice."

"I have friends here."

"Like that guy in the bar?"

"For your information, he's Bennie's boy-friend," I say dryly. "As in, there is *no way* he wants me in his bed."

He gives me a semi-baleful look. "Why didn't you say that before?"

"Was there any point?" I take a sip of the freshly squeezed grapefruit juice that came with our meal. "Look, Lucas. I need to figure out what I'm going to tell Bennie. I can't just *leave* him. He's been my best friend since we were kids, and he's basically been the sole constant in my life."

Lucas stares at me for a moment, assessing and weighing my words. Finally he says, "I feel like what you're doing is withdrawing from me."

From the way he immediately flushes, I know he didn't mean to reveal so much of himself. My heart aches. He's been so vulnerable to me in this room. And I don't want to hurt him by being evasive or dishonest. "No other man has been able to occupy my thoughts the way you do."

"Well...good. But Ava, that's not enough. I want more."

He's making it clear that he wants everything from me. But no matter how open he's been in the last few hours, I'm not sure if I'm ready to leave myself completely defenseless. The idea is simply too scary.

"We've just reconnected after two years," I say with care. "And the way we parted wasn't... ideal. We need to give ourselves some room— some *time*—and take this relationship slowly. Rushing...well, rushing might doom it."

"Don't even think that," Lucas says harshly. "It is *not* doomed. I am going to make this work."

I don't know if he can, but I know he's determined to try. So I turn the conversation to something that's been bothering me for a long, long time. "If I ask you to stop seeing Faye Belbin, will you?"

He pulls back in surprise. "Ava... She's my friend."

"But every time I see her, I feel like I wasn't enough back then. I already told you all this on the flight."

His jaw firms. "All right. I won't see her. She and I have certain mutual business interests, but she can deal with my assistant if she needs to communicate with me. There will be no direct contact."

"So this time, you and I will be *one hundred percent* exclusive, right? Not just sex. No more taking other people to functions and parties?"

"Right."

That mollifies me. We finish our meal quietly. Mostly I'm thinking. This is a huge adjustment, going from expecting to take a job in Thailand to moving back home. I can't believe it's been only five days since we ran into each other again in Chiang Mai.

"Do you know where you might want to live in the States?" Lucas asks suddenly.

"I…haven't thought that far. I mean, I guess I might go to Charlottesville for a little bit to see some people." I want to say hello to Darcy and Ray and hold Mia in my arms.

Lucas nods. "We can do that. I still have the place in Charlottesville."

"You do?"

"Yup. Never got rid of it. I did all my surgeries and rehab at the UVA hospital."

Unease settles over me. I take a few bites of the berries and then push my plate away. "I should get going before the traffic gets really bad."

It's a flimsy excuse. But I need some time alone to figure out exactly how my life with Lucas is going to be in the States.

Thankfully, he doesn't object. He calls the butler, asking her to bring my clothes back. He dismisses her once she's completed the task, and helps me get dressed. We walk down to the lobby together, our hands linked. The physical connection helps settle my nerves.

He puts me into a waiting taxi and hands the driver a five-thousand yen bill.

"That's too much," I say. "I can take care of the fare."

He shakes his head. "You're mine. Let me provide for you."

"But—"

"Don't fight me, Ava. I'll send someone to help you pack and we'll go out to dinner tonight."

He leans down and gives me a quick kiss on the mouth. When he pulls back, the taxi driver, mildly scandalized, closes the door. I turn and watch through the window as the cab carries me away from the only man I've ever loved.

Ava

LESS THAN AN HOUR AFTER I GET BACK TO THE apartment, Bennie barges in. His black-socked feet stomp on the floor like a raging rhino's. I stare, surprised that he's already home. Normally he has after-school club activities that require his supervision.

"Tell me where the son of a bitch is. I'm going to kill him!" Bennie yells, fists clenched and ready to throw.

I think I have a pretty good idea of who the *son of a bitch* he's referring to is, but I don't want to talk about that right now, especially when he's in this kind of mood. "What are you doing back so early?"

"Melissa the Aussie, who has a friend at your school, said that you were called into the principal's office and left with your things. And the rumor is apparently going around that you're a slut who went to a hotel room with a guy late on Sunday while *cohabiting* with another guy."

I cringe. God. It hasn't even been a full day. On the other hand, I'm certain Kouchou-sensei and Mishima-sensei wasted no time tarring and feathering me, most likely using elegantly passive-aggressive Japanese.

Bennie continues, "There's only one asshole who'd try to ruin your life this way."

"Do they know that you're the guy I'm living with?" Melissa works alongside Bennie, is totally fluent in Japanese and integrated into society here. I don't want his job to be affected by what's going on in my personal life.

"Not at the moment. But I wouldn't be surprised if that fucker reveals the information just because. He's out to win the Asshole of the Century award."

I sigh, my shoulders sagging. "You're safe. Lucas isn't going to tell anyone."

Bennie's face flushes. "You think I care about that? I'm upset for *you*. Now he's forcing you into taking that Thailand job."

Probably not the best time to mention the offer's gone, and thanks to Lucas. "I thought you wanted me to."

"I did, but only because I thought it'd be good for you to work for someone who values your professional capabilities, not like your Kouchou, who's a xenophobic bitch. But I wouldn't have pushed you to take it if it wasn't what you really wanted. Lucas isn't doing this for you."

"I know. He wants another chance." I give Bennie a quick summary of what happened between me and Lucas in the last few hours.

Bennie listens, his jaw slack. When I'm finished, he shakes his head.

"You *slept* with him?" He makes it sound like I've doused myself with gasoline and then juggled lit matches.

"Well…yeah."

"After what he's done to you?"

"Yes." Before my best friend can launch into a rant as to why what I've done is beyond the pale, I add, "It was the first time he made himself really vulnerable. I think he's changed. The accident and the two years apart made him different. And—foolish as it sounds—I want to try again."

"*He broke your heart!*"

"I know. And I'm scared that he's going to do it again. But you know what scares me more?"

Bennie's face is tight. "What?"

"That if I turn him down now, I may regret it for the rest of my life. You know, wondering *what if?* What if I'd been braver? What if I'd just let myself open up, just a little bit?"

"Ava, you're playing right into his fucked-up mind game. He *wants* you to feel all these things so he can con*trol* you. And despite his having been a contemptible fuckhead, you're going to reward him *anyway?*"

Placing a shaky hand on my forehead, I exhale long and hard. "You may be right. But I can't help that my heart believes he's sincere."

"Was he sincere when you told him about Mia?"

"Uh…not exactly…"

Bennie stares at me intently. "You haven't told him."

"No. Not yet."

"You won't have to tell him if you two stay apart. But if you get involved again, you'll have to. Have you thought about the fallout?"

No, I haven't. I've been too wrapped up in me and Lucas. Guilt knots my chest. What kind of person does that make me?

Bennie isn't finished. "If he doesn't care about Mia, then you've got the wrong guy. If he does, you're with the right kind of man, but...he's going to totally disrupt her existence."

My head starts to throb. *God, what a mess!* I don't know where to start unraveling it.

I rub my temples and finally say, "You're making this too complicated. I'm going to have a relationship with Lucas, not go to a confessional. He doesn't need to know everything." I exhale roughly. "Mia isn't even really his baby now."

Bennie keeps glaring at me. "You tell yourself that if it makes you feel better, but you and I both know the truth. What are you going to tell Darcy and Ray? Do they know what you're planning to do?"

"No." I place a hand over my twisting belly. "I haven't had a chance to tell anyone anything."

"If you want to keep things secret, you're going to have to cut Darcy and Ray out of your life, or you're going to cost them Mia. Losing her would be worse than the miscarriage."

I feel my vision dim at Bennie's negativity. I can't handle it right now. What I wanted from my friend was a bit of concern and a lot of "good luck". But it looks like I'm only going to get the concern.

Bennie knows I would never cut Darcy and Ray out of my life. They were the ones who showed me that I could be more than my parents. They took in a teenager with horrible attitude problems and turned her into something that could pass for a respectable human being. Without them, I would've ended up a crack whore or something.

But even owing them as much as I did, I stayed somewhat aloof, not asking for their help while in college because I was too scared of being turned down. It was nicer to pretend I had people who cared about me instead of putting that fantasy to the test.

It wasn't until I was adrift and pregnant that I had no choice but to turn to them. My lack of judgment…and only the sweetest understanding and support from them… Just thinking about it still makes my heart fill with gratitude and love.

Because I know what wonderful people they are and how much they wanted to have a child of their own, I let them adopt Mia so she can have the lovely life and opportunities that I never had growing up. And unlike some random adoption agency couple, if they raise Mia I can watch her grow up. I love seeing how she thrives, basking in their love and care.

"You're right. Things are not ideal," I say. "No matter who I end up with, I'm not going to have a perfect relationship. You know why? Because perfect relationships don't exist. I know you don't approve, Bennie, but it would mean a lot if you could just support me here. After all, you *are* my best friend."

Bennie's handsome face falls. He drags his fingers through his hair. "I know you want this to work. But I'm worried that if it doesn't, I'll be the one picking up the pieces and trying to put you back together. Like I did last time," he says pointedly. "I can't watch you suffer like that again."

"Bennie…"

"But, I guess… If this is what's going to make you happy…" He sighs. "Fuck it. You only live once, right?"

Fond emotions surge inside me. I wrap my arms around him. "Thank you. I couldn't ask for a better friend."

He hugs me back, enveloping me in his familiar, comforting warmth. "You're welcome. I think you're being very brave, and I admire you for it."

I close my eyes, grateful for his friendship. What would I do without him?

Suddenly something vibrates between us, and I pull back. "Is that a phone in your pocket, or are you just trying to make me happy to see you?"

"Har har." He takes the phone out, checks the screen and shoves it back.

"Go ahead and take it. I don't mind."

"It's no one."

The taut way he speaks lets me know who tried to contact him. "It's Drew, isn't it?"

Bennie shakes his head. "I told him I didn't want to talk to him. I don't know why he keeps bothering me."

My instinct tells me he should call back and listen to what Drew has to say. But after asking him to give me his approval despite his misgivings, I can't bring myself to criticize him for his relationship decisions. I reach over and squeeze his hand.

"Thanks for not nagging," Bennie says.

"I'm sure you have good reasons for doing what you're doing. I don't want to make you doubt yourself."

"I always thought I was the best friend a person could have, but you're not too bad yourself."

I elbow his ribs lightly. "And I thought my ego was the biggest."

Bennie laughs. But somehow I can't help but think that he's secretly miserable.

SEVENTEEN

Lucas

I FIND MYSELF IN FRONT OF AVA'S APARTMENT a little before six o'clock. I didn't plan to come so early, but I couldn't make myself stay away. She agreed to go to the States with me, but it's going to be impossible to relax until she's actually on the plane.

So you're being clingy. Just the way your mother always hated.

A coat of sweat films my palms, and I wipe them on my pants. I'm no longer the grubby, needy child that not even his own mother wanted to touch. And Ava isn't as cold as Betsy Ford. Probably no woman could be.

I knock on the door and wait, holding a bouquet of calla lilies. I saw them on my way to Ava's apartment, and I had to ask the taxi driver to stop so I could get them for her. The elegant white blossoms reminded me of Ava—her beauty and her grace.

The door opens, and instead of Ava's lovely smile, I'm confronted with Bennie. His face scrunches like he's just stepped in a pile of dog shit on the sidewalk as his eyes rake me up and down.

"What the hell are you doing here?"

"I have a dinner date with Ava," I answer evenly. Arguing with Ava's best friend probably won't earn me any brownie points. Knowing how important Bennie is to her, I want to have a good relationship with him as well.

"Really? Is that what you just *decided?*"

What's with this hostility? "No. She knows I'm coming."

"She didn't say anything about it."

"Why should she?" My temper starts to fray. "You're not her chaperone."

"No, just a good friend who had to watch you ruin her career." Bennie shoves his feet into a pair of dingy sneakers at the entryway and comes outside, closing the door behind him. "You're a self-ish SOB who's only out for Number One. Don't lie and tell me you care about Ava."

"You're half-right. I am a selfish son of a bitch, but contrary to what you assume, I care a great deal about Ava."

"Is that why you humiliated her at her school? You know what kind of rumors are flying around about her?"

It's a bit of a shock to realize that Ava has told him everything. At some level, I guess it makes sense since they're best friends. Still, the knowledge that he's this close of a confidant starts to burn like acid.

"Do they matter? We're leaving tomorrow," I say, even as guilt prickles my conscience.

"Without a goodbye party with her friends? I don't think so, buster." Bennie shakes his head. "Maybe this is just a game to you. I mean, you're rich, right? So who gives a shit about a few ruined lives along the way so long as you get what you want? But to her the job meant something. And if you don't understand that, you're just a prick who only gives lip service to the idea that you care about her."

Anger swells in my chest. How dare he accuse me of not caring about her? He knows nothing about me—how I feel.

Bennie continues. "Be honest. You want her because you think she's a challenge. Or maybe you figure she'll be easy to manipulate because her family was poor. How hard is it to dazzle a girl who grew up hungry?"

"If you think that, you don't know much about me at all. I care about her because I value her sweetness, her kindness, and her loyalty." All the things I saw when I first met her…and wanted for myself with a desperation that bordered on obsession. "I won't insult both our intelligence and claim that my feelings are purely platonic. I want her in my bed. But if I *only* wanted sex, there are much less challenging women."

"Then why are you using money to force her to take you back? Because that's what this is about, isn't it? You making sure she can't support herself without you?"

Because money's the only thing of value I can offer. Anything else would be unfair.

"I want to provide for her, give her things that she's never had before. It isn't wrong for a man to want to see the woman he cares for live in comfort."

Bennie sneers. "Like I said—with money. Just like—" He suddenly stops and shakes his head.

My eyes narrow. He was about to say something critical. *Come on, say it!*

Predictably, he doesn't. "If you ever bother to get to know her—really *know* her—you'll realize what you're offering to, quote *provide for her* unquote, will never be enough. It doesn't matter how poor she grew up. She doesn't care about money, not the way you think. Otherwise she would've kept on buying those stupid lottery tickets."

What the...? The Ava I know is careful with her funds. I can't imagine her pissing away what little she has on something as pointless as a lottery.

Bennie continues, "So take a moment to think about that before you do anything else to corner her into being with you."

The muscles in my left cheek tick as he hits my sore point. Deep inside I know she only consented to stay with me because she has no better option—I made sure of it.

If she had other choices, she'd never give me a second look.

Who cares about that? You can't let her go now.

Of course not. She's as vital as air to me. And I'll fight anyone who dares try to take her away.

EIGHTEEN

Ava

I T'S SILLY TO START GETTING READY FOR DIN-
ner when it's barely six, but I can't help it.
Lucas called earlier to get directions. He'll be
here soon, and there are butterflies fluttering in
my belly as the minutes tick by.

I apply a fresh coat of lipstick on my mouth.
It's a sexy shade of red, and I like the way it makes
my lips look plump and juicy. I check my appearance in the mirror one more time. Blush has
added some color to my cheeks, and my long-
sleeved wine-red dress with floral lace patterns
is fitted with a flirty, flaring skirt. I picked it up
on sale last year at a store in Tokyo. Although
back then I laughed at my own silliness for buying something I might never wear, I'm glad to
have it now. I put on the set of pearl earrings and

matching necklace that Darcy and Ray gave me at my college graduation. I chided them for being extravagant, but now I'm grateful. I don't own anything that can really be considered nice—most of my accessories are sale items from inexpensive stores—certainly not fancy enough to wear on a dinner date with Lucas.

A knock sounds at my door, and Bennie sticks his head in. "Your man's here. Says you two have a date." His tone makes it clear he isn't crazy about me going out with Lucas. "I parked him in the living room."

"Okay." I go over and lightly pat his back. "I know you're trying. Thank you."

"Sorry." He runs his fingers through his hair. "It's just… I want to be supportive, but seeing his face… *Fuck*. It reminds me of what you've lost."

"If you mean Mia—" I say, voice low.

"And more. He's cost you so much."

I squeeze his shoulder. "I didn't lose her. She's happy where she is, and I would've made a terrible mother."

"You're way too harsh on yourself. Shitty parents are people like your parents and mine, not you." He huffs out a breath. "Anyway, have fun."

The moment I step out of my room, I spot Lucas. My breath hitches at the perfection of his presence. He is impeccably dressed in a black button-down shirt and a jacket that accentuate

NADIA LEE

the strong lines of his chest and a pair of inky pants that fits perfectly around his hips and shows off outlines of his muscled thighs. His long dark brown hair covers the left side of his face, hiding the scar from view. The vulnerability that represents makes my heart clench.

What am I doing with him? Lucas is so beautiful, so perfect. And I...

I feel like a fraud.

He told me how he felt about me, but there's a part of me that wonders if it's just a dream, some kind of wish-fulfillment hallucination. What woman wouldn't love to hear a man like Lucas say that about her?

But it did happen. He feels so incredibly possessive about you, he values you and you should accept that if you want this to work.

He stands from my crappy couch. He walks over purposefully and pulls me into his arms, his head slanting down. Our noses brush, and his mouth fits over mine. I respond immediately, my lips softening underneath his. My heart hammers, knocking against my chest in a rapid staccato. I curl my hands around his biceps.

Some pointed throat-clearing pulls me out of the moment. Lucas gives Bennie a cold stare for a second before turning and going back to the couch. He leans over, reaches behind the far arm and produces a bouquet of calla lilies.

"Thank you," I say, taking the flowers. I bury my nose in the blossoms, inhaling their sweet scent. It reminds me a little bit of how things were when we were in Charlottesville. He would often come over with flowers back then, too. "Let me put these in a vase and we can go."

I kind of feel like a traitor, but I want to leave as soon as possible. Bennie isn't happy about my reconnecting with Lucas, and I'm afraid if we stay much longer there's going to be trouble.

Thankfully, since our place is so tiny, I'm able to keep an eye on both men. Bennie is staring at Lucas with his arms crossed over his chest, his stance overtly aggressive. Lucas merely gives him the cool, condescending smile of a man who knows he's won. I sigh inwardly. I need to talk to Lucas about being just a tiny bit gracious.

"Okay, let's go." I grab my purse. Lucas places a possessive hand at the small of my back. The touch is searingly hot, and I inhale sharply as liquid heat loosens my limbs and pools between my legs.

Lucas lowers his head so he can whisper into my ear, "As much as I would love to, we're not skipping dinner."

I look at him over a shoulder. "Who said anything about skipping meals?"

He grins at me. It's so unexpectedly light and carefree that I can't help but lean into him, knowing that I'm the one who put that smile on his face.

"Ava, I might be an insensitive Neanderthal, but I can sense when you're turned on."

"You mean you're a horny Neanderthal," I tease, running my fingertip along the exposed skin at his throat. I say to Bennie, "See you later."

"Sure." He opens his mouth then presses his lips together tightly. "Stay safe. Don't do anything I wouldn't do."

Too late. I'm already doing something he wouldn't do. He's worried at the moment, but once he knows things are different now it'll be okay.

A gleaming taxi is waiting for us outside. The driver opens the door, and we get in. He starts off without any instructions from Lucas.

"Where are we going?" I ask.

"A sushi restaurant the concierge recommended. But if you don't like it, we can do something else."

"Like room service?" I waggle my eyebrows.

"Possible…very possible. You know how much I love room service. It's efficient and we have a big bed to ourselves right next to the table." His gaze is hot as it traces the shape of my mouth. "Dinner in bed sounds even better than breakfast in bed, don't you think?"

I'm tempted to tell him we should go to the hotel then so we can be cocooned in each other.

On the other hand, I've made a big deal about not being his dirty little secret, the one he hides from the world.

"We can do sushi. The anticipation will make it even hotter."

"Mmm." He lowers his head and kisses me so fast that I barely have the time to feel the pressure. "You're a cruel woman, Ava."

"Not cruel." I place my head on his broad shoulder. "Just want to make it work this time."

The light mood slips, and he grows serious. "I do, too. I can't go back to what the last two years were like." He pulls me onto his lap and holds me like he's afraid I might vanish at any moment. He's not the only one who feels the anxiety of botching our second chance. You'd think it'd be easier on a repeat attempt, but it's much worse because now I know the exact shape and texture of failure.

We stop in front of a squat white building. It's only two stories tall, and in front is a small rock garden with pale, smooth pebbles.

I reluctantly leave Lucas's lap so he can pay our fare. The driver levers the door open, and Lucas steps out and helps me exit the cab, his warm, strong hand closing around mine. I smile at him and link my fingers tightly with his, not letting go even after I'm fully out and standing.

He lifts my hand and kisses the knuckles. The hot moist touch of his lips sends frissons of heat along my spine. He can do so many wicked things with his mouth, bring my body to immeasurable heights of pleasure. Shivers run through me. I want to be with him like that again, him devouring me then rising up and driving into me with his thick, hard cock. It's been so long since I've let a man possess me so completely.

"Keep thinking like that, and we aren't having dinner after all," he warns me, grazing my knuckles with his teeth.

"Blame yourself for being too sexy."

He gives me a light grin. "Too sexy, am I?"

"I see I'm inflating your head."

"Oh, you have *nooooo* idea."

I reach for the door, but Lucas is faster. He pulls it open and escorts me in. The entryway is elegantly appointed with a minimalist Japanese-style flower arrangement: a few maple branches framing a single, large autumn bloom.

The hostess is a young Japanese woman in a beautiful deep-pink kimono. The skirt portion has intricate patterns of bright yellow butterflies and red and purple flowers. She bows precisely, her movements neither slow nor fast, then welcomes us in a professionally girlish voice. "Irasshaimase."

Lucas gives her his name, and she says, "Hai," with an "I'm thrilled to be serving you today" smile and takes his jacket. Another young woman in a beautiful kimono, this one crystal blue, comes out and takes us to our table.

As we walk along the corridor, I glimpse other diners through bamboo screens hanging from dark wooden beams. Most of them are decked out in expensive suits and beautiful dresses. Rolexes flash on their wrists, and colorful jewels twinkle on their fingers and ears. One or two might be celebrities I've seen on TV.

Our table is in a secluded corner. The bamboo screen gives us an illusion of privacy. On one side is a window that faces an interior courtyard with more rock garden and a pair of miniature maple trees. The leaves are a shade between green and red; behind them, a bamboo fountain gurgles at the opposite end. Small spotlights embedded among the pebbles showcase the various features.

"It's beautiful," I say, sitting down as the waitress pulls out a plushy, high-backed chair for me. She's also in a kimono.

"Glad you like it." He grins and takes a seat. "I made it clear to the concierge that she had to select a place you'd never forget."

The waitress serves us warm fragrant tea. She then confirms the sake choices with Lucas and leaves. Everything at the table is perfectly minimalist. The chopsticks are gorgeous, lacquered black with golden fish motifs on the thicker ends, and rest on pale ceramic pieces shaped like crescent moons. A translucent green glass centerpiece holds a huge chrysanthemum in the most vivid shade of yellow.

I rest an elbow on the table and prop my chin in my hand. "You're taking my comment back in Chiang Mai seriously, aren't you?"

I don't have to say more. He shakes his head. "I'm not going to force you to get the most expensive items while being a dick about it. And I apologize. That was uncalled for. But…I want to spoil you. So why don't you let me?"

"All right. So what are we getting?"

"Omakase."

"So it's going to be a surprise?"

"For both of us. The concierge ordered. My Japanese isn't good enough to deal with all the details myself."

I smile wryly at his modest response. "I doubt that. You did some real damage at my school, and if you sounded barely literate, Kouchou-sensei wouldn't have taken you seriously."

His forehead wrinkles, his mouth tightening for a moment. "I…hired someone to make the call." He sighs. "Not exactly proud of that."

I raise an eyebrow. "I'd hope not."

"Another thing on the 'Lucas needs to earn forgiveness' list?"

If it were anybody else, I'd laugh as though it were a joke…or maybe tell him that yes, he'd have to work his ass off to earn my generous pardon. But Lucas… He is surprisingly vulnerable and sensitive, and I don't want to do anything to hurt him.

I reach over and take his hand in both of mine. "There's no list, Lucas."

The waitress interrupts the moment by placing our first course on the table—finely cut slices of various fish with miso sauce for dipping. The plates are stunning, with a delicate white glaze that seems to shimmer under the light. Warmed plum sake provides a perfect complement.

I have a slice of salmon and sigh, reaching for my drink. The fish is perfectly prepared, the coldness of the meat going well with the heat of the liquor. "This is so good."

He smiles. "Glad you approve." He takes a bite thoughtfully. "Just so you know, I hired a crew to come over to your place tomorrow. They're going to help you pack everything."

"So fast?"

"With the right incentive…"

"I can pack my own stuff. I don't have much." I didn't bring a lot to Japan—just clothes, shoes and a few personal items.

"I'd rather you relax tomorrow. I booked you a massage."

A massage? "You shouldn't have."

"Wrong answer. You're supposed to say, 'Lucas, I'm disappointed you only got me a lousy massage,'" he says in a falsetto voice. "Just so I can say, 'Actually, you can get whatever you want at the spa.'"

I feign irritation, but it's impossible when he's looking at me totally unrepentant. "I think you're the one keeping a list. 'Don't ever let Ava hear the end of it.'"

"I'd *never*. You said you wanted to be treated like a queen, and you're right." The light humor slips from his face. "Bennie told me you don't care about stuff like this—"

"I don't."

"—but you must've at least dreamed of it at some point if you were buying lottery tickets."

Oh my god, *how* could Bennie talk about that? Argh! It was a stupid thing I did when I was younger. I don't want to think about it ever again.

"I'm not judging," Lucas adds. "The odds are horrific, but people buy them to dream." He gives me a crooked grin. "Guess you were sick of PB and J sandwiches."

He is giving me a perfect deflection. I should seize it and nod and laugh and pretend I was a silly, fanciful child.

But I can't.

Lucas has allowed himself to be vulnerable with me, and I want our second chance to work. I'm already hiding a huge secret, and I don't want to lie to him about more things.

Sighing, I put down my chopsticks and reach for another small serving of sake. "I was young and stupid and didn't listen to my mother, who told me I would've been better off spending that money on snacks or something more immediately practical. I did stop eventually. I've learned my lesson."

"Ava…" Lucas pulls back, his concerned gaze on my face.

Damn. I sounded too bitter. I didn't mean to. I merely blame myself for not realizing what was going on sooner.

"When I asked my mom to get them for me, I had no idea what they were really for. I just knew if I won, Dad wouldn't have to work so much."

Lucas is quiet, but eerily still. His full attention is on me, like a lion looking into tall, waving grass.

"But the fact is, even if I'd won, Dad wouldn't have spent my birthday with me. Or Thanksgiving or Christmas or…"

I pause, trying to control my roughening breathing. I've never told anybody about this. People who know know because they either saw the whole thing blow up in person or heard from those who did. It's the ugliest chapter of my life.

I could stop now, and that would be that. I don't think Lucas would probe, but I don't want to stop, and it's beyond merely trying to be more open about myself with him. Do I *want* Lucas to become disgusted and leave me alone before he breaks my heart again? Is this a final attempt at testing him? I don't know, but I can't keep it inside anymore. "He would've found another reason for being away."

The lines of Lucas's face grow hard and unyielding. "Was he having an affair? Had a child he had to provide for or something?"

I flinch. Lucas is so close. If it didn't hurt so much, it would almost be funny how quickly he's put it together. My past isn't that unique—just a damn cliché. Suddenly I can't talk about it any-more—my childhood self as a laughable heroine in a tragic farce. "Forget it. It's a pointless story, and it doesn't matter anymore."

"Yes, it does, not if you can't laugh about it." He links his fingers with mine over the table. "Can you?"

I shake my head and toss the sake back. "He was a cheater, but not the way you think. He was a married man having an affair with my mom, but neither she nor I knew. She thought the reason why he didn't want to get married was because

I was a girl and he didn't want to jeopardize the benefits we were getting. Their combined income would've been too much to qualify for stuff. But if they weren't married, he could use his friend's apartment as his 'mailing address' and we could collect EBT and whatever else my mom qualified for."

Lucas's hold on me tightens. "I'm sorry."

"We found out only because there was an accident while he was driving with Mom. Miraculously, Mom was fine, but Dad didn't make it. I can't describe how it was then… I was…" I close my eyes for a moment, seeing the entire scene play in my head like a movie. "I was devastated, and so was Mom. But it was nothing compared to how we felt when his *family* showed up—a wife and a daughter. Sondra and Elle." I pick up a piece of fish, but discover I can't eat it. "They weren't anything like us—well-fed… well-dressed…well-groomed…"

The old humiliation burns through me. They wore designer clothes and expensive perfume that wafted from bodies toned from regular gym visits. Sondra's hands were soft and well-cared for—the total opposite of my mom's.

"It was clear they'd never had to eat peanut-butter sandwiches. Apparently, Dad was a banker. He left everything to his real family, and the only thing Sondra and Elle cared about was keeping his dirty little secret hushed up to save face."

"I'm sorry, Ava. I'm so sorry." He's squeezing my hand gently, but tension is twisting his face. "God, I don't know how you can give me another chance after an experience like that. You must've hated me when you said I was treating you as a 'dirty little secret.'"

I shake my head. "I didn't hate you, Lucas. I…I just didn't believe we could be together. I know about your family. How wealthy and important they are."

"The rich part is right, but they aren't important." His dark gaze meets mine directly. Its intensity is like a snare, impossible to pull away from. "*Nobody* is as important as you," he says.

I take his hand and lay my forehead on it. But it isn't enough. I need a deeper connection with him. "Do you think they'd mind if we left now?" I murmur.

"*I* would mind," Lucas says. "I want you well-fed, well-cared for. You can't possibly understand how much I want to take care of you."

My lips curve into a smile. He doesn't understand how irresistible he is when he speaks like this, how easily he can cut through all the protective layers I have and reach into my heart.

It doesn't matter what I told myself two years ago…or since. I'm still in love with this man.

This sweet and generous side is what I saw first in him—with me and with Mrs. Ling. He quietly loaned them some money—interest-free—so they could get through the year, and he paid off the lease on my apartment so I wouldn't be evicted after two of my roommates were arrested and expelled from the university for selling prescription drugs. The only reason I found out is because the landlord slipped up, not because Lucas ever wanted to take credit. He loathed talking about his own good deeds.

And that's not all. I found more and more little things he'd done to help out. And that selfless generosity…it really touched me. It felt so good to have somebody watching over me for once. Like I mattered.

"Why don't we compromise?" he offers. "After we eat, I'll give you everything you want."

"That doesn't seem like much of a compromise, horny Neanderthal," I tease.

"But it is, Ava," he purrs. "I plan to make you come as many times as you want…and then some more, but only after you finish your dinner."

I smile and lean over the table to kiss him on the mouth. "Deal."

NINETEEN

Lucas

I'M SURE THE PROPRIETOR OF THE RESTAURANT would be horrified if I said I'm not really noticing the food that much.

I have the feeling it's pretty good—there's no urge to spit it out or anything—but I'm riveted by Ava, her obvious enjoyment, the way she licks her lips and laughs at the jokes I make. My body's hot and hard, and I feel my blood heat as we get closer to the inevitable conclusion of the night, but I try not to let it color my interaction with her. My need for Ava isn't just sexual. It's…everything.

As annoying as Bennie was, I'm grateful he made me probe about her background. Otherwise I might've never known.

You didn't want to know.

That's true enough. When I first met Ava, the last thing I wanted was to become overly entangled. Even as I craved her, I fought against feeling too much for her—that would've only ended in utter disaster…or so I told myself.

What a fool I was. I missed out on discovering a lot of Ava's most critical aspects. If I'd known back then… Well, I'm not sure precisely what I would have done…but I would've acted differently.

My patience is slowly running out as we approach the dessert, but I ignore the lust bubbling in my blood. It's only one more course, and Ava deserves to enjoy everything.

She spoons the sweet custard paired with rich vanilla and chocolate ice cream. "This is so good," she moans as she licks the spoon clean off, her pink tongue flickering.

Jesus.

My dick engorges further as I imagine her licking it the same way. I have to remind myself she's just pleased with the dessert. I have no idea how it tastes; every cell in my body is incapable of processing anything but her—her presence, her scent, her smile, her warm gaze.

Long, thick eyelashes lowered, she spoons another bite. A lovely flush colors her cheeks. When she lifts her gaze, I see the want seething beneath those ice blue eyes.

"Are you really going to make me finish dessert?" She ends her question with a slow smile.

I toss my spoon on the table. "No. We can have a private dessert."

"Finally!"

I hand my credit card to the waitress, and as soon as we pay our bill we're out of the restaurant. It's a bit chilly outside, the wind nipping. I take off my jacket and drape it around Ava's shoulders.

"You're going to be cold," she says.

"Nope. I have you to keep me warm."

I pull her close, fitting her in front of me, and wrap my arms around her. When I hold her like this, I can let myself relax a little bit. I've *got* her, and she can't go anywhere.

She relaxes against me as a taxi pulls in. "Mmm," she hums, rubbing her ass against my stiff dick. "Sure you don't want your jacket back?"

I bite her earlobe gently, feel her shiver. "You can be my cover."

When the taxi door swings open, she and I climb inside together. I give the smartly uniformed driver the name of my hotel, and he shuts the door and merges into the traffic on the road.

I don't let go of Ava. Instead I settle her between the V of my legs, and run my fingers along her soft, silken thighs under her skirt.

"Lucas," she whispers, her voice thready.

"I know, baby."

"The driver can see us."

I flick my gaze his way for a second before returning it back to her. "He isn't paying attention."

"But—"

"Shhh. Who cares? We'll never see him again."

I press my lips against the bare skin at the base of her neck. Her breath hitches, and I tighten my hold on her. My cock feels as heavy as iron now. I grit my teeth as she squirms in my lap.

When the ride is finally over, I toss the money at the driver and drag Ava out, keeping her in front of me to hide the tent in my pants. The whole building could be crumbling down in front of me, and it wouldn't lessen my ardor a bit.

Ava takes my hand and presses it against her belly. And we're off.

Ava

MY FINGERS LINKED WITH HIS, I TROT AS FAST AS I can in my heels across the impeccable lobby. Lucas maintains speed, his long legs eating up the distance.

Call me shameless, but I want to kiss Lucas silly in the privacy of an elevator. My body is tingling all over after feeling him pressed against me in the taxi and his hot breath on my neck. Sizzling need throbs with my every pulse; it's all I can do not to pant.

Disappointment crashes down when we reach the elevators. There's a crowd waiting—women in traditional kimonos and men in black suits. *Crap.*

"Don't despair," Lucas whispers against my ear. "We'll find a way."

"A way to what?" I whisper back, feigning ignorance although running my tongue along my lips probably betrays me.

"Another sneaky"—a sharp nick at the ear-lobe—"naughty way." A lick to soothe it.

I gasp. "You're shameless."

"Shamelessly desperate for you."

Hearing those four words, my clit throbs as though they physically rubbed against it. I clench my legs so I don't behave like a total hussy and devour him right here in front of the elevators.

When a car arrives, we manage to get in first, mainly because Lucas pushes through the crowd. We settle into the back of the elevator, and the people fill in. I'm standing in front of him, his jacket draped around my shoulders and his left hand still linked with mine and pressed against my belly.

As the car moves, I feel his right hand slipping under the skirt and roaming all over my ass, lightly and teasingly. Even though my body is heating with need, I pull away. I'm already about to blow. I don't need him to stroke...

A finger caresses along my folds through the damp panties. My entire body goes rigid. I dig my teeth into my lower lip to stifle a moan, gripping his hand so hard it almost hurts.

But he is undeterred. The elevator stops every so often to let people out, but his fingers continue to trace the slickness between my thighs. Three floors away from our room, the last people get out and we're finally alone in the car. He pushes underneath the hopelessly wet fabric and rubs against the bundle of nerves.

"Lucas," I hiss. My knees are threatening to buckle.

"I've got you," he whispers in my ear.

I close my eyes. "The security camera."

"Can't see what we're doing unless you move."

That's true enough. My skirt covers his hand from view, but oh my god...

"You're so wet for me, Ava. I can't wait to have you."

I lean back against him and pant. "I can't wait. I want you inside me. Now." I punctuate that by grinding myself against him. The feel of his erection twitching against my ass is gratifying, but nowhere near enough.

The elevator finally opens on our floor with a sharp ding. We both stagger out. I'm drunk with need, and from the dark glittering look in Lucas's eye, so is he. He spins me around so he can kiss me deeply as we slowly edge toward the suite. I pull him into my mouth, stroking and sucking his tongue, my fingers digging into his hair and my nipples rubbing painfully hard against his chest.

It takes three tries before he gets the door unlocked. He sticks the card into the slot and the suite lights up. Our mouths still fused, we kick off our shoes. His jacket falls on the floor. He finds the zipper in the back of my dress and pulls it down, while I fumble with the buttons on his shirt.

The second he drags the dress over my hips, I shimmy out of it. His hot gaze sears me, taking in my black lace demi-bra and tiny panties. He rips his shirt off, buttons flying, and tosses it over a shoulder like a worthless rag.

Before I can gasp at the violent reaction, he grabs me and kisses me again. I make quick work of his belt and the rest of his clothes. His cock springs out and presses against my belly. I wrap my hand around it and squeeze, watch the pre-cum bead at the tip, and lick my mouth.

"Jesus," he mutters.

"You. Inside me. Now," I pant.

"Wrap your legs around me."

I do so instantly. He adjusts so his thick, pulsing shaft is nestled between my folds. I rock against him, unable to stop myself. He grits his teeth.

"You might want to wait until I get a condom."

"Hurry," I demand, my fingers digging into his hot flesh.

He carries me to the bed and deposits me in the center. His cockhead is glistening and I lick my lips. He curses under his breath. "You're trying to kill me."

"Is that an objection?"

He grins. "Nope."

He supports himself on his elbows, resting one on each side of my head and kisses me again. I breathe in his scent—soap and male and a hint of musk—and I wrap myself around him, totally primed.

His greedy mouth traces my jawline, my neck and my collarbones. He moves lower, kissing the soft swell of my breasts, and tugs at the bra cup until he can wrap his mouth around one of my bared nipples.

He sucks hard, trapping the pointed tip between the roof of his mouth and the flat of his tongue. His cheeks hollow, his hot eyes on mine. Bliss spreads through me, leaving my body heavy and languid with sensual delight. My fingernails rake across his back and dig into the thick muscles. His chest rumbles as he chuckles like the sexy devil he is. He switches his attention to the other nipple, and I writhe underneath him as blistering pleasure streaks along my veins. I feel like I'm burning from inside out, and if he doesn't drive into me, I'm going to die in the next two seconds.

He licks the smooth skin along my belly, going lower and lower and lower until his breath fans my clit. Shamelessly, I spread my legs as wide as I can.

"Please, Lucas!" I beg, uncaring what comes out of my mouth so long as he takes me. "I want you inside me, thick and hard, fast and strong. I've been dreaming about this for two years. We couldn't do it last time, and as satisfying as it is to have you down there, I want you pounding into me more. Don't deny me. And don't make me wait any longer."

The muscles in his jaw flex. I know from the way he grinds his teeth that his control is slipping dangerously.

He pushes himself off the mattress and reaches into the drawer by the bed. He pulls out a foil packet and rips it open with his teeth. With an elegant deftness that I can't help but adore, he sheathes himself in the rubber and links his fingers with mine, pushing my hands up until they're above my head.

"Ava, you're the only woman who can shatter me like this."

He drives into me in one smooth stroke. Although I'm slick and ready, I feel his invasion with a tinge of mild discomfort. He is so big and so damn hard. But it doesn't last long. He keeps himself still to give me the time to adjust, but the ache that his immobility starts in my belly is too much to bear.

"Please," I whisper.

He starts to thrust, creating that delicious friction that only he can. Hot liquid pleasure unfurls inside me, spreading in sweet ripples.

I grow even wetter, more desperate for him. We breathe in the same air, staring into each other's eyes. Even through the lust relentlessly driving both of us, I feel a deep connection forming. It is as though my soul is entwining with his every time he sinks into me, finding his bliss and giving me mine.

An orgasm erupts within me. I arch my back, screaming his name.

A harsh groan tears from his throat. Sweat forms along his hairline and spine, but he doesn't stop. He's a man possessed, determined. He keeps going, each drive somehow different—somehow better—than the one before.

"I'm so close. Oh my god, I think I'm going to—" My fingers tighten around his.

He breathes harshly against my neck, placing a hot kiss against my jawline. "That's the point.

I want you to come again with my dick in your pussy, and I want you to feel me come, feel me inside you long after."

I meet his gaze with mine. "I'm never going to forget anything. You're the only one." He's always been the only one.

He drives more powerfully into me. I climax again. "Lucas!"

Tendons stand out starkly on his neck as he thrusts into me one final time. "*Ava.*"

He shudders within me as a powerful orgasm finds him. And I hold his hands as tightly as I can.

Because this moment? This is so damn sweet, so damn powerful. He said I shatter him, but he's the one who shatters me.

When he can breathe normally again, he lifts his head and looks at me, presses his lips to my forehead. "Stay."

I close my eyes and nod. "Okay."

TWENTY

Ava

"GOOD MORNING, SLEEPY HEAD."

"Ugh. Too early, you sex fiend." I start to turn away from Lucas's cheerful greeting, but then smell coffee. "Is that…?"

"Yes."

I open my eyes. The first thing I see is him—freshly showered and in a casual white cotton shirt and old faded blue jeans. His dark gaze is soft and bright, and the morning light hits the beautiful, straight blade of his nose and the sharp angles of the cheekbone I can see. My breath catches. I've never experienced waking up with him. And I like it. Too much so.

Suddenly shy and discomfited by the thought, I sit up and extend a hand for the coffee. I inhale the deep aroma and take a sip. It flows over my tongue like an elixir. "This is really good."

"Only the best for my girl." Lucas sits next to me. "As much as I'd like to have you sleep as long as you want, it's already ten. And you have a spa appointment at eleven."

"*Ten?* I never sleep that late."

He grins at me, entirely too happy. "Well, I kept you up."

I take another sip. "And I kept *you* up. Insatiable beast." As I shift, my body protests, making every little ache and soreness known. Still I can't complain. It was for a good cause, and I feel like I just conquered Mount Everest.

I get out of bed carefully, holding the mug. "I'm going to finish this coffee and take a shower."

Lucas checks out my naked body, scraping his lower lip with his teeth. Even though the heat in his look sends a pang of lust through me, I wag my finger.

"Remember the appointment at eleven?"

He sighs. "You might want to shower first. I ordered room service about ten minutes ago."

I nod and chug down the coffee as quickly as I can while starting the water. Steam fills the bathroom. Placing the empty mug by the sink, I hop into the shower and wash efficiently. The moist heat helps loosen my muscles, and I feel much better.

By the time I'm out and finish applying some lotion to my skin, I hear dishware rattling around outside. Gotta admire Japanese efficiency.

"Food's here," Lucas announces from the living room.

I go out, tying the sash around my robe. "What did you get?"

"A couple of egg omelets and ham and sausage."

"A man after my own heart. And croissants too?"

"Of course. And apricot jam." He pulls out a chair for me.

Taking my seat, I give him a small smile. "How did you know?"

"When we were flying, you didn't touch anything except the apricot jam with your bread and croissants." He sits across from me and twists the jar open.

"I won't have much time to linger over our meal."

"If you're calculating travel time, don't. The spa's inside the hotel."

I give him a stern look. "Do you have any idea how much it costs to go to a hotel spa?"

"Do I look like the type to care?" His smile is completely unrepentant. "Now, say thank you and enjoy your meal."

"Thank you. But you really didn't have to." I lower my eyelashes. "I could cancel it and spend the rest of the morning in bed with you..."

"Much as I appreciate the gesture, I'm not letting you cheap out on me." He reaches over and takes my hand. "I want to spoil you, Ava. I haven't been able to do anything for your birthday or holidays in the last two years. So let me."

Gifts. *Things.* I can't help but feel sort of blah about them. "Okay."

I can sense him withdrawing at my rather tepid response. *Oh come on. He's trying. And isn't this what you wanted? Give him a chance. He isn't like your father.*

I muster a high-wattage smile. "A spa does sound like fun." I take a bite of the egg omelet, which is excellent—fluffy and light, almost like a soufflé. "But now I have to think about what I'm going to get you."

Relaxing a bit, he says, "You don't have to give me anything."

"But I haven't gotten you anything for your birthday for two years either."

He gives me an odd look. "It's enough that you're with me."

Surprised, I study him. It's obvious he means what he said. It's sweet, but it won't be enough for me personally. If we apply this logic, then being together should be enough for both of us. I'm not sure why I'm so reluctant to just accept all his extravagant gifts, but somehow I am.

"Be gracious and say thank you, Ava," he says with mock sternness.

"Fine. Thank you," I say as ungraciously as possible, which elicits a laugh.

I manage a smile. But I can't shake off the unease.

Ava

DESPITE MY WORRIES, I END UP WITH AN EXTRA five minutes before the appointment. Lucas has thought of everything. He had the concierge bring up my favorite face lotions and took my wrinkled dress and hung it in the bathroom while he showered so it was presentable again. That was considerate, since I don't have anything else to wear, and I didn't think beyond being with him last night.

The spa reception area isn't huge, but it's airy with bright cream colors, soft leather couches and oval glass-top tables. High-quality herbs and spices scent the air, and numerous vases with fresh roses and lilies occupy various nooks and crannies. A young, slim receptionist in a dark blue and cream dress informs me in excellent English to wait a bit and serves me my drink of choice—hot lemon tea with milk—in an elegant bone china cup with a saucer.

I take a quick sip of the tea. It's great, made with real lemon, not the cheap imitation goop you often find in Osaka supermarkets. I pull out my phone and text Ray and Darcy.

I'm coming back home soon, probably this week. Don't know exactly when yet. Will let you know. Miss you. Give Mia my love.

A couple minutes later, I get a call. "Ray! I didn't know you were still up."

"Mia's been a little fussy today. Darcy was with her, and I told her to get some sleep."

I wince. "Sorry she's such a difficult child." The apology slips out before I can stop myself. Every time she gets sick or acts in a manner that makes her less than perfect, I feel responsible.

"Ah, she's an angel. Even princesses have bad days." He chuckles. "Listen, I just wanted to make sure you're all right. Darcy said something about asking you to come home for Thanksgiving. But your vacation probably isn't gonna be long enough to make it worth your while to fly all the way out here, right? So what's going on?"

"Kind of a long story, but I think I'm moving back home. Permanently."

He's quiet for a moment. "You are? Did you resign?"

"Something like that."

"Okay. Well… Do you have a place to stay?"

Probably Lucas's place in Charlottesville, but... "Yes, I think so."

"It's a man, isn't it?"

"What?"

"You hesitated, and there's no way you just quit your job like that. The Japanese are bad about quitting."

It was Ray's expertise in Japanese history and culture that got me interested in working in the country in the first place. "Yes."

"He must be something special."

"He is." I turn away from the receptionist checking the computer and lower my voice. "It's Lucas."

"The Lucas from two years ago?" Ray asks sharply.

"Yes."

"Well... I suppose I should say I'm glad you're getting back together."

My hand clenches and unclenches around the phone. "Ray."

"Does he know?"

"No."

In the silence, I can see Ray pinching his steel-gray eyebrows together. "So. You aren't one hundred percent certain about him, but somehow you quit your job to be with him."

Put that way, it does sound pretty crazy.

"Darcy's going to worry," he says.

"I know."

Ray sighs. "Can you send me your flight information as soon as you know? I'll pick you up from the airport."

"You don't need to—"

"I insist. So will Darcy. We've missed you, and Darcy's going to want to keep you under our roof and spoil you for a while."

And when Darcy wants to spoil you, you get spoiled. "Thank you." We'll discuss where I'm going to be living later—that's not a battle I want to fight at the moment.

"No need for thanks. That's what family's for."

My eyes prickle with tears. Ray and his wife, Darcy, are the ones who treated me like their own. Without them for foster parents, who knows how I might've ended up?

The receptionist smiles to signal that they're ready for me. I turn my attention back to the call. "I have to go, Ray. I'll text you the flight info as soon as I can."

"Great. Love you, Ava."

"I love you, too, Ray."

Lucas

SINCE I KNOW AVA IS GOING TO CHEAP OUT ON me—I don't trust that she'll get more than a foot massage—I call the spa and instruct them to give her the works. I want her happy, relaxed and glowing when she comes back.

I lean against the headboard and smile to myself. I wish I were there to see it when she realizes she's going to be pampered whether she likes it or not. Mostly so I could kiss away her annoyed scowl and taste that adorable pouty mouth.

My phone buzzes with a text. *Ava, writing about my high-handedness?* I should probably send her something inappropriate. Maybe a pec shot...or something more risqué. I snort with a suppressed laugh, but my humor vanishes when I see who it is from—Blake.

When are you available? Found the perfect woman for you.

The message is so bizarre, it takes me a moment to process. It isn't like him to give a damn about my love life.

Not interested, I text back.

Already find a bride? Is it the woman you wanted to talk about earlier?

I scowl. Ava is none of his business. *I'm not marrying her for the painting,* I write, referring to the fucked-up proposal from our father.

Then what?

I hesitate. I want Ava for reasons other than the damned paintings. And I want her to crave me the way I crave her…the way I love her.

Another text comes in. *You are marrying, right?*

I already told you guys no. As I hit send, I feel a pit growing in my belly.

Dad is a borderline sociopath, but he's no dummy. He knows the only way to make us all jump is to make sure everyone gets punished if even one of us disobeys.

I can live without the painting. My siblings believe Grandpa saw our greatest potential and put that into the portraits he did of us when we turned eighteen. It might be true for them, but it isn't for me. He saw something in me that didn't exist. He only saw what he wanted to see, and when there wasn't anything there, he imagined it.

People think that Elliot and I are geniuses and that we founded and nurtured the company that made us rich together. But it was really Elliot who protected it from the embezzler—I didn't know the money was missing since stuff like that isn't my forte—and he's the one who courted our investors. I was always a bit too shy and awkward. Or, as Elliot would put it, "Hard to get to know."

The more precise verdict would be "wears his heart on his sleeve unless he's careful" delivered in a female voice dripping with contempt.

You know this is going to devastate Elizabeth.

I glare at the phone screen. Blake knows my weak point. Other than Ava, my half-sister, Elizabeth Pryce-Reed, is the only woman I'd take a bullet for. She isn't Catholic, but she should be canonized anyway for all the good work she does for the destitute and disadvantaged in the world. I've seen the difference she's made in people's lives. If I died today, it wouldn't make the world any sadder, any less bright. But Elizabeth? The world would be a poorer place.

That's a cheap shot. She'll get over it if I donate a few million bucks to her foundation to make up for it, I respond even though I know that isn't true. Even though Grandpa's portrait couldn't capture all that's good about her, she adores the work since she loved that man. She'd grieve if she lost it.

Is that what she said? Blake texts back.

She doesn't have to. I know.

I tip my head backward, banging it against the headboard a few times. I don't want to disappoint Elizabeth, but I can't bear to hurt Ava. She deserves nothing less than true love, a fairy-tale wedding…the works.

I'm not asking her to marry me for some fucking oil and canvas.

TWENTY-ONE

Ava

MORE THAN THREE HOURS LATER, I emerge from the spa. At first, I was a little annoyed that Lucas went overboard—and rather sneakily too, getting the spa people to give me what *he* wanted. But with my muscles feeling like warm clay, my skin scrubbed and glowing, and my nails shiny with a coat of gorgeous pink lacquer, I can't complain. He was right to give me the works.

I claim my purse from the locker and check my phone. I have a couple of texts from Bennie.

First: *Guess you had a good time. Don't make it too good for him. He deserves to suffer a little for what he's done to you. And good god, why did he have to send the moving crew so early? They showed up before coffee.*

Second: *Lucas said you were leaving today, so I'm going to host a party starting at seven for you. Tell him to hold the damned plane until midnight or something.*

I frown. I had no idea we were leaving today. Lucas said he sent people to get my things today, but...*flying out* today?

When I reach the suite, Lucas opens the door and says, "Wow. You look amazing."

"Thank you. I feel great." I give him a smile. I've never been so thoroughly spoiled before, and not even Bennie's text can take away my glow. "But what is this about us leaving today?"

"Where'd you hear that?"

"Bennie."

Lucas mutters something under his breath. "Yes. I told him that, but only because he was pissing me off. But like I said before, I can't linger too long."

"Okay." I breathe out shakily. "You're right. Why delay it?"

He takes my hand and kisses the back of it tenderly. "I swear you won't regret this."

"I know you'll do your best. You promised."

A man who allowed himself to be as vulnerable as Lucas isn't a man who intends to screw up.

"Thank you."

"Apparently there's a going-away party tonight. I want you to come with me."

His eyebrows rise. "Me?"

I nod. "You should. I'd love you to meet some of my friends before we leave."

He shifts his weight a bit. "If you'd like."

"I'd like." I press myself against him. "So… what should we do until then?"

"What do you have in mind?"

"I think you know." I give him a wicked smile, rocking against him.

His gaze glitters. "Do you now?"

I let my hand brush against his cock. "It's a bit too obvious." I grip his broad, thickly muscled shoulders and steer him toward the bed. "And I think you're too tense." I run the back of my fingers along his shaft through his jeans.

"I think you're right." His voice is taut.

"You should be pampered too."

"Most definitely. For the sake of fairness."

"Equality."

"Good for the goose."

"Lemme take a gander." I stop at the threshold between the living room and the bedroom. Does it matter where we are when I know exactly how I want to pamper him?

Going on my toes, I kiss him. He dips his head, fusing his mouth with mine. He tastes of mint and Lucas—an amazing indescribably sexy flavor that's uniquely his. The scent of clean, warm male skin and a trace of soap that I'll forever associate with him is tantalizing, arousing. His hands dive into my hair and clench the back of my head, not hard enough to hurt but forcefully enough to make his presence known. We breathe the same air and drink each other in as though somehow we can be one.

I let a hand drift lower, caressing the hard planes of his chest through the shirt. Though he seems to believe that his injuries have marred him, I marvel at the beauty of his body, its inherent strength. It's heady to know this is all mine.

My fingers flick over the nipple piercing.

A low groan tears from his chest. "Ava."

"Shhh…" I push the shirt upward. He helps, sliding it over his head and tossing it somewhere behind me. I lick my lips at the rippling muscles that are revealed. A medium amount of hair covers his pecs; his abs are taut and ridged, every line lean and clean. The silver ring on his nipple glints, and I flick my tongue over it, unable to stop myself. I *love* toying with that thing—the response it elicits from his body.

My tongue isn't enough. My teeth and lips join, tormenting that small nub, while my hands are busy running all over his perfect physique. Heat pulses between my legs. Every time he groans, I feel the vibration all the way to my clit, and my thighs clench reflexively.

I undo the buckle of his belt and unbutton his

jeans and push them down along with his boxers. His cock juts forward, the plum-shaped tip slick. I lick it teasingly as I sink to my knees before him. Gripping his narrow hips with my hands, I look up at his flushed face.

"Let me," I say.

He nods.

I kiss his thighs, loving both of them equally, scarred and unscarred. I cup his sac in my hands, feeling its heavy weight, and luxuriate when he inhales sharply.

Tenderly I stroke his thick, hard shaft with my fingers, then trace the throbbing veins with my tongue. He groans, the sound deep and harsh, but keeps his fists by his sides.

I reward his restraint by taking him into my mouth. The large and pulsing feel is amazing. I hollow my cheeks, pulling him deeper.

His chest heaves. "Ava, baby, make yourself feel good too." He pulls out.

I moan in protest. "But I already do."

"I want you to come when I do. I want to feel your scream muffled against my dick."

My cheeks heat at the unabashedly carnal idea. Slipping a hand between my legs, I take him back into my mouth. I'm already slick, my clit swollen and ready. I grip his ass with my free hand and bob my head while pleasuring myself to the same rhythm.

I feel his cock get bigger, his balls contract. His breathing is shallower, and the muscles in his abs go taut. The precum coating my tongue is slick and salty, and I watch his face, wanting to savor the moment, needing him to know what he means to me.

"I'm so close," he rasps.

I suck harder, pulling him deeper, my tongue stroking him, wanting him to climax in my mouth. The beginning of an orgasm wraps around me, tightening my core, ready to rip me apart at any second.

He throws his head back, his body tensing. A guttural cry tears from his throat. "Ava—!"

He spurts hotly, the salty cum flooding my mouth. Swallowing, I shudder as my own orgasm barrels through me, leaving me breathless and weak.

Lucas drops to his knees and wraps his arms around me. His lips find mine, and his tongue meets mine in a crazy hot kiss of gratitude, affection, trust and something else I can't name.

In that moment…scarily enough, I feel truly and utterly loved.

Ava

Lucas decides we might get too hungry
before we get to eat later that night, so we munch
on some snacks from room service. Well, I snack
on fruit and yogurt, while Lucas polishes off a
roast beef sandwich and fries.

"How can you eat like that and maintain your
body?" I ask.

"Genetics?"

"Is that what you call it?"

"I exercise too."

I cup my chin. "Do you?"

"Uh-huh. Mostly weights. Don't run much
anymore…obviously." He shoots me a rueful grin.

I place a hand on his left leg. "Don't be too
hard on this guy. It's incredible that you survived
the crash and the leg's still working."

His numerous scars tell me everything I need
to know. I wonder briefly how things would've
turned out if I hadn't left after Blake's vicious
words. The bastard denied everything to Lucas,
but I know what was said…and so does he.

"By the way, do you know when we're going
to arrive in the States?" I ask.

"I had our pilot schedule a red-eye, and
he's estimating that we'll land in Charlottesville
around eight thirty p.m."

"Great." I pull out my phone and text Ray
with the time.

"Who's that?"

"Ray—my foster dad. He wants to know."

"I'd like to meet him," Lucas says.

My mouth forms an O. "You would?"

"You like him, so he must be a great guy." Before I can ask him how he knew, he flicks the tip of my nose. "You were smiling fondly."

I didn't realize. "It's difficult not to. He *is* a great guy. And his wife is lovely. They live in the same neighborhood you do."

"Really? You never told me about them," Lucas says.

"We never talked about a lot of things."

We had sex, we had fun, but we didn't spend any nights together, and we didn't pry. I was afraid if I did, he'd disappear—he seemed so aloof and private. And I didn't want to talk about myself, worried that it might come across as a ham-fisted attempt to make him feel obligated to share in return. Plus, my past is mostly pathetic.

Lucas looks pensive. "I should've made an effort."

"We were both skittish."

"Yeah, but… That's no excuse."

"So we can do better now." I wipe a bit of ketchup from the corner of his mouth with his napkin. "I have faith in us. Don't you?"

He takes my hand, kisses each fingertip tenderly and presses his lips against the center of my palm. "I do."

TWENTY-TWO

Ava

THE PLACE BENNIE MANAGED TO SNAG IS A popular expat bar. The owner is an Irish guy who married a Japanese woman five years ago. He and his wife manage the place.

Lucas and I walk inside, hands linked. The place is already half-full with familiar faces. I'm stunned as I look around. I didn't realize so many people would show, given the short notice and the fact that it's a Thursday evening.

"My god, Ava, I can't believe you're leaving! It's so sudden!" Barbara says, hugging me. She's a freckled redhead from Scotland with a Sean Connery accent. Fortunately, her voice is a good octave higher than his. Always down to earth, she's in a simple plaid dress and chunky boots, although she said the garment isn't at all authentic—she picked it up in Shibuya. She looks at Lucas curiously. "And who is this fine specimen?"

"Barbara, say hello to Lucas. He's my, um—"

"Boyfriend," Lucas says.

Pleasure unfurls at the designation. We never called each other boyfriend and girlfriend before. We never really had the chance, since we were rarely out in public where we could run into people we knew.

"Hadn't the slightest you were dating." Barbara winks. "No wonder you didn't show him around. He's a catch, he is."

I sense him stiffen through our linked hands, but she seems oblivious.

"Good for you," she continues. "The two of you going back together, then?"

"Yes." I look up briefly at Lucas who smiles his distant smile. His aloof attitude bothers me, but maybe he just doesn't know how to behave around people who are really gregarious. "Have you seen Bennie? I want to say hi."

"Aye, sure. The laddie went back there"—she gestures toward the shaded area near the kitchen and storage—"with Drew."

Oh no. My spider sense tingles, and not in a good way. Bennie doesn't do well when he feels cornered, and Drew going with him may not be the best thing for either of them.

I turn to Lucas. "I'm going to go say hello. Can you get me a beer?"

Lucas's forehead creases, and I smooth it with my left forefinger. "Anything in particular you want?" he asks.

"I'm not picky." I grin. "Surprise me."

While Lucas moves through the crowd to get the bartender's attention, I head back to look for Bennie. If things are going well between him and Drew, I plan to retreat quietly. Otherwise I want to stop Bennie before he does anything he might regret.

I spot them easily in the back. Bennie is in his favorite black long-sleeved shirt paired with frayed black jeans. His hair is sticking up like he hasn't combed it in days. Meanwhile Drew is smartly dressed in a button-down gray shirt and navy blue jeans. The Converse sneakers on his feet are fire-engine red, lending a splash of color to the otherwise conservative ensemble.

They're facing each other, their bodies slightly angled away from me. Bennie's hands are fisted, and he looks like he's about to throw a punch. Drew doesn't seem to be close to violence, but he isn't relaxed either.

"I told you already," Bennie hisses.

"No, you didn't. You walked out and started ignoring my calls and texts. That is *not* telling me anything. *That* is being an arse."

"Do I have to explain everything?"

"Yes. You don't get to storm out on me and then shut me out."

"You're abandoning me."

Drew pulls back. "What? I am not. I asked you to come with me to England!"

"What the hell am I going to do there while you..." Bennie rolls his wrist rapidly in the air. "... do whatever it is you do?"

"What does that mean?"

"You're the son of an earl!"

Holy crap. Drew is an *English peer?*

Drew's jaw slackens. "Is that what this is about? I simply can*not*—" He throws his arms up in the air. "Yes, I'm the son of an earl. The *third* son."

"So?"

"I'm not going to inherit the title. It's my oldest brother's. What does it... Wait. Are you upset about that?"

"No." Bennie bristles. "I'm upset that you didn't tell me from the beginning."

"It's not something I talk about. It would be ostentatious and obnoxious to brag about something that has nothing to do with me."

"Nothing to—!" Bennie's voice rises, then as though he's realized that they aren't in private, he lowers his head...and hisses forcefully, "You were born to aristocracy!"

"It doesn't define me."

"You know what? Forget it. You don't get to decide how I feel." Bennie shakes his head. "You've talked enough. Just go. Go back to London and your...your life!"

He spins around. I step backward into the shadows, and he doesn't notice me as he storms out. I sigh, my heart breaking. Poor Bennie. This explains so much.

Bennie doesn't do well when he feels inferior. Although Drew's right about what he said, Bennie won't see it that way because he is keenly aware of where he came from—a messed-up family with an alcoholic dad and a clingy mother who just couldn't recognize how toxic the marriage was, not only for her but for her child. She even lost a baby when her husband got wasted and pushed her down the stairs in a violent argument. To this date I don't know how Bennie's dad avoided jail.

Drew curses under his breath as he sticks his hands into his hair. I wave at him from where I am. He jerks back but recovers his aplomb quickly. "Lurking in the shadows, are we?"

"Sorry. I was coming to say hi to Bennie."

"I suppose you got more than an earful."

"Sort of." I walk slowly toward him. "Sorry," I say again.

His shoulders droop. "It doesn't matter. He would've told you anyway."

I stop a few steps away from him. "Actually he didn't say a word about what's been going on between the two of you."

"He would have eventually. You're like the sister he never had."

"Maybe. He's really upset about…" I gesture around. "This."

He sighs roughly, digging the heel of one palm into his brow.

"He cares about you, Drew." I pat his back. "He worries that he may not be good enough." The exact type of fear I understand all too well.

"I know, but he'll never know that he *is* good enough if he never gives us a chance." He shakes his head, then forces a grin. "Look at me, whining about my love life when you're going home. Big change, eh?"

I smile. Drew is popular, and I'm certain he's heard about the fiasco at my school. Osaka is a large city, but its expat community is small.

"It is, but I think it'll be good for me."

"I hope everything works out for you."

I hope so too. "Thanks."

We go to the main area where the crowd has gathered. Lucas watches me and Drew questioningly, and I give him a quick shake of head. Before I can introduce them to each other, Drew makes his excuses, hugs me and leaves. He's probably not in the mood to mingle after that fight with

Bennie, who is at the bar glaring at him like he's the reason polar bears are dying.

Lucas hands me my beer. "What happened?"

"Too long to get into now," I say. "Let me talk to Bennie for a moment. We didn't get to say anything."

"I thought you went back there to talk to him."

"That was the idea, but he and Drew got into a fight, so I sort of cowered away."

Lucas kisses me on the mouth. "I doubt that. You aren't the type to cower."

"Thanks, but I generally try to stay out of people's love lives." I press my lips over his chin, then walk toward Bennie.

My best friend is sitting on a stool. He knocks back a shot, his wary gaze on me. Maybe he did see me in the back, but didn't want to blow his dramatic exit by acknowledging me.

"Okay, stop," he says, morose over the tiny glass. "You're leaving tonight, and I don't want to fight."

"Why do you think we're going to fight?"

"Oh, come on. You're here to tell me why I was wrong to act that way to Drew."

"Maybe. Maybe not. You don't know what I'm going to do."

"I know you're on his side."

I sigh and slide onto the empty stool next to his. "Bennie, if I take anyone's side, it'll be yours."

His shoulders slump. "I know. And I know I'm disappointing you."

"You're not. You're worried and maybe a little…apprehensive. I know you better than you think. We grew up together, remember?"

His lips are pressed tight, but he nods.

"I want you to be happy. I do think you should give Drew a chance, even if it's scary. You may regret it if you don't."

"But if it doesn't work out, what will I do?"

I squeeze his shoulder. "You'll pick yourself up and keep going. The Bennie Monsanto I know is no quitter, and he's a survivor."

He turns his torso toward me, his mouth twisting into a rueful smile. "When the hell did you become so insightful?"

"When I decided to be your friend."

The smile he gives me this time is open and radiant. He hugs me tightly, and I put my arms around him. Now it's up to him to decide, and I hope he follows his heart rather than allowing fear to overwhelm him.

"Go to your man," Bennie says, tilting his chin behind me. "He's new and attracting attention. And he looks *really* uncomfortable."

I look over my shoulder. Sure enough, a few people are introducing themselves, and Lucas is doing his signature aloof reception, his gaze cool and assessing. Shaking my head, I go over to introduce him to everyone. He might believe that being friendly doesn't matter because we're leaving, but I want him to get to meet the people I've hung out with over the last year.

As I get closer, he comes forward and puts an arm around me. We fit together like one of those yin-yang symbols, and I make the introductions.

He thaws a bit and engages in a little small talk. I know he's making an effort for me, and I smile up at him softly as my pulse scatters for a moment.

Am I doing the right thing? Probably. Am I scared? Yes.

But I know if I don't give us one more chance, I'm going to regret it for the rest of my life.

Because my heart? It wants me to follow Lucas.

Lucas

THE FAREWELL PARTY DOESN'T END UNTIL TEN p.m. despite the fact that tomorrow is a working day. More than thirty people came, all genuinely sorry to see her go but at the same time thrilled that she has another opportunity opening up.

As we ride in a taxi, speeding toward the airport, I pull her close until she's pressed tightly against my side. "Did you have fun?"

"Yes. Did you?"

"It wasn't as excruciating as I thought it was going to be." I smile into her hair. "Mainly because all those people adore you."

"I'm going to miss them."

Guilt squirms in my chest. I'm taking her away from them because I want her. Not only that, I forced her into this situation.

Am I fucking things up? Will she be all right away from all those people who care so much about her?

I want to believe I'll be enough...but who the hell am I kidding? That's not...

I clench my jaw. I have to get my shit together, become worthy of Ava. Questioning myself isn't the way to go.

"What?" she whispers.

"Hmm?"

"You're tense."

I force a small smile. "Perceptive woman."

She tilts her chin and looks up at me. "Are you okay?"

"I'm fine. Just not looking forward to the long flight." That's the least cause of my discomfiture, but I need to give her something.

"Nobody ever does."

She rests her head on my shoulder. It feels so right to have her lean on me like this.

Don't fuck this up.

I won't. I can't.

TWENTY-THREE

Ava

THE PLANE LANDS EXACTLY AT EIGHT thirty p.m. Everyone around Lucas seems to devote their lives to making sure his schedule stays uninterrupted. As the jet touches down, he shows me a small black thing.

"Lemme see your phone," he says, his palm up.

"What's that?"

"A new SIM card. I noticed your phone isn't locked, so I got this for you so you can use it in the States." He swaps the cards, takes his phone out and rings someone. My unit vibrates. "I'm saving this into your contact list. It's my personal number and you can call me anytime."

Handing me my phone back, he doesn't comment on the fact that it showed up as an unknown number. I deleted his digits when I left the States. "Still only eight people have this number?"

"Once again eight. Seven and you."

The plane comes to a complete stop, and the captain makes a short arrival announcement. The cabin attendant opens the door, and I stand up first. Lucas winces as he pushes himself up.

"You all right?" I ask.

"I'm fine. Just a little stiff from sitting for so long."

I run my hand over his shoulder, wishing I could do more. Lucas isn't old enough to start to feel bad after a flight—even a long one—and I know his injuries are bothering him. From the hard set of his jaw, it's obvious he doesn't want me to fuss, so I step back and give him some space. It doesn't take much time before he puts a hand at the small of my back, ready to deplane.

We step out together. I stop for a second and inhale deeply. The familiar stretch of road, the cool kiss of the evening breeze and autumn-spiced air...

I'm home.

"We have a car waiting," Lucas says, putting an arm around my shoulder.

I nod. "Let me text Ray to let him know I've arrived." I start typing on my phone and hit send.

Where are you? Ray texts back. I almost slap my forehead, because I forgot he planned to pick me up. *We just landed. Let me get my bags and I'll meet you right outside.*

The Charlottesville airport is small, and there's no way I'm going to miss him.

"Where are our bags?" I ask.

"They should be in the car by now. Why? Need something?"

"It's Ray. He's here."

Lucas frowns. "Why?"

"He wants to…um…pick me up."

Lucas's expression grows darkly speculative. "And I suppose he wants to take you to his home."

"Yes."

"Do you have to go?"

"He's like my father. Actually he's more of a father than—"

He holds up a hand. "Okay. You don't have to say more." He sighs. "He has the right."

"Thank you."

I can sense he isn't thrilled about spending the night apart. And to be honest, after yesterday I feel the same way.

Lucas rings his driver, instructs him to bring the car around to the main entrance, and we leave together. I see Ray standing by himself.

His hair prematurely gray, he looks distinguished and intelligent, his pale blue eyes observant yet warm. He's in a salmon-colored button-down shirt, a brown vest and chestnut-colored slacks. A pair of worn loafers peeks under the hems of his cuffed trousers. Although he isn't a tall man—only five-ten—he's slim from staying active. Combined with his excellent posture, he seems taller than he is.

His lightly tanned face brightens when he spots me. He walks forward and wraps me in strong, wiry arms.

"Ava! So good to see you."

I hug him back. "I missed you so much, Ray."

And that is true. No matter how many video chats we have, it's not the same.

After three beats, he pulls back. "And this fellow?"

"Ray, meet Lucas. Lucas, Ray."

Ray gives Lucas a thorough inspection, from head to toe, then back up as though he were studying merchandise before a purchase.

If that bothers him, Lucas doesn't show it. He merely smiles politely—but not openly—and extends a hand. "Nice to meet you, sir."

"Likewise," Ray says, pumping the offered hand vigorously. If he were younger, he probably would've tried to crush every bone in Lucas's hand. He turns to me. "Where are your things, Ava?"

"In Lucas's car."

"It'll follow us to your place," Lucas adds.

Ray nods, and we walk out to the short-term lot to claim his car. He's still driving the same dark gray SUV.

Lucas opens the rear door for me, and we climb inside. The interior is as neat as ever, and if I didn't know any better, I would never suspect he has a seventeen-month-old child.

Ray takes the car out of the garage. One hand holding mine, Lucas texts his driver, and I note a black SUV tailing us.

"How was the flight?" Ray asks.

"It was very nice," I say.

"My plane has a bed," Lucas adds.

Ray's eyebrow cocks. "A bed?"

"We, um, flew private," I say, while giving Lucas a "what are you doing?" look.

He pointedly ignores me. Instead he mouths, *Call me tonight.*

I nod, then turn to Ray. "So where's Darcy?"

"Home. She couldn't come. She was disappointed, but I told her she could wait an hour."

Charlottesville isn't a big town, and its traffic isn't as terrible as some of the larger metropolitan areas in Virginia. Finally, we drive through the gates manned by old Mr. Jackson—the "security guard". The community is immaculately maintained, all the autumn leaves ruthlessly gathered up and disposed of, shrubs trimmed and lawns mowed.

Ray and Darcy live in a three-story house with a sizable two-car garage and a shed in the back. Darcy told me they bought it because of its proximity to the golf course—in Ray's universe, no day is complete without a round or two of golf.

I don't see Darcy's Infiniti in the driveway, but there are lights on in the house. Ray parks out front, and Lucas helps me step down. The black SUV stops, engine idling, and the driver comes out to grab my suitcases and take them all the way to the porch.

Lucas cups my face and gives me a hard but brief kiss. "Don't forget to call."

My mouth tingles, and I nod, my fingertips brushing my lower lip.

He inclines his head at Ray. "Nice to meet you, sir."

"Have a good drive home."

Lucas climbs into the car. The SUV gets smaller and dimmer down the tree-covered road before the taillights vanish around a curve.

Ray squints. "So. That's the man."

"Yeah."

He just grunts, which is slightly surprising. I expected him to have more things to say about Lucas.

The door opens, bathing us in warm light coming from inside the house.

"Ava!" Darcy cries out. "My goodness, you're finally home!"

I spin around. "Darcy!" I run over and hug her tightly. "I missed you."

"I missed you too, love." She pulls back and cradles my face between her hands. "Let me look at you."

I smile. Her sleek bob has more silver in it, and her skin is paler now that the weather's colder and she isn't playing tennis as much. But her bright gray eyes are the same—warm and twinkling—and she's in the same simple sort of clothes I remember: a light blue sweater, denim jeans and white tennis shoes. You'd never know she's a trust fund baby.

"You look lovely, but tired. The travel must've been horrendous." She squeezes me again. "Come on in. My goodness, Ray, help with her bags, will you?"

He laughs. "Yes, dear."

She herds me inside, an arm around my waist. She's only five-four, and it isn't easy for her to reach up to my shoulders. "I wanted to go to the airport too, but Ray didn't think it was a good idea."

She doesn't have to say more. It's about Mia, and neither Ray nor Darcy is sure about what's going to happen now that Lucas is back in my life.

Ray helps me drag my two suitcases into the house and closes the door. The high-ceilinged foyer is bright, and Darcy's put up fall decorations: pinecones, miniature pumpkins and acorns, gold and silver ribbons. She adores holidays and all the festivities.

She leads me to the living room with its comfortable couches and a fireplace, not yet lit.

"Where's Mia?" I ask.

"Sleeping. Would you like to see her?"

The nursery is on the first level. Darcy thought it prudent not to risk stairs. "I'm not so young anymore, and my knees do creak a bit," she said, laughing heartily.

The room is dark except for a small nightlight by the crib. I don't need it to know that the walls are pastel pink and cream, and the one to Mia's right has a rainbow, a unicorn and clouds painted on it because everyone knows a little princess deserves rainbows and unicorns—something I never had growing up, but want for my daughter very much.

The floor is covered with soft cork, but I tiptoe anyway.

Mia is sleeping soundly, her breathing fast but easy. Her mouth is pursed like a fresh rosebud, and I carefully brush my fingers along one plump cheek and breathe in her sweet, toddler smell. Hot emotions surge through me, and I blink away tears.

"She's beautiful," I whisper.

"Just like her mother," Darcy murmurs.

I shake my head. "No. She's not going to be anything like her mother. She's going to be exactly like you."

Darcy runs a gentle hand down my back. "My dear, you're an incredible woman. Mia will be fortunate if she ends up as smart, resilient and strong as you are."

Another fresh wave of tears stings my eyes. I look up at the ceiling for a moment, then sniffle once.

I kiss Mia on the forehead and leave the nursery. Ray's already taken my suitcases upstairs.

"Something to drink?"

Darcy goes into the big, open kitchen. It has four burners, a griddle for pancakes and two ovens. Ray loves to cook, and he shows off his skills on Thanksgiving and Christmas.

"Water would be great."

Darcy hands me a bottle of water from the fridge. "I'm surprised you're back with…him."

"Lucas," I say, sliding onto a tall chair at the breakfast bar. "His name is Lucas Reed."

She takes the seat next to mine. "I see." A moment of silence. "Are you going to tell him?"

I shake my head, picking at a nonexistent hangnail. "No. I don't think so."

"He has the right to know, dear." Darcy puts a hand over mine.

I flinch. "You'd have me tell him, even though he might try to take her away from you?"

"It would be tough if he insists on taking her. I'm not going to lie about it, but maybe—"

"I'm scared."

"Ava…"

"There are so many things at stake now." I swivel the chair so I can face her directly. "I don't have a job anymore, and he has so much power over me—to hurt me. But at the same time…when he's open and loving… My god, he's amazing."

"Do you love him?"

I stare at her.

"It isn't a difficult question."

Maybe not, but it's a damn scary one. "I… yeah. I do."

"Then let's trust that you wouldn't have fallen in love with a man who isn't worthy."

Staring at the hand in my lap, I nod, but her faith in me only makes me feel worse. She doesn't understand what a terrible judge of character I can be—that falling for a man who's prone to making you miserable and doing terrible, irresponsible things because of that man runs in my family. Just look at my mother.

"I'm sorry, Darcy," I murmur.

"For what?"

"For complicating everything. If I were less selfish—"

"Ava, everyone deserves to try to find happiness."

"I promise I won't let Lucas jeopardize the adoption."

She pats my hand. "You've had a long trip, so let's let you rest a bit. I'm beat too." She smiles. "We should have a picnic tomorrow, if the weather's nice." Darcy loves spending time outside.

"Sure."

"Good night, dear."

"Good night, Darcy."

I watch her disappear into the newly done master bedroom on the first level. Guilt niggles at me, and I can't help but feel like I'm taking something from her that I have no right to.

Even if Mia is really mine.

TWENTY-FOUR

Lucas

I HANG MY KEYS ON THE HOOK IN THE FOYER, and shut the door. The house is dark and slightly cold. My housekeeper Gail doesn't heat the main area unless I'm in town.

Tonight the place feels larger and darker... bleak, even. I scowl into the hall as a knife twists in my gut. Jesus. This is always how it is coming back from a trip. What the hell is the matter with me?

I hit the switch by the kitchen, and light pours over the granite countertop and the fridge. A couple of bottles of excellent red await me, along with two wide-rimmed glasses. I instructed my assistant Rachael to get them so Ava and I could enjoy ourselves tonight.

The sight of them only makes the knife inside my gut dig deeper.

For some reason, I never expected her foster father to actually show. Well…I didn't expect anybody to show. Nobody picks me up from airports or calls to see if I'm all right. Nor do they expect texts letting them know I'm okay.

I have an absurd urge to text Elizabeth, because she's the only one who won't mock me for feeling the way I do.

Jesus. Stop being so clingy. Nobody likes immature, needy…

I go to my bedroom, stripping down along the way and discarding my clothes in a long trail. It doesn't matter if Ava's not with me at this particular moment. She's on the same continent, in the same country, the same state, the same city. Hell, her foster parents' place is in the same gated community. *This is not a big deal.*

I remind myself of that again as I slip into the cool sheets, phone clutched in my hand.

The grandfather clock out in the living room ticks, and I can hear it through the closed door. Or perhaps I'm imagining it; my brain's going at two hundred miles an hour.

Why isn't she calling? She said she would.

Oh please. Don't tell me you really believed that. People say what you want to hear, but at the end of the day, they do whatever they want. Haven't you learned that by now?

I have. I've learned it especially well.

If you behave, maybe I won't have to send you away to camp. My mother, standing with her arms crossed.

If you behave, maybe you won't have to go to boarding schools like your half-siblings.

If you behave, maybe I'll take you with us on our trip to Italy.

And it wasn't just Betsy. There were others.

You're important to me. How can you not know that?

Of course I'll come by to see you.

The only one who never played that game is Elizabeth, but she's above such petty bullshit.

So is Ava. She's never said she'd do something then broken her word.

What about Blake?

I frown. If she claimed Blake said that shit to her, he probably did, even if he denies it. He probably forgot because he says shit to everyone he meets, kind of the way most people wouldn't remember a particular meal from six months back. When you eat all the time...

I close my eyes and imagine an invisible metronome is in my room, slowly ticking away. The trick always helps me fall asleep, no matter how agitated I am.

Bit by bit my muscles loosen. My eyelids grow heavy and my brain starts to drift. Air fills my lungs, then leaves in a steady rhythm.

The phone in my hand vibrates, jerking me out of drowsiness. I stare at the text.

You asleep?

I blink myself fully awake, then smile. *Yes.*

The phone rings. "Good lord, woman, can't a man get any rest around you?"

"Rise and shine."

Her tone is light, but I can sense some tension running underneath. "Are you all right?"

She hesitates. "I'm fine. Just tired…and I miss you."

"Miss you, too." I make a face even though she can't see me. "I wish you hadn't called your foster parents. We could've spent the night together, then surprised them tomorrow."

I hear nothing but the sound of her slow breathing for a minute. "Probably a bad idea," she says finally. "They hate surprises."

"Even if the surprise is good?"

"Even then."

There is a hint of listlessness in her voice that's making my scalp prickle. "Did something happen?"

"No." She sounds genuinely confused. "Why do you ask?"

Damn. So if that's not it, then what? She seemed fine on the flight home. God, I'd give my left foot to have her with me right now, so I could look into her eyes and make sure she's really all right. I hate having the feeling that something's going on, but not being able to act on it, make things better for her.

Suddenly I'm not certain that bringing her home was such a great idea. I didn't factor her foster parents in. They weren't much of a presence two or three years ago, and I assumed it would be the same again.

"Hoping for a reason to get you to come over," I say finally, deciding to make a joke of it, rather than get really serious when she's too far away to hold in my arms.

She snorts, then giggles quietly. "You're awful."

"If by 'awful' you mean 'desperately horny', then yes…"

"Are you? Horny?"

"Yeah. But the real problem is I miss having you by my side," I answer honestly. Being with her, just holding her hand and sitting in silence, is incomparably preferable to an orgasm…unless I'm climaxing with her.

"I miss you, too."

I can hear the smile in her voice, and it loosens another bit of my tension. "Listen, are your foster parents going to insist on being old-fashioned about us?"

"Maybe. They know how things fell apart between us. They're worried."

Jesus. Protective parents. I'm grateful she has them, but I have zero experience dealing with them. My dates' parents didn't care since they were more concerned with my money—which is why I mentioned my plane to Ray, although he didn't seem that impressed—and *my* parents... Well, they don't exactly qualify for any conscientious caregiver awards.

"If they're worried, they can always talk to me."

"They just might."

"Good."

I'd love a chance to explain myself, let them know things aren't going to be like before. Mentally I pencil that in on my calendar for tomorrow. Then I decide my weekend is empty. If it's not empty, Rachael can make it empty.

"I'll be there tomorrow to say hello."

"And try to seduce me while you're at it?"

"Sure, why not? Getting naked with you is my new purpose in life. If your folks happen to be in the same room, well..."

She chuckles. "Is that all you ever think about?"

"If I were to create a diagram of what's in my head, you'd occupy ninety-five percent."

"What's taking up the other five?"

"Breathing. Eating. Occasional personal hygiene. Remembering how to tie my shoes."

She laughs. "Please. Are you telling me only five percent of your brain was needed to make your fortune?"

I'm quiet for a moment. "You know about that?"

"Of course. I Googled you after…you know. That was pretty impressive."

"Well…I didn't know you then. So I was able to free up more of my brain. I'm lucky we didn't meet until after I made my money. I wouldn't be able to spoil you."

"You don't need money to spoil me, Lucas. All you need to bring is yourself."

And just like that, she makes my heart so full it aches.

"I'll see you tomorrow," she murmurs.

I swallow the lump in my throat. I place a hand over my chest, wishing she were here so I could grasp her before she vanishes. "Good night, sweetheart."

"Dream of me."

"Always."

Long after the line cuts off, I keep the phone to my ear so I can pretend we're still connected.

Lucas

HARSH WINDS WHIP THE GRASS, COMBING THE field this way and that. The cliff juts over dark, churning water, and far beyond my right is an olive tree. Its branches are barren of fruit. What olives that fell, are all gone.

Black clouds move over the ocean, the briny air charged with electricity. My left leg aches as I brace the wind and march forward.

Come back, Lucas. It's dangerous out there.

Muted voices call from behind me, but I ignore them. Ava is out there…somewhere. I have to find her.

The sky splits open and water pelts down, drenching me instantly. The temperature is freezing, and my teeth chatter. The old injuries seem to harden, the muscles knotting and gnarling painfully.

Still, I have to find Ava. I can't go back to safety without her.

There.

I see her standing at the edge of the cliff. Her platinum tresses and all-too-slim body are unmistakable. The hair is stringy with rain, and the flimsy white sundress sticks to her like wet tissue.

"Ava!" I bellow.

She looks at the dark horizon beyond the sea. I force my legs to move, even though the wind is unbearably strong now. How is she able to just stand there, her back as straight as a steel rod?

"Ava!" I call out again.

This time she turns. Her face is pale with cold, except for the eyes. They're electric, so hot and bright they appear like tunnels of blue fire through the rain.

Her lips move. She isn't speaking loudly, but somehow I can hear her clearly over the raging wind and rain.

"You're despicable."

"Ava…"

"Why did you ever think you'd be good enough?"

Crippling fear surges within me, but I clench my legs and extend a hand. "It's dangerous out there. Come with me. Please."

"No." She turns to the ocean. "I'd rather be there than with you."

"Ava."

I push forward, using every drop of strength in my body. But the distance between us seems to grow wider.

Fuck.

Suddenly she turns, facing me again. "You can't have me, Lucas. You never deserved me." She steps backward, beyond the cliff, her dress and hair fluttering like streamers as she vanishes over the edge.

"Ava!"

Panic slams into me, and I jump forward only to crash against an invisible wall. Sharp pain slices through me.

"*No!*"

Breathing hard, I jackknife into a sitting position. Sweat covers my skin, and my heart is hammering against my ribs with such force that my chest throbs.

I run a hand over my face. *Jesus.* What the fuck was that?

Just a dream…with fragments of Grandpa's *Landscape of Tuscany* tossed in. It doesn't mean anything. I reach for my phone, ready to dial Ava's number, but the screen shows it's after three a.m. I toss it on the sheet and bury my face in my hands. It's good that it's too late for me to call. What would I say?

I lie back, but sleep doesn't come.

TWENTY-FIVE

Ava

I'M UP BY FIVE THIRTY, WHICH IS WAY EARLIER than normal. Despite the very comfortable travel, jet-lag has struck.

I stay in bed and read a mystery novel that I downloaded a couple months back. It's an okay book with a cute librarian as the lead. Around the time I hit the end of the fifth chapter, the house starts to stir.

After a quick shower, I put on a blue sweater and jeans and make my way downstairs, my sneakers quiet on the hardwood floor. Ray and Darcy are sharing coffee by the breakfast bar in the kitchen. Ray looks like he's ready to go out for a round of golf. A navy blue zip-neck sweater with horizontal stripes across his chest lies neatly on

his torso, and well-fitted dark brown trousers—
as well as his golf shoes—look brand new. Darcy,
on the other hand, doesn't seem interested in any
particular activity. She's in a bright yellow cotton
shirt with a cream-colored cardigan thrown over
it, and her favorite plaid angle-length skirt hangs
on her slight body. A pair of plushy brown slip-
pers covers her feet.

"Good morning," I say with a cheery smile.

"Morning. Sleep well?" Darcy asks.

"I was up a little early because of the flight,
but yeah. I did."

I head for the coffee maker and pour myself
a big mugful. Ray is a connoisseur of the brown
stuff, and my foster parents have some of the best
coffee in the world.

I wrap my hands around the mug and take a
sip. "This is so good."

"I got some new beans from Colombia," Ray
explains. "They're excellent. Much better than I
expected."

Darcy smiles. "If they weren't good, you
would've sent them back."

Laughing, Ray gets up with his empty mug.
"Of course. No reason to pay good money for bad
coffee." He looks at both me and Darcy. "Do you
ladies have any special requests for breakfast?"

"Belgian waffles?" I ask, licking my lips.

Ray is an excellent cook, and his specialties

are waffles and pancakes. I don't know what he puts in them, but it's highly addicting.

While Ray gets busy in the kitchen, Darcy and I check the nursery. Mia is already up. When she spots Darcy, she extends her fat little arms, silently asking to be picked up.

"Hello, baby girl," Darcy coos as she slips her hands under Mia's armpits and pulls her upward, settling the small child against her chest. "Aren't you a sweet little thing? You were so quiet in here, we didn't even know you were awake."

Mia chortles. Then she swivels her head toward me, her mouth parted in an open smile.

I step forward and brush my finger tenderly along her cheek. "Hello, Mia."

"'Ello," she says.

"Mia is quite a talker," Darcy says. "She speaks surprisingly well for her age."

"Is it all right if I...?"

"Of course." Darcy hands me the child.

I cradle her against my heart, feeling her slight precious weight. Mia was born small, and if it hadn't been for Darcy and Ray's assistance, I'm not certain she would've gotten the medical care she needed. The labor was very difficult, and I was too young and too out of it afterwards to figure out what needed to be done. It also didn't help that I felt so alone, knowing that I could never depend on Lucas for support. In many ways, Ray and Darcy have been better parents to Mia than I ever could have. What I feel for them extends beyond mere gratitude.

With prickling eyes, I look at Darcy over Mia's head. My foster mother gazes back at me with a sweet smile that says she understands.

The sound of the doorbell breaks the moment. Darcy and I look at each other. The digital clock on the wall says it's barely eight a.m. Who could be visiting so early?

Darcy marches out of the nursery, me following closely behind. As she walks past the kitchen, she calls out, "I got it."

"Thanks, hon," Ray says, whisking something in a bowl.

The second Darcy opens the door, she stiffens. I gasp when I spot Lucas over Darcy's head. He's freshly showered, his hair slightly damp, his face carefully shaved. A black untucked button-down shirt fits over his strong, muscled shoulders and chest, and a pair of well-worn black denim pants and suede leather shoes complete the darkly foreboding look.

"Lucas," I say.

Darcy shoots me a quick look over her shoulder, then turns her attention back to him.

"What are you doing here so early?" she asks, her tone neither polite nor impolite.

"I wanted to take Ava out for breakfast," he says.

Whoa. I knew he would visit, but I didn't realize he meant to come by so early or monopolize my time because—despite what he told me yesterday—there's no way he popped up merely to say hello to my foster parents. I search his face. Fatigue has etched lines in the corners of his eyes and his mouth. *What happened?* He sounded fine when we talked last night.

His gaze lands distractedly on Mia in my arms. "Pretty girl."

My insides freeze. Before I can respond, Darcy pulls Mia away from me, her hands gentle but slightly shaky. "Lucas, meet Mia. My daughter." The second she's done, she purses her lips and lifts her chin. Most people wouldn't pick up on her mood, but I know she's flustered. She wasn't prepared to have Lucas see Mia, at least not yet.

Lucas says, "Hi Mia," even as he glances back and forth between Darcy and Mia a couple of times. My mouth goes dry. No matter how you look at it, the chances of Darcy and Ray having a child as young as Mia are almost nil.

For a moment it looks like he's about to say something, but he doesn't…which only unnerves me further. What is he thinking?

"And I'm afraid Ava's not available to go out to breakfast," Darcy continues. "She's eating with us."

A muscle in Lucas's jaw ticks. He shifts his weight forward.

"But you're welcome to join us. I'm sure it's not too late for Ray to make extra batter for his Belgian waffles."

Lucas's visible eyebrow scrunches. "I'm…" He recovers. "Thank you. That would be nice."

Darcy nods once and goes to the kitchen to announce to Ray that we have an additional guest. I lean closer to Lucas and whisper, "I didn't realize you were coming this morning."

"I wasn't planning to, but I missed you." He gives me a reproachful look. "You could've just told them you can't eat with them."

"That would've been unbelievably rude since I already told them I would." I give him an impish smile. "Don't worry. You'll be able to charm them, and if everything goes well, we can spend some time together after breakfast."

"All right. After breakfast, we're going for a long, long drive far away from here, just you and me."

Something's really bothering him, and it puts a damper on my mood. Even though I made tentative plans to have a picnic with my foster parents, I nod. "Deal."

Lucas

BREAKFAST TAKES PLACE IN THE DINING ROOM. The cherry-wood table is set for four, with a high-chair-plus-tray contraption for Mia. I guess that means the girl's eating with us. The idea is somewhat surreal; I don't remember dining with my parents until I was old enough to use napkins and utensils properly. Mom has always hated dealing with messiness, and children are inevitably too messy for her taste.

Ray serves waffles, pancakes and crispy bacon with a jug of Canadian maple syrup and a small white pitcher that turns out to have honey in it. He even has a dark navy and orange apron wrapped around him.

It's odd to see the man of the house cook and serve things. The last time I saw that was when I was eighteen and staying with my grandfather. When he wasn't busy painting he dabbled in Italian cuisine…and forced us to eat what he made, no matter how badly it turned out.

As for my parents… Dad couldn't find the kitchen in any of the fancy houses he's lived in—that's what the cook's for. Mom also acted as though she didn't know how to turn an oven on, even though I'm certain she didn't grow up in wealth. The only time I see people cook and serve food these days is when I happen to flip by Food Network.

Ava brings out a thermos of hot coffee, while Darcy cuts waffles into small pieces for Mia on a plastic plate. I remain standing, unsure what to do. Mia flutters her fat little fingers in my direction, and I waggle mine back at her.

Ray takes a seat at the head of the table, and his wife takes the place to his right. I pull out a chair to his left for Ava so I can sit next to her and as far away from her foster parents as possible. Of course, this arrangement leaves me sitting opposite the girl. She chortles in my direction, waving her plastic fork around. I give her a small smile, unsure precisely what's expected of me. Small children are not an area of expertise.

"Try the waffles," Ava whispers in my ear, dragging my attention from Mia. "Ray's a great cook. You won't be sorry."

I glance at her face, noting the smile. I take a small forkful of waffle and put it in my mouth. It's surprisingly good.

"How do you like it?" Darcy asks.

"Excellent," I say. "Better than anything I've ever had…and I've been to a lot of fancy places for breakfast."

Ray beams. "Waffles. The love of my life."

"Other than golf," Darcy says. "If Ray could make waffles with a four-iron, he'd expire from joy."

Darcy, Ray and Ava laugh. I watch them with a small smile, glad that this is what Ava had after she lost her parents.

Darcy and Ray ask Ava about her life in Japan. She answers in general strokes, until they ask about Bennie. She tells them about his love life troubles in detail, and how she wishes things would work out.

"He won't accept that he deserves better," Ava huffs. "It's so frustrating."

"He didn't have an easy childhood," Darcy says sympathetically.

"I know, but right in front of him—we're not talking hypotheticals here—he has this perfect man mooning over him. All he has to do is give in…just a little." Ava shakes her head.

"I hope you were able to talk some sense into him," Darcy says. "The boy could use a bit more."

"Speaking of which, what made you leave Osaka so suddenly?" Ray asks.

I tense. The truth would get me shot—or brained with one of Ray's golf clubs—but I don't want Ava to lie for me. Not to these wonderful people.

She takes a long, slow sip of coffee before responding. "The principal was never too fond of foreigners. And when she had a chance to get rid of the only gaijin teacher she had, she took it."

"Then who's going to teach English at her school?" Darcy asks.

Ava shrugs. "I don't know. Not my school anymore, so not my problem. I just feel bad for the students."

Sharp guilt over the fact that Ava is forced to lie to cover for what I did makes me fidget. I still would've found a way to bring her home, but I wish I could go back in time and spend more of my energy convincing her to quit on her own rather than forcing her into it. I was so focused on my goal that I didn't think about the consequences of putting my desire first.

Ava deftly steers the conversation to a few funny anecdotes about her friends in Osaka. I listen vaguely, while feeling Darcy and Ray's eyes on me every so often. Maybe it's just me, but their gazes seem full of judgment. Can foster parents see through bullshit from their kids too?

Darcy turns to me all of a sudden. "So Lucas, what do you do?"

The question is a little unusual for me. Most people in my circle ask about how my investments are doing, not about my job. "These days, I make speeches, mostly of inspirational variety, or I consult." Neither of which I've done much of recently since I've had very little drive. Nor do I particularly need the money. "And I have some investments. I've funded a few tech startups that look promising."

"I see. Your family seems to live quite a ways from Virginia, except for your father."

Wariness courses through me. The woman has done some homework, and most likely she found something she didn't like.

"Darcy," Ava says quietly, shooting a quick uncertain glance in my direction.

I nudge her leg under the table to let her know I can handle this. "That's true."

"Is it also true that your family is quite…wild?"

Wild doesn't begin to describe some of my siblings, but if she has something to say, she can just say it. "I'm not sure what you mean."

"Your brother Elliot—your twin, actually—has a certain reputation. I looked him up. Sex tapes, marrying a stripper, and I'm sure that's not all."

"Darcy!"

"Your mother has the right to know," Darcy says blithely.

Ray gives me a sympathetic look. "Darcy's mom was worse with me."

Ava slumps in her seat, and I reach over and pat her hand.

Darcy continues, "Then there's Ryder Reed, the actor brother, who of course has his own playboy reputation."

"So are you saying that I'm like two of my brothers?"

"I didn't say anything of the sort. I'm just pointing out some of the things I found out about you."

"Actually," I say pleasantly, "you haven't found anything about me. You've discovered something about two of my siblings. And you've conveniently left out my oldest half-brother, who has never had a scandal attached to his name, and my half-sister, who does quite a lot of work in charities and other social programs."

Darcy assesses me. Very deliberately, I push my hair out of my face so she can see the scar. The sight of my imperfection elicits a gasp.

I give her a cool smile. "Anything else you'd like to know? My dating history? My blood type, maybe?"

"Actually, yes," Darcy says, refusing to be cowed. "Faye Belbin."

Jesus. Did Ava tell them about her too? "She's an old friend and a business partner."

"That…isn't how it looked. We saw photos," Ray interjects.

"She came with me to a few social functions I couldn't really attend alone. I didn't think Ava would want to take time off from school to go to those things, most of which are mindlessly dull. Now I see that I should've asked."

Ava stands up. "Does anybody want more food?"

Darcy and Ray shake their heads.

"Then we should clean up," Ava suggests—rather more forcefully than necessary—to Darcy. "Ray cooked."

Darcy shoots a long look my way before nodding. She gets up to join Ava, but says, "Lucas, you're a guest, so please sit and...perhaps enjoy some coffee if you'd like?"

Ava shakes her head subtly, while glancing meaningfully in Ray's direction.

I hide a smile. "If you wouldn't mind."

Sighing, Ava takes the pitcher and pours me a fresh cup. "Tried to warn you," she murmurs before turning away.

She and Darcy take stacks of empty plates and head to the kitchen. Ray studies me, his expression bemused although there's a hint of smile on his lips. But it's more of an "I'm trying to decide what I think about you" smile rather than genuine friendliness.

"Ray, I know you have something you want to say. Let's get it out of the way."

He steeples his hands and leans back in his seat. "I'm trying to decide if I can trust you with Ava a second time. You left her when she was vulnerable and needed you."

My face heats. He's not saying anything I wouldn't if our positions were reversed. But at the same time he only knows things from Ava's point of view.

Needing to convince him that I didn't ditch her, I say, "At the time, I was stuck in the hospital after a motorcycle accident. I didn't know she needed me…much less that she thought I'd abandoned her."

"If you didn't want to break up, why didn't you come see her when you were out of surgery?"

"She left a box with my nurses. It had all my stuff in it."

Ray's eyes sharpen. Obviously he didn't know this part.

"Yeah. A pair of sunglasses I'd left, a book she'd borrowed. And all the things I'd given her during our time together. What would you have thought?" I give him a little time to get the picture. "Then there are my scars. I have them on other parts of my body as well, and they're not particularly pretty. All from the accident. So I figured that maybe she didn't want a guy who was all mangled up."

Ray nods, but his forehead is furrowed. "Okay, I get it. But in that case, why are you back now?"

"In spite of my best efforts to stay away, I happened to discover where she was, and I couldn't stop myself anymore." I lean forward, holding his gaze. "When she left, she took something from me."

Ray goes very still. "What do you mean?"

"Ava took all that was warm and good in my life. After she left, I…well, I couldn't really feel much of anything."

Ray picks up his coffee and has a sip, but his hand is shaking a bit. "I see. Well, that clarifies things." He flashes a quick, empty smile in my direction.

Something's off here, but I can't quite put my finger on it. Ray doesn't seem like the nervous type. Before I can ponder any further, though, Ava and Darcy return.

"All done," Ava says, squeezing my shoulder.

I take her hand. "Since I couldn't take you out for breakfast, I want to take you for that drive instead."

Darcy's mouth immediately flattens. But Ray says, "Of course."

Worry and apprehension cloud his eyes, and I know that he still doesn't quite approve of me. I mentally shrug away his concerns. I have Ava. That's all that matters.

TWENTY-SIX

Ava

W E DRIVE FOR A GOOD THREE HOURS IN Lucas's Mercedes. Before leaving I told Darcy I probably wouldn't be back for the picnic, and she agreed to take a rain check.

Lucas picks scenic routes through the valleys and fields. Trees are in various stages of change—their leaves transforming from vibrant, lush green to deep yellow, red and every shade in between.

The sun sits high in the impossibly blue sky, and I stretch my arms over my head, loving the warmth coming through the sunroof. The sound system plays a bright classical tune by Mozart.

"How far are we going?" I ask after a while.

"As far as we can."

I glance at his profile. He looks outside, his

shades reflecting the changing scenery. The wind ruffles his hair.

I reach over and tuck an errant strand back behind his ear. "Are you kidnapping me?" My tone is whimsical.

"What if I am?" The question is conversational and surprisingly casual despite the sudden weight behind each word.

I run my thumb along the shell of his ear. "I'd say drive faster."

His mouth curves into a crooked smile. He takes my hand and kisses the knuckles, his lips taking their sweet time.

I shiver. It's been less than twenty-four hours since we've been apart, but from the way I long for him, it might as well have been weeks. It isn't just his body that I want but the closeness, the intimacy when we're together...just the two of us.

Finally he pulls over by a field with a small lake in the center and we get out. The breeze trails fingers along the surface, creating small ripples I watch until they're lost in the reflected sun. Trees rustle, a few red and yellow leaves twirling away like dancing fairies.

"It's beautiful," I whisper, afraid to break the moment.

Placing his sunglasses in his shirt pocket,

Lucas cups my cheek. "Made more beautiful by your presence."

The wind whips by, lifting the hair that covers his scar. I cradle his face, my bare fingers touching the raised white tissue. He flinches, but doesn't pull back. I rise on my toes and kiss him on the mouth. "Made perfect by your presence."

He perches his butt against the hood of his Mercedes and pulls me between his legs. "Every day you destroy more of my walls."

"I want nothing between us."

Even as the words slip from my lips, I feel like a fraud. I still haven't told him about Mia.

Tell him. He'll understand.

He's seen Ray and Darcy are good people, protective and fully capable of taking care of the child we created two years ago. If he wants to be part of Mia's life, surely he wouldn't be so vindictive as to try to take her away from them.

I open my mouth, and suddenly a low growl stops me.

"What's that?"

He winces. "My belly."

"Didn't you eat enough?"

"It was a little difficult with Darcy watching me like she wanted to gut me and use my intestines for garters."

I chortle. "She did not."

"She so did. Is she descended from the Torquemadas?"

"Ha!" With a great deal of reluctance, I pull away from him. "All right. Let's get you fed." I cast one more glance over my shoulder at the beautiful view. It seems cruel to have to leave this paradise when we just arrived.

"Great idea." He grins, not at all perturbed by the fact that we're about to go. Then, instead of opening the driver's door, he pops the trunk and drags out a cooler and basket.

"Ta-da!" He spreads his arms and bows like a magician.

I laugh. "When did you prepare all this?"

"I had Gail pack us something before I went to pick you up. And before you get jealous, she's my housekeeper and she's in her sixties."

I punch him lightly in the bicep. He wraps an arm around my shoulder and pulls me closer. "Don't pout. I think it's adorable when you're possessive."

"Do you now?"

"Yes. It means you think I'm worth keeping."

My heart shatters a little. I don't understand what made him think that he isn't worthy, but if I ever find out who did this to him, I will beat them to death with my bare fists. "You're definitely worth keeping, Lucas. You don't know how much I've regretted the last two years."

He gives me a lopsided grin, boyishly beautiful in its openness. Pulling me even closer, he kisses the top of my head.

We stroll over to the lake and pick a spot under a spreading oak. I help him lay out the blanket and take a quick peek into the basket and cooler. I assumed they would mostly contain breakfast stuff, but no. There's a bottle of wine, thinly sliced roast beef, a few pieces of fried chicken, cheese, bread, some Caesar salad, cut fruit...

"You were planning on a picnic all along," I say, pulling out the items and laying them on the blanket.

"Yes. I didn't have you with me last night, so I was determined to have you with me today."

Quietly, we eat. To be more precise, we feed each other. Every time he takes a bite from my hand, he licks my fingertips, making my muscles clench. I do the same to him and enjoy the way his nostrils flare.

I sip the excellent California rosé and run my tongue along my lips.

"Keep doing that and we may not finish eating."

"You're still hungry?" He's already polished off most of the beef and half the chicken.

His gaze drops to my wine-moist lips. "I'm always hungry around you."

"Then let's clean up."

I start putting stuff away. He helps too until the only things left are the bottle of wine and our glasses.

I pat the blanket. "Lie down."

His eyebrow arched, he does.

I take his arm and stretch it out, then lay my head on the bicep. It makes a very comfortable pillow as I snuggle next to him. "You know what I realized?"

"What?"

"That we didn't take any photos when we were together. I mean, of us. As a couple."

An odd look crosses his face. "No, we didn't."

"This time we should." I take out my phone and position it over us. "We should capture every happy moment together so we never forget what we have."

The reflective screen shows us lying on the blanket, my face relaxed and his tight. I lower the phone. "You don't want to?"

He shakes his head. "No. I'm just…" He turns his head toward me. "Nobody's ever wanted to do that with me."

"Maybe they weren't very good at preserving memories."

"Honestly, I never wanted to, either," he says, kissing me softly on the mouth. "I never had a reason."

Oh, Lucas. "But now?" I ask lightly.

"Now I do." He grins and takes my phone and positions it above us himself. "Smile."

I do.

The shutter clicks.

He isn't finished. He takes many, many more, all of them featuring us smiling, kissing, laughing.

Happy.

The sun starts to dip lower, and the wind is definitely getting a slight bite to it. I move closer to him. "I don't want to leave." I would give anything to preserve this moment in time.

"Neither do I."

Two beats. "But we probably should." As much as I'd love to, we can't stay here forever, especially with the temperature dropping.

"We're not going anywhere. I kidnapped you, remember?"

"Yes, I do. But I forgot to warn you that I'm a pretty high-maintenance hostage. I need a bed and a hot shower—at least—from my kidnapper."

He shakes his head. "A total princess. Lucky for you, I'm a kidnapper with high standards." Standing up, he extends a hand. "Ready to be wowed by your accommodations?"

I grasp it. "Yes."

TWENTY-SEVEN

Ava

THE PLACE HE FINDS TURNS OUT TO BE A rustic B&B not too far from the lake. It has five guest suites and is run by a ruddy-faced woman with a big apron around her that reads *Sweet Lakes Bed 'n' Breakfast*.

She welcomes us when we walk in and introduces herself—Doris Penn. Do we have a reservation? No? But aren't we lucky since she just happened to have a cancellation. But we have to check out by Monday if that's all right. Other guests are coming in.

Lucas hands her his plastic, and she shows us to a room with a view of the woods. The place is nowhere near as fancy as the suite he stayed in in Osaka, but country charm more than makes up for the lack of glitzy opulence.

Clean, soft sheets cover the king-size bed, and an armchair and love seat occupy the living room along with a small table. The TV is large and new, and the bathroom is well-stocked with basic toiletries including toothbrushes and toothpaste. It also comes with a tub big enough for two adults.

"It's lovely," I say to Doris.

She beams. "This is the best one we have. Just renovated, too. Hope you enjoy your stay."

"We sure will," I say.

She hands us the key to the room and leaves. I look at the actual metal key and smile at Lucas. "This is very good, Mr. Kidnapper."

"I agree. Sometimes I'm so awesome I impress even myself."

"Is that so? I also should've told you that I demand clean underwear during captivity as well."

"Surely you jest. The whole point of kidnapping is to keep you naked in my room."

"How will I go out to eat?"

"That's what room service is for."

"Does this place have room service?"

He taps his lower lip. "Hmm… Maybe not. All right. I suppose I can get you some clean things to wear. Something super lacy. In fire-engine red." He shoots me a comically lascivious leer.

He is, however, deeply disappointed when the only store we find is a general merchandise place that sells all sorts of things, including some clothes. He looks at the blue plastic carts with horror. I bet he's never set foot inside a store that requires him to push one around. Given the wealth and social position of his family, he's probably never shopped for groceries either.

"What the hell are those?" he whispers hoarsely when I dump a few packages of panties into the cart.

"Underwear."

He picks one up and reads the label. "White," he says sourly. "*Cotton?* C'mon!"

I press my twitching lips together. "If you wanted something fancier, you should've warned me first. Then I could've packed."

"What kind of kidnapper warns his victim?"

"The kind that doesn't like plain white cotton underwear?" I grab a few men's boxers and toss them into the cart. "There."

He sighs, but doesn't comment further. I bite my lip so I don't laugh out loud and grab a few clean shirts and pants while I'm at it. He gives me his size, and I dump stuff for him too.

"Who does your travel planning for you?" I ask as we wait in line to pay.

"My assistant. I tell her what I want and she does it."

"I guess she didn't take part in your criminal activity today."

"No, I didn't think to make her an accessory. Should've."

"Eh, not too bad for your first time on your own." I smirk as the cashier scans our goods. "At least we've got acceptable dental floss."

"Thank the lord," he says with mock sincerity, then pulls me into his arms and dips me dramatically like in a black-and-white romance flick and kisses me on the mouth. "Next time, I'm abducting you to Paris."

My eyes widen. "Paris?"

"Uh-huh. *Much* better lingerie." He grins as he straightens me and swipes his card.

"You can abduct me anytime"—I kiss him back breathlessly—"even if you aren't taking me to Paris."

Lucas

WE'RE FORTUNATE THAT DORIS PROVIDES US with dinner—a homey beef stew served in the dining room. Actually *I*'m feeling lucky since I was leery of finding a decent place to eat after our shopping experience. All the women I've dated before would've been horrified at the lack of five star establishments. Ava, on the other hand, seems amused and content to take what comes, for which I'm grateful.

When I initially visited her at Ray and Darcy's house, I didn't mean to spirit her away like this, but I just couldn't bring myself to give her up for another night. Given the way Ray and Darcy have been, I'm certain they would've objected if Ava spent the night at my place, and I'm not sure which way she would've jumped. She's so damn loyal to them.

If only I could be certain of her devotion.

I'll have to earn that of course, but I don't know how. I've never successfully earned anyone's love.

You are marrying, right?

You know it's going to devastate Elizabeth.

I shunt aside the memory of Blake's cool words. Portraits or no, I would've gone after Ava. I'm not going to marry her for a damned painting, and if that decision costs my siblings, I'll make it up to them somehow. But I can't use Ava like that.

"This is really good." Ava soaks up her last bit of stew with a piece of bread and pops it into her mouth.

"Glad you like it," Doris says. "Sammy had to leave early to go to the hospital, and I hate eating alone." She laughs. "Sammy's the handyman, works himself up a pretty good appetite most days, but he's gotta go see his grandson born."

"Wow. That's awesome. Congrats to him," Ava says.

"Oh, he's thrilled. Loves him some children." Doris smiles, revealing the small gap between her front teeth. "Who doesn't, though, right?"

Ava's gaze rests on me, and I look back at her. Her brow is furrowed as though she's trying to weigh something that can't be weighed.

Apparently having noticed the odd vibe between us, Doris stares at me. I feel a dull flush rising from the base of my neck.

"Children are interesting," I mutter finally, re-experiencing the particular embarrassment I felt when I forgot my line in a school play.

Doris beams. "'Course they are. Fascinating, when you come right down to it."

I nod with a neutral smile, but Ava is looking at me like I'm an alien. Damn it. Is "interesting" not the right word? The first word that pops into my head when I hear "children" is "grubby." And "grubby" elicits "untouchable" and "to be avoided." I thought "interesting" would be better.

Thankfully, the awkward moment is broken when Doris announces it's time for something sweet. It's hard to be anything but happy when presented with a dessert as American as apple pie with huge double scoops of vanilla ice cream.

"Amazing," Ava says after a bite. "I feel a little disloyal for saying this, but it's better than Ray's."

"Is there anything he can't make?" I ask.

"Hamburgers." She snorts, then laughs. "It really drives him nuts that he can't master them for some reason, and Darcy can." She takes another big bite. "God, I could eat like this every day."

"Want to?" I turn to Doris. "Would it be a huge imposition if we asked you to cook us dinner for the rest of our stay? I'd be happy to pay extra, of course."

"Wouldn't mind at all." She pronounces it *ah-tall.* "I love cooking."

"Excellent. Thank you."

"Just so you know, I make a different pie every day," she says. "Hope that's all right."

"Variety makes life interesting," Ava says.

Doris smacks a thigh with a loud laugh. "Ain't that the truth!"

We return to our room, and while Ava texts Ray to let him know she won't be coming home for a few days, I run the bath for her. Doris has provisioned us with a bottle of some scented bubble concoction, and the bathroom soon smells like tropical flowers.

"Mmm," Ava says, looking at the thick layer of frothy bubbles in the tub. "A man after my own heart."

Wrapping an arm around her waist, I pull her close. "Never let it be said that I don't know how to take care of an abductee."

She's already shucked her shoes, so I help her out of her outfit, laying her clothes on the toilet seat cover. She sinks into the hot water.

"Ah, this feels sooo good."

"If only you had some wine," I say.

"What do you know about bubble baths and wine?"

"All women drink wine when they take one." I strip, dropping my stuff on the floor, and join her in the tub. "It's like a law."

The warm water sinks deep into my muscles. As I settle behind her and spoon her against my chest, she murmurs, "You're going to smell like flowers."

"I'd risk smelling worse if it meant being with you."

She snorts a laugh. "We're so sappy."

"Sappy's good. We deserve to be happy after two years." I take her hand and kiss it gently. "All I ask is that you give me a chance, Ava."

"I know."

But somehow, watching her cheeks flush with heat, I can't help but think that she's holding back something important, something without which I can never be truly close to her. Unease dips its chilly finger into my heart, and I will myself to be rational. *Don't get clingy*.

I fist my hand into her golden hair and pull her head back for a deep, lush kiss. She obliges, her mouth soft and eager. I take her with my mouth, my tongue, leaving nothing of her untouched. One of her hands digs into my hair while another finds the pierced nipple. My cock hardens, and she turns around and adjusts herself until she's cradling my dick between her slick folds. I curse under my breath, and she laughs breathlessly against my mouth.

"I love what I can do to your body." She wraps a hand around the shaft and squeezes.

I groan.

"What I can do for your body," she adds in a pant.

"Ava."

I brush my fingers over her sensitive beaded nipples, one after the other. She arches her back, pushing them toward me. My mouth clamps over one, pulling it in deep and hard. Her breasts aren't the largest I've ever seen, but they're the most sensitive…and sensitivity trumps size any day.

Her breath hitches, and she rocks harder and faster against me. I grip her ass to hold her still. She has no clue how amazing her bare flesh feels against my throbbing dick. Or maybe she does and doesn't care.

"Condom," she whispers. "Tell me you have a condom."

"In my pants pocket," I say.

She gets out of the tub and bends over to fish it out, treating me to a nice show along the way.

I rise out of the water and grab a towel to dry the pertinent part, then help her sheathe me. Her fingers are shaky, but surprisingly dexterous.

"I'm going to be on top," she says, her voice low and husky.

I pull her in for a hot, open-mouthed kiss. "You can be anywhere as long as you get there soon."

She pushes me down and positions herself. Her fingers digging into my shoulders, she slips lower…lower…finally taking me deeper inside. The hot muscles contract around my dick, and I thrust, wanting the connection to be deeper, hotter. She throws her head back; the water slaps the edges of the tub around us. I take a rosy nipple into my mouth, and suck hard as she increases her tempo, taking me in, then pulling almost all the way back, determined to drive me out of my fucking mind.

Who the fuck am I kidding? I'm already out of my mind. I lost it the second I met her.

"Lucas…" Ava pants. "Oh my god…"

Water drops cling to her flushed skin and spikes the dark lashes framing her lust-darkened eyes. She looks fucking amazing as she climbs higher and higher, ready for a blinding climax. I slip a hand between our bodies, find the swollen clit. She cries out, and her fingers dig even harder into my muscles. From the way her pussy contracts around my shaft, I know she's close.

"Come for me, babe," I grate out between clenched teeth. "Let me feel you come."

"Not alone. Together." Her gorgeous glazed eyes meet mine, and I feel like I'm being sucked into her. "Come with me."

She could tell me to follow her to hell and I'd say okay. Her body tightens as the orgasm rips through her, her spine arched, her mouth parted in a scream. Nothing could be more beautiful than Ava in climax, and that's all it takes to push me over the edge.

I spurt into her hotly, my entire body so tense it feels like I'm made of stone. My hands grasp her tiny waist, holding on as pleasure spirals through me, as sharp and uncontrollable as shrapnel.

When I can breathe again, I pull her close and whisper into her damp hair, "Let's stay here as long as we can."

She nods.

TWENTY-EIGHT

Ava

IT RAINS THE REST OF THE WEEKEND, BUT I don't mind as we stay cocooned with each other. We turn off our phones and don't let anything intrude on our time. When Monday rolls around, the rain has finally stopped but it's still heavily overcast.

My mood is as low as the clouds. I hate leaving the humble bed and breakfast. It's been such a haven for us—to reconnect and spend time together. I still haven't told Lucas about Mia. I'm not certain yet what I'll tell him or how he'll react, especially after that comment about children being "interesting." I'm pretty sure he was thinking something other than *interesting* when he said it.

If it were only me, I would've told him by now, but I worry about Darcy and Ray. She miscarried three times, and if anything were to happen to Mia…I don't know what it would do to her.

"Do you honestly intend to take these with you?" Lucas asks, hoisting up the plastic bags stuffed with the underwear and clothes we bought.

"Yes. Why would you want to toss them?"

"Because." He kisses me behind my ear. "I'll buy you something sexier."

"You mean you're going to ask your assistant?"

"She can send us the whole catalogue, and you can model for me and we can decide together."

I elbow him in the side. "We won't be doing much picking then."

"If we can't get through everything in thirty days, we'll just keep all of them."

I laugh. "You're terrible."

We settle our bill with Doris. I look around as she and Lucas go over the items to make sure everything's right. I'm going to miss this place. Maybe we should come back, make our stay here an annual event. I'd like that.

The drive home is quiet. Lucas maneuvers with his left hand, holding mine with his right for the hours it takes us to reach Charlottesville. I feel the weight of real life growing with every mile.

I don't understand why I'm so uneasy. We can't live in that bed and breakfast forever. But for some bizarre reason, the real world feels like a wedge that's coming between us.

My hold on him tightens, and he looks at me questioningly.

"Nothing," I say. "I just wish the weekend were longer."

"Me, too." He smiles. "But I meant what I said about abducting you to Paris."

"I look forward to it, but not over Thanksgiving. I definitely need to spend that with Darcy and Ray." I hesitate. "Do you have any plans?"

"For what?" He blinks. "Thanksgiving?"

I nod.

"No… No plans."

The slightly bemused tone speaks volumes. He doesn't celebrate the holiday—or at least his family doesn't. "You're welcome to join us."

The eyebrow rises. "Are you sure?"

"Of course."

"Well…okay. Thanks. Let me know if I need to bring anything."

"I will."

"And speaking of things—do you want your Lexus back?"

My head swivels so fast I almost sprain my neck. "My what?"

"Your Lexus. The car. You left it."

"I didn't *leave* it. I gave it back to you."

"Well, I've got it in the garage."

"Why?" It's not like he doesn't have a car of his own.

He shrugs, then clears his throat. "In case you changed your mind."

"Lucas."

I place my forehead against his shoulder. My gut clenches painfully as I realize maybe I should've stuck around and confronted him directly rather than have his hateful brother drive me away. Even though Google showed how different we were—his wealth, his family, his connections—I should've at least given him a chance to explain. Even if there was a possibility that it might add to my already painful humiliation.

"I'm not a total idiot, Ava." He lets out a rough laugh. "I knew you weren't planning on coming back. But getting rid of it felt too…final." The corners of his eyes crinkle as his lips twist self-deprecatingly. "I suppose it's the reason some people keep their children's rooms the same after they move away."

"You got me back."

"Yes, thank god." He sighs. "So, the car…"

I want to say no, but I can tell that accepting it matters a great deal to him. "I'll…take it back. Thank you." I squirm.

"You're uncomfortable," he says.

"Because it's too extravagant! It's a whole *car*."

"If we're going to be together, you have to get used to extravagance."

I sigh and finally nod. "Okay. You're right." It wouldn't be fair for me to ask him to drastically lower his living standards just to suit me. Besides, there's no car he could've bought that would've made me feel comfortable taking it.

When Lucas drives through the gates to the golf course community, he turns the opposite way from Ray and Darcy's home and follows along the immaculately maintained winding road. At the end is a one-story house that sprawls unlike my foster parents' home.

He pulls into the driveway and cuts the engine. Another car is there. Glossy, black, expensive looking. Everything inside me freezes when I see a woman climb out of it. Inky black hair, alabaster skin, amber eyes and lush carmine lips paired with the fabulously voluptuous body of a pinup girl from the fifties. Incredibly, horrifyingly, Faye Belbin is even better in person than in her photos.

The red dress she's wearing looks painted on. It leaves absolutely nothing to the imagination and seems almost indecent, despite the fact that its hem reaches mid-shin. Her hips sway seductively as she walks toward us in red shoes with skinny high heels.

"Ah, fuck." Lucas yanks on the door and gets out.

I climb out, too. I'm not going to sit inside the car when my man is about to interact with his ex or…something. I'm still not sure what to label Faye.

"I am so going to fire Rachel," Lucas says.

"Now, now." The woman has a purring husky contralto that belongs to a phone sex operator. She barely spares a glance my way. Suddenly I feel small and inconsequential in her presence. "Don't be irritated. Come give me a hug."

She comes forward with arms spread, but he raises his hands, palms out.

She stops. Her focus remains zeroed in on Lucas. "All right, so you're upset with Rachel, but she didn't do anything wrong. I told her I had to see you, especially in light of what's going on with your family."

Lucas huffs out a breath. "Elliot or Ryder?"

She laughs. "It's Elliot, and you know how it is. Got tangled up in another juicy scandal."

"Marrying a damn stripper isn't enough?"

"Apparently not."

He curses viciously. "All right, so why are you here? What's so damned important?"

She looks mildly surprised. "Lucas, I know you want to beat your father at his little game. I wanted to offer my help, but couldn't reach you by phone. So…"

That reminds me that we turned off our phones while we were at the bed and breakfast. Apparently Lucas forgot too; we both fish our phones out and turn them on. As soon as mine finds reception, it starts vibrating with numerous alerts.

Most of them are Facebook messages and emails from Bennie. I open the latest one on top of my inbox.

Subject: WTF

Where are you? Are you still with that son of a bitch? What bullshit is he feeding you? Girl, you need to get the hell away from him. HE IS FUCKING POISON, AND HE DOESN'T DESERVE YOU.

There's a link attached at the bottom of the email. The URL makes it clear it's some kind of celeb gossip website, and my stomach churns with apprehension. This cannot be good.

The site loads. The headline reads: *Greedy Billionaires Want More.*

A knot tight in my throat, I skim the article. The more I read, the more nauseated I become.

This is so much worse than I thought. All the stuff Lucas fed me, the sweet words about how he couldn't live without me, that I took something from him—warmth and all that is good and great about his life—was all lies. He didn't mean any of it.

What he wanted was a portrait worth several million dollars that his grandfather created before dying. Lucas has to marry soon—and for a year—in order to inherit. And it's the same for his siblings as well.

I just happened to be a gullible, easy-to-impress target.

I clench my teeth as nausea roils through me. I'd rather slit my wrists than throw up and show him how he's gutted me.

A silly little fool, that's what you are.

He must be inwardly laughing his ass off about the Lexus. I chided him for overindulging me with a car when all this time I've been helping him get something that's worth millions.

Suddenly I'm grateful I didn't tell him about Mia. It would've been a disaster to have her in the middle of this mess. I don't doubt for a moment that he'd use her as leverage to force me to do what he wants.

The skin around my eyes feels hot with tears. "You son of a bitch."

"Ava," Lucas whispers. He clutches his own

phone in one white-knuckled hand, his face bloodless.

I raise my phone, screen facing him. "It's all true, isn't it?"

He doesn't answer. He reaches for my mobile, but I step back quickly. I'm not letting him touch me or blind me to the truth.

"*Isn't it?*" I yell. I need to hear him say yes. I deserve that much.

"It's not like that. Nobody is expecting me to get married."

I shove a fist against my mouth to stifle a sob. He doesn't have to say more. I'm smart enough to piece things together.

Slowly and carefully as though he's reaching for a wounded wild animal, he extends a hand. I stumble back, not wanting him to touch me. If he does, I might crumble and humiliate myself. "You're despicable," I choke out.

"Ava, please. Listen to me—"

"I'm *not interested.*" I gesture wildly at Faye, who's watching with an unreadable look on her face. "Why didn't you ask her to marry you? After all, she was your first choice when you needed to go out in public!"

He's shaking his head. His expression beseeches me, but that too is a lie. "Ava, don't. That's not—"

"We're *done." The past ten days...all lies.*

I steel myself against him. I slash the space between us as though with that simple action I can sever everything. "Don't follow me. I know my way home."

Then I turn around and run as fast as my legs can carry me.

TWENTY-NINE

Lucas

AVA DISAPPEARS RAPIDLY DOWN THE ROAD. Soon she makes a turn, and I can't see her anymore.

That, more than anything else, jolts me out of my paralysis. I can't let her go like this. I can't repeat the last two years again, this time with no end. The weekend showed me what Ava and I can have. *I'm not giving that up without a fight.*

I start to move forward.

"Lucas, we have to talk."

I shrug Faye off, not bothering to look at her. "Not right now."

She wraps a hand firmly around my wrist. "Before you go after her, you need to think about what you're going to do next. She's not the priority. Everybody knows about the deal between you and Julian. And if that's not bad enough, they know what happened between Elliot and your third stepmother. Some tabloid published all the sordid details."

That makes me pause. "My third stepmother?" I didn't see anything about her in the article I just skimmed on the phone.

"I guess she's technically your second stepmother. But your father's third wife. Annabelle Underhill."

What the...? "What about her?"

"She and Elliot had an affair. They apparently were...dating before she married your father and they had a...reunion of sorts at the wedding. Who knows how many other times they cuckolded Julian."

I close my eyes and run a rough hand over my face. I love my twin. Despite the fact that our mother clearly preferred him, he himself has never purposefully done anything to hurt me. It wasn't his fault that Betsy loved us unequally.

But this? This makes me *hate* him. It's obvious the scandal that exploded between him and Wife Number Three is what's motivating Dad, who doesn't exactly embody magnanimity or great fatherhood. There's no doubt in my mind that Dad's the one who leaked the deal to the press to purposely humiliate us and make our lives more difficult.

"I know how much you loved your grand-father," Faye begins, letting go of my wrist and coming closer to put a hand on my chest. "And I can help out. I don't mind marrying you for a year so you can get the painting. That girl who just ran away? She's not the type who would understand."

If this were any other time and if this were before I reconnected with Ava, I might've welcomed her suggestion. But now things are different. I can't go back. I can't imagine a life without Ava and I can't marry Faye, even if it's only for a year. If I do, there will be no redemption for me in Ava's eyes. Zero.

"Thanks for the offer, but what will help is if you stay out of the picture," I tell Faye, stepping away.

"'Out of the picture'?" She pulls back in surprise and presses her lips together for a moment. "You'd honestly throw away our friendship over her?"

"If that's what it takes to win Ava back... She's the most important person in my life."

"She doesn't want you, Lucas. Look how she ran off without giving you a chance to explain."

What Faye's saying cuts deep, not just because it's true but because as far as Ava is concerned, what happened doesn't even warrant an explanation. And I can't blame her for coming to that conclusion, either.

"Well," she continues, "I'm not a fickle friend. I'll be waiting for you when you realize what you've just done. And unlike her, I will listen and we'll be friends again." Without waiting for a response, Faye climbs into her car and drives off.

I shove my hands through my hair. How in the hell am I going to end this nightmare? There has to be a way. Failure is simply *not* an option.

My phone vibrates. My heart jumps—*maybe it's Ava*. But no. It's Elizabeth.

I don't want to answer, but I can't ignore her either. She's the diplomat in the family, and if she's calling now, it's because she has information and a way to defuse the situation. "What is it, Elizabeth?"

"I guess you saw the news."

"Who hasn't?" My voice drips with sarcasm. "It's all over the fucking internet."

"We're going to have a conference call to figure out how to control the situation. We can't have it hanging out there like this, you know that."

"Damage control? Now?"

"Yes."

My molars grind together. It takes a great deal of effort to unclench my teeth. "The time to do something was *before* it leaked. To make sure that it *didn't* leak."

She sighs. "Sometimes things don't work out the way you want, and you just have to roll with the punches."

"How the hell am I supposed to do that when it's already ruined the one thing that matters to me?"

"I'm sorry."

"How fucking stupid are you people to let this thing become public?"

As soon as I say it, I feel awful. Raging at Elizabeth is like kicking a puppy. She probably has nothing to do with the damned article, and she's just trying to help.

"I'm sorry, Elizabeth. I didn't mean *you*. I'm just…"

My throat closes up, and I can't talk anymore. The fact that I may have just lost Ava forever is sending such a huge surge of panic through me…

"It's fine," Elizabeth says in a warm, soothing voice. "I know you're upset, and I would be too in your shoes. But can you please join the call? I'll email you the details. We have to present a united front if we're going to minimize this thing."

I nod, then remember that we're on the phone. "Okay," I croak out.

"Great. Talk to you later." She hesitates. "Take care of yourself, Lucas. This too shall pass."

She hangs up.

She believes that bullshit about this all passing because she isn't the one losing somebody important.

Flexing my clammy hands, I climb into my car. I have to go to Ava. I *have* to fix this.

THIRTY

Ava

B Y THE TIME I REACH RAY AND DARCY'S
house, I'm completely out of breath.
Perspiration drips from my face and soaks
my clothes. The door is locked; I pull out the key
and go inside.

Just in case, I call out, "I'm home!" Only cool
silence greets me.

Letting out a long shaky breath, I lean against
the wall. My legs feel like soggy noodles. Tears
I've held back until now stream down my cheeks,
mingling with my sweat. My chest shakes, and an
ugly sob rips from my throat.

Slowly I slide down to the floor until I'm
crouching and crying. Lucas isn't worth it.
Intellectually I know that. But my heart doesn't
want to listen. It breaks and breaks and breaks,

and I don't know how I'm going to pick up the pieces and make everything okay again.

I need to get a hold of myself before Ray and Darcy come home. I don't want them to see me like this. It's just too humiliating to think that I fell for him—twice!—when he's never loved me or cared about me. He's had an ulterior motive, just the way my dad had an ulterior motive when he stayed with Mom. Her body, plus the cheap thrill of doing it with someone who wasn't his wife. Except Lucas is smarter than my father because he's playing for a multimillion dollar inheritance in addition to the cheap thrills.

I don't know how long I stay there crying, but a sudden loud thump on the door jolts me. My spine reverberates from the forceful bang as I jump to my feet, spinning around. I look through the peephole and suck in a breath.

Lucas.

Quickly, I lock the door before he realizes he can just walk in.

"Open the door," he roars.

"Go away," I say.

Much to my disgust, I sound like a frog with a cold. Damn it. He's going to know I've been crying. And that thought enrages me, giving me the strength to get through this confrontation.

I wipe my face with the sleeves of my shirt. "You've done enough. Get out of my life."

NADIA LEE

"Ava, you didn't give me a chance to explain."

"*Explain?* I read the article! I saw your reaction. I know what they printed is all true."

"Yes, it is all true, but it has nothing to do with us!"

"*Really?*"

"I didn't come back to you for a damn painting."

"Right. You don't care at all about a painting worth millions. And you just happened to run into me when you needed to marry someone to get it, because you just happened to be in Chiang Mai, halfway around the fucking *planet*, at the same time I was. Wow. That sounds really believable."

"Damn it, it's not like that."

I slam my palm against the door as loudly as I can. "I don't *care* what it's like, *go away!*"

"Ava, talk to me face-to-face. *Please.* Five minutes. That's all. Let me make you understand."

What more am I supposed to understand? That he thinks I'm a pathetic sucker? "If you don't leave, I'm calling the police." I swallow a bitter ball forming in my throat. "Stop harassing me, Lucas. I don't want to listen. There's nothing you can say that's going to change my mind. You blew it."

"Ava!" His fists slam against the door again. "Then one minute."

"You're not getting another second. Go away before Ray and Darcy come back. Or are you going to try to explain to them why you did what you did?"

"I don't care what they think. The only thing that matters is what you believe."

"I believe the worst. There. Go away. If not, I *will* disappear again. And this time you won't find me."

"Don't even think about it, Ava," he threatens in a voice so awful and dark that it sends shivers down my spine. "The only reason I didn't find you in the last two years is because I didn't try. But this time I won't just sit on my ass and do nothing. I'll hire a platoon of private detectives if that's what it takes."

It's more than a threat. It's a promise, and it sends cold terror through me. If he digs too hard and too much, he'll find out about Mia.

No. Anything but Mia.

"Lucas... you need to go. *Please*," I add, feeling utterly defeated and drained.

There's a pause that feels interminable. Then he quietly says, "I hate doing this, but I'm going to leave now and give you a chance to calm down. Once you do, I hope you realize what we've had over the last week was all real—what we had at the bed and breakfast was real. We can have that for the rest of our lives, and you want to throw it all away because of something you read on the internet. I'll be back, though. Tomorrow, and the day after, and the day after that, until you give me a chance to explain. *I'm not giving you up without a fight.*"

Pressing my lips together, I blink away another wave of tears. How dare he say that after shattering my heart?

He has no right.

Another eternal moment passes. Then I hear the sole of his shoe turn on the concrete porch, footsteps as he walks away, a car door open and shut, the engine start. It's Lucas leaving...as he said he would.

Feeling like the weight of the world is on my shoulders, I drag myself upstairs to my room and message Bennie. *Hey.*

Oh my fucking god. There you are. Holy shit. What took you so long? Were you digging a ditch deep enough to bury him?

I let out a watery laugh. Leave it up to Bennie to lighten the mood even when everything feels bleak and hopeless. *No. I didn't kill him. I didn't even know anything was going on because my phone was off until about half an hour ago.*

You should've killed him.

I wipe my tears impatiently. *I should've listened to you.*

I'm so sorry. I wish I could be there for you.

I do too, I type, fighting a sob. I miss my best friend so much. *I wish you were here too.*

Stay tough. You can get through this. Lucas isn't strong enough to destroy you.

I close my eyes as another shard of pain digs into me. Bennie is wrong, and it's too late. Lucas has already destroyed me. I gave him that power when I gave him my heart.

THIRTY-ONE

Ava

TRUE TO HIS WORD, LUCAS DOESN'T GIVE UP. For the next seven days, every day, he comes by at nine thirty sharp. Thankfully, Ray and Darcy act as a barricade. They've seen the social media furor, and they're incensed on my behalf. But they don't ask me to talk. I think they knew better when they saw my face swollen with tears.

Not willing to brave the world quite yet, I stay cooped up in my room. I need to answer an email I received while Lucas and I were away—some medical center in L.A. wanting to interview me, thanks to my old roommate Erin's recommendation—and I need to take care of myself, but at the moment everything just seems like too much.

Within a day of the ugly exposé, Lucas's twin, Elliot, makes a social media post about how stupid it is to believe the bullshit since there is no way anybody can assume he's the type to marry merely for some lousy inheritance. From the ensuing reaction, it seems like it worked. Then Lucas's more famous half-brother, Hollywood superstar Ryder Reed, goes on an interview to promote his latest film and addresses the matter publicly. I watch the segment on my phone.

"Get real. The idea that I married Paige for a painting is silly. I mean, my reputation's a little on the wild side, and I've done a lot of over-the-top crazy stuff that most people would never do." He gives the camera an impossibly handsome and winning grin. "But I'd never marry someone I didn't respect and love."

"But it's understandable that people are skeptical," the interviewer says. "Your wife isn't like most women you've had…er…relationships with."

"You mean because she isn't an actress, or because she isn't a size two?"

The interviewer has the decency to flush. "A little bit of both."

"So I used to date a lot of actresses"—Ryder shrugs—"so what? I didn't fall in love with any of them. Looking at it now, I think I was always meant to fall for Paige.

"Furthermore—and I want to get this out publicly, because no matter how many times my staff and I try to stop this stuff, people just don't seem to want to listen—a woman's attractiveness has nothing to do with how much she weighs. One number doesn't determine a woman's worth, okay? It's sexist, it's demeaning, and it says more about the people who think that than it does about my wife. I don't care about her weight or dress size. The only thing I care about is what's inside, and Paige is the most genuine and caring and loving woman I've ever met."

Ryder is utterly convincing, his expression somber, his voice earnest. I wonder if his wife knew about the deal between him and his father from the beginning, and if not, what she thinks about it now. Or maybe she doesn't care, because she has Ryder Reed and she's in love with him.

Maybe if I could just pretend that I never saw the article, I might be able to relive the happiness from my weekend with Lucas for as long as our relationship lasts. But I have my pride. I will *not* be deceived or used.

I still don't understand why Lucas didn't just go to Faye. The woman is absolutely gorgeous, and I'm sure she'd be more than willing to marry him. I saw the way she followed him with her eyes. He might believe what they have is platonic, but how she looked at him just isn't how a woman looks at someone in the friend zone.

Maybe he doesn't want to ask Faye because she's not that kind of woman, just like my dad didn't leave his wife, Sondra, hanging because she isn't the kind of woman men treat that way. She's the kind men woo and marry and treat like a queen. It's like this aura she projects.

When Bennie and I chat on Skype, I tell him this. He shrieks and glares at me. "Ava Huss, you did *not* just say that!"

"Calm down, Bennie."

"Don't tell me to calm down! I'm not going to sit quiet while you bad-mouth yourself!"

I cringe. Maybe I should've mulled things over in the peace of my own room.

"For fuck's sake, Ava! Why the hell would you think shit like that?" He raises a hand, palm out. "No, don't answer. I know why. That *fucking* Lucas. I'm so going to send a platoon of ninjas to gut his ass!"

"Okay, Bennie, I ge—"

"Your asshole dad treated you and your mom that way because *he was an asshole*. Not because there's something wrong with *you*. You've been moping for a week now, girl! What are you going to do? Just curl up and wait for a man to treat you right, or say fuck all this and treat *yourself* right? Huh?" He finally starts to calm down a little. "Nobody loves you like yourself. Well, except me. I love you."

"I know." I smile wanly.

"You've lost weight. Don't starve yourself over that worthless piece of shit." Bennie takes a breath. "I swear, we need better cuss words for assholes like Lucas."

"You swear that you need better cuss words?"

"Shut up." But he finally smiles. "Look, do what you need to feel better. But don't forget you're a fantastic, worship-worthy woman. If Lucas can't see that, it's on him, not you. Don't let some brainless fool destroy your self-esteem. You're a fabulous human being!"

Bennie's the really fabulous one here. "Oh, Bennie, if only you were hetero. We'd make beautiful music together."

"Or if you were gay. No, wait. That wouldn't work." We laugh and hang up.

The next day—which happens to be day number eight since the article was published—I get up early, shower and put on a pink long-sleeved shirt and jeans. They hang loosely. Bennie's right about the weight loss, but I just haven't had any appetite.

But that's all over now. No more Pathetic Ava. I didn't come back to America to leach off Ray and Darcy. I want to be someone they'll be proud of. And I want to be a role model for Mia, even if she never knows I'm her mother.

Hiding in my room is not going to achieve any of these things.

I fire up my computer and answer the medical center email with an affirmative for a phone interview. I don't think anything will come of it—there must be a qualified candidate who's closer—but why not? Then I upload my résumé to a few more places.

Once I'm done, I go downstairs. Ray and Darcy are reading next to each other on the couch and they look up almost simultaneously in surprise. I haven't been downstairs much in the last week.

"Good morning," Ray says in a careful but cheery voice. "You want some breakfast? We have coffee and I'm about to make pancakes."

"Both, if you don't mind."

Ray beams. "Of course not. I'd be delighted."

Darcy immediately jumps to her feet and offers me a fresh mug of coffee. Ray whips up breakfast quickly, as though he's afraid that if he takes too long I'll change my mind. Their kindness brings a fresh wave of tears, and I wipe them away. I'm going to be okay—I have amazing people in my life. I don't need Lucas to make things work.

One step at a time. And surely I'll be happy on my own.

After breakfast, I ask Ray, "Is there a pot I can use?" He and Darcy maintain a bountiful herb garden in the back. "Just a small one. I want to plant something."

"But it's fall, love," Darcy points out.

I force a smile. "It's fine if it doesn't survive or do well. I just want to try."

"There's an old terra-cotta pot in the shed," Ray says. "It's pretty small, but if you just want to experiment, it might be enough."

"That'd be perfect. Thank you."

I walk into the shed and see the pot Ray was talking about. It's old and slightly discolored, a sun-faded reddish orange. But it's exactly what I need. I take it to the backyard garden and fill it. Thankfully the pot's small so it doesn't require much time or dirt. I'd hate to leave a big hole.

When I bring it inside, Darcy looks at it curiously. "What are you trying to grow?"

"A very special something," I say.

"A mystery, huh? Well, hope it works. It's such a pleasure to watch something grow and thrive under your care."

"I hope so, too." I speak with more confidence and verve than I've had in days. This little pot is going to make my point crystal clear to Lucas.

At nine thirty sharp, Lucas shows up, knocks on the door and waits. Ray gets up from his armchair, ready to tell him off yet again, but I rise to my feet.

"I'll deal with him."

Ray's eyebrows go up a notch. "You sure?"

"Yes."

"Okay." He stands there, clearly wanting to go with me. "If you need reinforcements, we're right here."

I give him a small smile. "I know. Thank you."

I take the pot and go to the door. Before Lucas can knock again, I open it.

There stands Lucas. A white button-down dress shirt and black slacks look good on him. Some men are made by clothes, but Lucas isn't one of them. He makes the clothes. But no matter how well cut, they can't hide the weight loss. His facial bones are sharper and starker. Concern stirs inside me, but I quash it immediately.

I don't care, not anymore.

"Ava," he murmurs, his voice low and soothing as though he's afraid to spook me. He wets his mouth. "Are you ready to listen?"

"I'm ready to give you five minutes, but only if you do something first."

"Name it," he says, his Adam's apple bobbing.

I hand him the pot, careful not to let our

hands brush. I don't think I could bear it if we touched skin-to-skin. "Take this."

He does, eyeing it warily. "What is it?"

"I want you to take care of it for the next two weeks."

"Then what?"

"Then bring it back."

His squints slightly. "Is this some kind of test?"

"If you want to think of it that way… Sure."

"All right." He's having a hard time deciding whether to look at me or the pot. "What is it? A tulip? Some kind of herb?"

I shake my head. "Just take care of it for two weeks. You'll know."

"And then I get my five minutes?"

"Absolutely."

He studies me as though he's looking for some kind of trick. I stare back, willing him to not see how much I'm bleeding inside. It feels like I'm cutting off my own arm, but I have to do this in order to be free to move on.

"Fine. I'll be back at nine thirty a.m. two weeks from now." He lifts the pot. "With this baby."

"Okay. See you then."

I close the door. He thinks that this is going to give him a chance to talk to me. What he doesn't know is that it will convince him of how hopeless we are.

Once I hear his car engine start, I go up to my room and sink to the floor, arms around my legs, forehead on my knees. This…this will be the end of me and Lucas.

Hot tears soak my pants.

THIRTY-TWO

Lucas

I TAKE THE OLD POT BACK TO MY PLACE, DRIVing with care, then cradle it in my hands like it's the most fragile and important thing in the entire world as I bring it inside. And it is.

It represents a chance…and possible redemption. I don't know why or how she came up with this "test," but I'm certain she expects me to fail. I'm not going to. I'll set an alarm to remind myself to water it and take care of it to the best of my ability. Not to mention, if I need to, I'm going to ask my gardener. Scott will know—he's a plant whisperer. Two weeks from now, something wonderful is going to sprout from the dirt and I'll get my five minutes with Ava—a chance to show her that things are not what they seem.

However, taking care of whatever seed is in the pot isn't all I do. I drive by Ray and Darcy's house every so often. Actually at least twice a day. I want a glimpse of Ava, just so the vise around my chest will ease and I can breathe again.

I'm aware of the possibility that this could be a ploy to distract me so she can vanish again. But her disappearing isn't what makes my palms and spine slick with sweat. What I'm really afraid of is that she might meet someone else…and forget all about a fucked-up damaged guy like me. Jesus, not even my own mother wants anything to do with me.

If my obsessive driving by the damned house makes me a stalker, so be it. The only people who would mock me are ones who never had someone like Ava to lose.

After a week, I notice that something isn't right with the pot. Although I'm taking care of the seed as well as I can, nothing's coming up through the dirt. I don't think it's supposed to take this long. A Google search tells me most things sprout in four or five days. And something should definitely show by the end of a week.

I have a little conference with my gardener. Scott shakes his head, agreeing that it is indeed odd. He asks me how I've been taking care of it and gives me a few pieces of advice. I take them all into consideration, and keep the room where I placed the pot extra warm, just in case.

Still nothing.

As the end of the two weeks approaches, panic mounts. Did I somehow do something to kill the seed, and nothing is going to sprout? Have I fucked up again?

By the last day I'm practically frantic. Scott and I have a conference. "Look," I say. "It's just dirt. Nothing is growing. What the fuck's going on?"

He huffs a breath, his cheeks going poofy. "I don't know." He scratches the tip of his chin. "It's really strange."

"Maybe the soil's bad?"

"I doubt it."

"Then what? You think it's my fault?"

"No. You've been doing everything right." He shrugs. "Could be just a bad seed..."

"No." I shake my head. "She wouldn't have given me something bad on purpose. Ava isn't like that."

"That's not what I meant. Sometimes seeds just don't sprout."

But I'm certain that's not it. The universe simply can't be that cruel. And Ava would never have knowingly given me a seed that wouldn't grow. She isn't like my mother. It's me. I did something wrong.

All night long I stay up, staring at the damned pot, willing something green to push through the layer of dirt before I have to see Ava.

But my hopes and prayers go unanswered. By nine o'clock I'm pacing in front of the fucking thing, my hands shaky with panic. I can't go back to her like this—a total failure.

So just get something from a local nursery. Who cares? All young plants probably look the same anyway.

But I can't. That would be lying, and she's already upset about the fact that I didn't tell her everything. I can't add lies to what I've done.

Damn it. *Damn it!*

Fucking Elliot and his fucking mess with Wife Number Three.

My hands clammy and my heart thudding, I somehow manage to drive to Ray and Darcy's house without totaling the car. My eyes are gritty from the lack of sleep. I'm running on adrenaline and nerves, and it's all I can do to keep myself together.

I hold the pot against my chest and knock on the door. After a few moments, Ava appears on the other side. Her long platinum hair hangs loosely around her slender shoulders and down her trim back, her sky-colored eyes unreadable. The dark half-moons underneath her eyes are gone, although she's still a bit too pale for my taste. Still, she looks so beautiful in a red shirt and old blue jeans that it hurts.

My heart thunders. *Boom, boom, boom. Can't lose her. Can't lose her. Can't lose her.*

I swallow. "Ava."

"Lucas."

Her gaze drops to the pot cradled in my arm. She raises her eyes back to my face. She doesn't invite me in. Instead, she steps out and closes the door.

"Nothing?"

That single word guts me.

Blood roars in my ears, and I can't stop the horrible, nasty feelings from gelling in my gut like milk gone sour. "Ava, I did everything. I talked with my gardener and I did everything I could. You have to believe me."

"It doesn't matter what I believe."

What the fuck? "Of course it matters! It matters to me. It matters that you believe in me, have faith in me." Her face is closing; she's shutting me out. Panic spikes. "If you can't give me the five minutes because nothing grew, then give me another chance. I swear to you—"

"Nothing was going to grow."

It takes me a moment to process what she just said. "What?"

"There's nothing but dirt in the pot."

I shake my head, feeling like I'm in some kind of dream. "So I was supposed to fail?"

"Not fail. Be convinced."

"Of what?" I stare at her, willing myself to read her thoughts. "Are you trying to punish me?"

"If anyone's being punished, it's me—you keep picking at my old wound."

Suddenly, the lack of sleep and panic push my emotions over the edge. "*Bullshit!* That's called bad faith."

"Is it? I've done the same thing to you that you've done to me."

"I've never acted in bad faith with you!"

Her cheeks turn red and rage erupts in the icy blue of her eyes. "You haven't? You didn't get me fired from my school? You didn't have my new job offer rescinded? You didn't withhold some pretty damn important information about what's been going on between you and your father? About your *inheritance?* You didn't do *any of that?*"

My mouth parts. I've never considered… I didn't think about how my desperate drive to have her back would look.

She isn't finished. "Right. So instead of acting *in good faith*, you used your time to try to seduce me with empty words and gestures. What you've given me is *exactly* like that pot—nothing in it except dirt. But I would've believed, Lucas. I would have believed something wonderful could grow from it, and I would've poured my heart and soul and life into it…only to end up with nothing. Because you've never felt anything real for me."

"That's not…" I put down the pot. Some dirt has gotten on my palms, but I barely register that before reaching out and holding her hand in mine. It's so warm and sweet against my bare skin. "I'm in love with you, Ava." *Tell me I'm enough. Tell me you love me, too. Tell me I'm not some craven bastard for saying this to you, wishing that you'd say it back.*

Her face crumples for a moment. Hope stirs within me, but then the voice drowns it. *When you say things like "I love you" you're trying to get the other person to say it back.* A vise tightens around my chest. I can't draw in any air, but I try to keep myself together. This is the most important conversation of my life.

You're being needy.

My head pounds, and I can barely think. I'm so fucking nauseous, I'm barely standing up, but I do. I have to salvage this…have to save what I have with Ava.

Abruptly a hard mask descends over her face. "Don't say things you don't mean, Lucas, just to score a point."

"Seriously? You think—" I haul in a lungful

of air and struggle for control. "You think I'd say that to a woman I didn't love?"

"Yes." She pulls her hand out of my grasp, brushing her palm against her pants. When she looks back up at me, her gaze is as hard and sharp as a guillotine. "I do."

Don't touch me.

What did I say about touching me when you're dirty?

A cacophony of noise rolls through my head. I open and close my grubby hand.

She takes a half step back, shakes her head. "You're toxic, Lucas…"

The ugly sounds grow louder in my ears, but her voice is crystal clear, cutting through it all like a machete. "Ava," I whisper, my tongue thick and clumsy. *Please stop, please stop, please sto—*

"…and that is why I'm done with you."

Lucas and Ava's epic romance continues in *An Unlikely Bride*. Join my mailing list at http://www.nadialee.net to be notified when *An Unlikely Bride* comes out in summer 2017!

ABOUT NADIA LEE

New York Times and *USA Today* bestselling author Nadia Lee writes sexy, emotional contemporary romance. Born with a love for excellent food, travel and adventure, she has lived in four different countries, kissed stingrays, been bitten by a shark, ridden an elephant and petted tigers.

Currently, she shares a condo overlooking a small river and sakura trees in Japan with her husband and son. When she's not writing, she can be found reading books by her favorite authors or planning another trip.

To learn more about Nadia and her projects, please visit www.nadialee.net. To receive updates about upcoming works from Nadia, please visit www.nadialee.net to subscribe to her new release alert.